Barefoot in White

The Barefoot Bay Brides #1

roxanne st. claire

Critical Reviews of Roxanne St. Claire Novels

"St. Claire, as always, brings a scorching tear-up-the-sheets romance combined with a great story: dealing with real issues starring memorable characters in vivid scenes."

— *Romantic Times Magazine*

"Non-stop action, sweet and sexy romance, lively characters, and a celebration of family and forgiveness."

— *Publishers Weekly*

"Plenty of heat, humor, and heart!"

— *USA Today's Happy Ever After blog*

"It's safe to say I will try any novel with St. Claire's name on it."

— *www.smartbitchestrashybooks.com*

"The writing was perfectly on point as always and the pace of the story was flawless. But be forewarned that you will laugh, cry, and sigh with happiness. I sure did."

— *www.harlequinjunkies.com*

"The Barefoot Bay series is an all-around knockout, soul-satisfying read. Roxanne St. Claire writes with warmth and heart and the community she's built at Barefoot Bay is one I want to visit again and again."

— *Mariah Stewart, New York Times bestselling author*

"This book stayed with me long after I put it down."

— *All About Romance*

Dear Reader,

The resort and spa that grew out of the hurricane-ravaged Barefoot Bay is now home to the *Barefoot Bay Brides*—a destination wedding service specializing in dreamy "I do's" on the beach. The company is run by three women who are gifted in the art of creating a perfect wedding day...but haven't found their own happily ever after. *Yet.* All that's about to change...

First up, Willow Ambrose, who has fought a battle with the scale for much of her life, but has finally won the war. By putting her past behind her and cutting off all contact with anyone who knew her before and, of course, controlling everything she can, Willow has carved out a new body *and* a new life. But when she comes face to face with someone who left an indelible mark on her heart years before, all that threatens to crumble.

Navy SEAL Nick Hershey is on medical leave, doing a friend a favor as a stand in "man of honor" at a beach wedding. He might not be that interested in the nuptials, but the wedding planner catches his eye the minute they meet. When he realizes Willow is really a girl he knew in college—and a girl he unintentionally hurt to the core—he knows he has some making up to do.

Willow has learned how to beat every temptation...but Nick's sweet as candy kisses just might be the one thing she can't resist. But the closer they get, the more the past threatens to tear them apart. Together, they have to discover if they can overcome their history in order to have a forever future.

I need to tip my hat to the crew who makes this all possible for me: outrageously talented editor Kristi Yanta whose delicate touch is on every page; as well as eagle-eyed

Critical Reviews of Roxanne St. Claire Novels

"St. Claire, as always, brings a scorching tear-up-the-sheets romance combined with a great story: dealing with real issues starring memorable characters in vivid scenes."

— *Romantic Times Magazine*

"Non-stop action, sweet and sexy romance, lively characters, and a celebration of family and forgiveness."

— *Publishers Weekly*

"Plenty of heat, humor, and heart!"

— *USA Today's Happy Ever After blog*

"It's safe to say I will try any novel with St. Claire's name on it."

— *www.smartbitchestrashybooks.com*

"The writing was perfectly on point as always and the pace of the story was flawless. But be forewarned that you will laugh, cry, and sigh with happiness. I sure did."

— *www.harlequinjunkies.com*

"The Barefoot Bay series is an all-around knockout, soul-satisfying read. Roxanne St. Claire writes with warmth and heart and the community she's built at Barefoot Bay is one I want to visit again and again."

— *Mariah Stewart, New York Times bestselling author*

"This book stayed with me long after I put it down."

— *All About Romance*

Dear Reader,

The resort and spa that grew out of the hurricane-ravaged Barefoot Bay is now home to the *Barefoot Bay Brides*—a destination wedding service specializing in dreamy "I do's" on the beach. The company is run by three women who are gifted in the art of creating a perfect wedding day...but haven't found their own happily ever after. *Yet.* All that's about to change...

First up, Willow Ambrose, who has fought a battle with the scale for much of her life, but has finally won the war. By putting her past behind her and cutting off all contact with anyone who knew her before and, of course, controlling everything she can, Willow has carved out a new body *and* a new life. But when she comes face to face with someone who left an indelible mark on her heart years before, all that threatens to crumble.

Navy SEAL Nick Hershey is on medical leave, doing a friend a favor as a stand in "man of honor" at a beach wedding. He might not be that interested in the nuptials, but the wedding planner catches his eye the minute they meet. When he realizes Willow is really a girl he knew in college—and a girl he unintentionally hurt to the core—he knows he has some making up to do.

Willow has learned how to beat every temptation...but Nick's sweet as candy kisses just might be the one thing she can't resist. But the closer they get, the more the past threatens to tear them apart. Together, they have to discover if they can overcome their history in order to have a forever future.

I need to tip my hat to the crew who makes this all possible for me: outrageously talented editor Kristi Yanta whose delicate touch is on every page; as well as eagle-eyed copyeditor Joyce Lamb and stellar proofreader Chelle Olson. They join brilliant cover artist Robin Ludwig, formatter-to-the-stars Amy Atwell, the amazing Rocki Road street team of promoters, especially assistant Marilyn Puett, and my precious family who do so much for me so I can write for you! This book had some extra Navy SEAL research support from wonderful author and friend, Marliss Melton. (Do read her books!!)

Like every book set in Barefoot Bay, this novel stands entirely alone, but why stop at just one? All of the books and series are listed in the back. There are plenty of opportunities to go barefoot and fall in love!

— *Roxanne St. Claire*

Barefoot in White

roxanne st. claire

Dedication

This title is dedicated to my dear friend and fellow writer,
Leigh Duncan,
whose generous spirit, golden heart, and everlasting support
has carried me through many difficult days at the keyboard.

Chapter One

"This one..." Willow sniffed her phone. "Yep, this one smells..." She sucked in a breath so deep it quivered her nostrils. "...like a whole bunch of trouble."

"Her texts stink?" Gussie looked up from her place on the floor, where she sat surrounded by about a hundred different swatches of fabric.

"Like Limburger in the sun." Willow exhaled and scrolled through the last five messages from the high-maintenance bride-to-be, clearing her throat to imitate this ass-pain of a bride. "My MOH and I will arrive at Casa Blanca on the fourth to do a full resort inspection and interview the wedding planning team, please include all amenities, especially all spa treatments."

"So, no groom?" Gussie asked with a derisive snort. "Just the bride and maid of honor to do a resort review and planning session? Sounds like an excuse for a girls' weekend of pampering and freebies, then they'll probably end up holding the wedding at a different resort."

"I doubt she'll find a place that fast." Willow kept reading. "Oh, this is my personal favorite. 'Our villa must have two bedrooms and baths with direct ocean view.'" She rolled her eyes. "Can she not read a map of Florida to see that Barefoot Bay is on the Gulf of Mexico, not the Atlantic Ocean?"

"I don't know if she can read a map, but I can tell you from the swatches she sent, she's color-blind." She waved some flesh-toned material.

"Oh, yeah. How are you doing with her 'all tones of sand' color palette selections?"

Gussie lifted a section of pale lace, the material barely covering the purple bangs of today's colorful wig. "You call this a palette? I call it beige, a dull and dangerous state of mind."

"Told you. This..." She squinted at the bride's name again. "Misty Trew is trouble." Willow locked the screen and set the phone on her desk. "Not only does she come with no referral, but who chooses a destination resort a month before the wedding?"

"Someone pregnant," Gussie suggested.

"Or someone the last bridal consultant dropped."

"Or someone"—the third member of the Barefoot Brides wedding planning team popped into the office doorway, her whole face covered by a giant gift basket—"with a mongo budget who can get what they want." Ari inched the basket to the side, her midnight eyes and jet-black hair contrasting the cream-colored bow around the cellophane wrapping. "Which is why I made this over-the-top welcome basket. Any volunteers to take it over to their villa? Bride and maid arrive in a few hours."

Willow pushed back and stood. "I'll go. I need the exercise."

Ari choked softly. "Says the woman who ran two miles this morning."

"Should have done four," Willow said as she took the

basket, eyeing the mouthwatering contents. "Especially if I knew I'd be left alone with this box of truffles." She caressed the cellophane, giving a playful gasp when her fingers found an open seam. "Ooh, easy access, too."

"As if you'd touch a truffle," Ari teased.

"I have my moments. And our bride-to-be has a long list of demands, er, requests she sent, so I better make sure Artemisia is fully stocked right down to the Rosa Regale champagne that is, and I quote, '*The only thing I can possibly drink.*'"

"Spike it with Prozac while you're over there," Gussie suggested.

Laughing, Willow gathered the basket to her chest and headed out of the Casa Blanca Resort & Spa administration area where Barefoot Brides had its one-office headquarters. The upscale resort hummed with the activity of a typical Friday morning, gearing up for a busy weekend in Barefoot Bay.

Outside, the sun was high enough to make the gulf—*not the ocean*—sparkle turquoise, the water laced with white froth on a picture-perfect late-April morning. Bright yellow umbrellas spilled over the sand like lemon drops in the sunshine.

Willow chose the shady red-brick path that cut through the resort and led to each of the private villas, all named for different North African flowers in keeping with the Moroccan-inspired architecture. With each tap of her feet on the walkway, she let herself slip deeper in love with this piece of paradise.

They had to make this work, no matter how many high-maintenance brides put them through the wringer. Pooling their individual wedding consultant businesses to form Barefoot Brides had been her idea. The three of them moving here to run destination weddings at Casa Blanca was not only a unique selling point for clients…it was the key to Willow's personal happiness.

And she was happy, she reminded herself, humming a little, as though that soundtrack would prove the very thought to be true. So very happy and healthy and three thousand miles from California. New woman, new life, new everything.

Happy, happy, happy. The humming might be a little over-the-top, though.

Instead, she inhaled the briny bay air, stopping at the wrought iron gate that opened to Artemisia. Positioned on a rise, and angled so that the patio and pool faced the Gulf of Mexico, this butter-yellow villa was one of Willow's favorites on the property. Setting the basket on the terra cotta steps that led up to the front door, she pulled her resort ID that doubled as a master key out of her pocket, unlocked the door, and scooped up the goodies to go inside.

The living area was darkened from sunshades on the windows, cool and quiet, with the welcoming aroma of sweet gardenias left by the Casa Blanca cleaning staff. Heading to the kitchen, Willow froze mid-step at the sound of…was that running water? No. A footstep? She listened for a minute, heard nothing, then—

"Will ya…will ya…be my girl?"

Singing. Someone was singing. Well, more like howling. Woefully off-key.

"Gotta know if it's real, gotta know it's forevah!"

Willow's heart dropped so hard and fast the basket almost went with it. Was this some kind of joke? *That song*? That crappy, tacky, mess of metal that…that *pretended* to be a love song and paid for college and cars and everything else she'd had?

No one at this whole resort, on this island, or, hell, in the whole state of Florida, except for Ari and Gussie, could possibly know—

"No foolin' around, for worse or for bettah!"

Son of a bitch, who'd found her out? Did Ari or Gussie tell someone that Willow's father was a rock 'n' roll household name? They'd *promised* not to.

Gripping the basket so tight she could crack the wicker, she marched into the hallway that separated the two bedrooms, calling out, "Excuse me!"

"Will ya...will ya...be my..."

"Hey!" She lowered the basket to peer over the top and...oh. *Oh.*

Back.

Ass.

Muscles.

Ink.

Ass again. It deserved a second look.

"*Girrrrl!*" Tanned, muscular arms whacked the air, and a dark head of wet hair shook, sending droplets all the way down to...oh, really, that rear end was the most beautiful thing she'd ever seen.

"Come and take it, don't ya fake it, we can make—"

She opened her mouth, but nothing came out. The words caught in her throat, lost as her gaze locked on the bare-naked man air-drumming like a raving lunatic in the middle of the bedroom, totally unaware she stood behind him.

"Luh-uuuuve..." He destroyed the note, and not in the good way her father intended when he wrote the song. No, Donny Zatarain would probably weep if he heard his signature rock anthem being butchered by this idiot wearing nothing but noise-canceling headphones.

"Excuse me!"

His arms never missed a beat of the drum solo she had memorized before she was five years old, each stroke tensing and bulging muscles she hadn't even known existed. She opened her mouth to call out again, but that was a waste of time. Anyway, this particular feast for the eyes was way too good to pass up.

"Will ya, will ya be my *girrrrrl?*"

But that song *had* to stop. She reached into the basket and grabbed the first thing her fingers touched: a nice ripe Florida orange. Yanking it out, she lobbed it as he hit the high C on "girl," except he didn't come anywhere near C, and the orange didn't go anywhere near him.

Still, he spun around, jumping into a wide, threatening stance, both arms out like a warrior ready to attack. She blocked her face with the basket, peeking through the top spray of cellophane, silently thanking Ari for choosing clear.

Whoa, that was a big…man.

"What the…" he muttered after a second, whipping off the headset. "I didn't hear you come in. You can put that down out there. Thanks."

She didn't move. Not even her eyes, which were riveted to…his…his…him.

"Thanks," he repeated, the word tinged with impatience. "You can leave now."

What if her client had come face-to-face with this? With that exposed…giant…breathtaking… She'd think this took "welcome package" to a whole new level.

"No, *you* can leave, because you are not in the right villa," she said.

He scowled. Well, she assumed he scowled. It was difficult to see his face because she couldn't stop looking at the rest of him.

"I'm in the right villa. Isn't this Art..Arte…some flower that starts with an A?"

Was she in the wrong place? No, of course not.

Get a grip, Willow. He was just a naked man—okay, an exceptionally stunning naked man—and she had a job to do here. Which was to get him out of the villa.

"Artemisia," she supplied, her arms starting to burn from holding the basket high enough to cover her face but still see. "And, yes, you *are* in the wrong villa, because we have guests booked to arrive soon, and you're not one of them."

He turned his hands skyward in a less threatening gesture, not that his hotter-than-a-thousand-suns body wasn't threatening enough. "Yes, I am," he said. "And if you will please turn around, miss, and leave that in the living room, we're cool."

"No, we are not cool." There was an understatement. "Because I'm pretty sure you have more, um, body hair than the bride or maid of honor we're expecting."

He took a step closer, and she hoisted the basket high enough to completely cover her face.

"Man," he said

"Excuse me?"

"I'm a man." With two hands, he lowered the basket. "As you've obviously noticed. *Man* of honor. Not *maid*."

The words registered, but not the meaning, because she was face-to-face with his broad chest and wide shoulders and a deep-purple tattoo of…oh, really? Was this God's idea of a joke? That was the earth and star on the cover of *Zenith*, the number-one best-selling Z-Train record of all time. "Really?"

"Really. I'm the man of honor in Misty Trew's wedding." His tone was a mix of waning tolerance and growing amusement.

She finally lifted her eyes, finally coherent enough to process what he'd said, and realize the mistake was hers. "I get it," she whispered, meeting cocoa-colored eyes as rich and inviting as the truffles in her arms, and a mouth that could be forgiven for whatever sour notes he'd hit with it, and...

Once more, the world slipped out from under her, this time because recognition nearly buckled her knees. "You're..." Her throat closed.

"The man of honor."

"No, you're..." The one who...the boy who...no, now the man who...crushed her spirit.

"A male version of the maid."

"You're..." Nick Hershey.

"Naked," he supplied, adding a slow, sexy, sinful smile. "But you're not."

She clung to the basket as if it were the last logical thing on earth because right now, it was. "I'm not..." How long had it been? Ten or eleven years since she'd lived in a dorm at UCLA? And he'd been right down the hall. "Thinking straight."

"Clearly." He laughed and reached for the basket. "Here, let me take your junk so you can stop staring at mine." Placing the basket on the dresser, he held up a hand. "Just a sec. I'll get your tip."

"No tip, I'm not with the resort." The rote answer fell out of her mouth as he took a few steps, forcing Willow to stare some more at that round, hard handful of Nick Hershey's world-class ass before he disappeared into the en suite. "That ought to be illegal," she murmured on a sigh.

"So should breaking into a hotel room," he replied.

"I wasn't expecting...anyone. Or at least, not a man." Buck-naked. And she sure as hell hadn't been expecting the guy she'd tried to give her virginity to one slightly tipsy night after finals. *Tried* being the operative word, because he…

A dose of shame and a splash of self-pity mixed into a cocktail of humiliation, rising up to choke her. He'd turned her down cold and flat.

Willow rooted for a coherent thought, trying to center on the present. The bride was from New York. Nick was from California. How was it even possible that he was standing here in Mimosa Key, Florida?

It didn't matter. He was here, and a key member of the wedding party she was coordinating, so Willow would have to maintain professionalism and get control. She closed her eyes, willing her body and brain to get in line, the way she always did when she wanted to be stronger than whatever temptation or distraction threatened her well-honed control.

"So, you're a friend of Misty's?" she asked.

"Not exactly. Her brother is supposed to be here, but he's still deployed." He stepped back into the room, a towel wrapped around his hips, tied low, exposing a trail of dark hair that ran from his belly button down to his…no, no one could ever call what she'd just seen *junk*. "I'm doing him a favor and acting as Misty's second-in-command."

"She doesn't have a girlfriend to be the maid of honor?"

His brow quirked. "Have you met Misty?" he asked.

"No, not yet."

"Well, you'll understand when you see her. She's a model," he said, like that explained it. And, having been raised by one, it kind of did. "She's not exactly swimming in female companionship."

He crossed his arms and took another long, slow look at her, his gaze leaving a trail of heat, followed by goosebumps, and more heat. Still not even the slightest shadow of recognition. No surprise there.

Very few—actually none—of the people who knew her in college would recognize Willow Ambrose as Willie Zatarain. Not even someone who'd always said hello and made a point of being kind to her...but not *that* kind. Not kind or even drunk enough to sleep with a woman who outweighed him by more than a hundred pounds.

That was then, and this was...getting awkward.

"You know," he said, as if suddenly aware of how much time had passed while they looked at each other. "In the military, there's a rule that once you've seen someone naked, they get to see you naked."

Suddenly, a flash came back to her. Nick, friendly and even flirtatious when they were in college. His voice—at least when he wasn't singing—still had that smooth, silky quality that poured over her like hot fudge on cold ice cream. And like sundaes, he'd always been a temptation.

But Willow had long ago learned how to conquer temptations, hadn't she? "Good thing I'm not in the military, then. I get a pass."

The vaguest hint of disappointment darkened his eyes, giving her a surprising jolt of satisfaction. "Hey, can't blame a guy for trying. Lieutenant Nick Hershey." He extended his hand for a shake. "You don't work for the hotel, so are you one of the planner girls?"

"The planner girls?" She coughed a soft laugh, mostly to cover the certainty that he didn't remember her. The question was, should she refresh his memory? See the look of utter and abject shock on his face? Endure the questions, the litany of congratulations, and the embarrassment for both of them?

"Sorry, that sounded demeaning as shit, didn't it? I meant are you working for Misty as her wedding consultant?"

"Yes." She finally lifted her hand to slide into his,

fighting a shudder when his warm, large fingers closed over hers.

"And you're…" he prompted.

"I'm…" *A girl you knew a long time ago.* Not that she could blame him. Most days, she didn't recognize herself. "Willow Ambrose."

"Willow." He let the word roll around on his lips, tasting it, nodding as if he liked it a lot, smiling as though meeting her for the first time. Well, wasn't that why she'd ditched the shortened nickname and lopped off her world-famous last name?

"The pleasure is…well, I guess the initial pleasure was yours." He winked, and it hit her heart like a red-hot spark.

"Not the singing part," she teased.

He laughed, a low rumble in his chest that she *knew* could curl toes, melt hearts, and vacuum up phone numbers. "I suck, I know. But that's how I relax. Does your job mean I'll be seeing a lot of you this weekend?" The little bit of hope in his voice tweaked her heart, still not grasping the fact that *he* was flirting with *her.*

"Depends on how much wedding planning you and the BTB are going to do."

"BTB? Wait, don't tell me. Bride That Bitches?"

It was her turn to laugh. "Bride To Be, but your version is often dead-on, too. I thought you and Misty weren't going to be here for a few hours."

"We came from different places, and I got bumped to an earlier flight, and she's…somewhere." He put his hands on his narrow hips, the move accentuating his chest and pecs and stunningly cut abs. "Want to show me around until she gets here?"

Could she…not tell him? The thought landed in her head with a thud. It would be dishonest not to tell him they'd known each other a dozen years…and a hundred and twenty pounds ago.

Except, he'd known Willie Zatarain, the fat girl in Sproul Hall who had few friends and famous parents. He didn't know Willow Ambrose. And by the way he was looking at her, he wanted to.

The powerful, dizzying, irresistible pull of temptation tugged at her insides. This time, just this one time, temptation kicked her ass.

"Yes," she said softly. "I'll show you around."

Chapter Two

Nick tightened the towel, even though it was exactly the opposite of what he'd like to do with this lovely surprise who couldn't hide her admiration. He was probably looking at her with a similar kind of interest, memorizing the pewter tinge in wide eyes tipped with thick lashes. He was already imagining getting a handful of long, blond hair that was ten different shades of the desert, and tipping her head back to sample the sweet skin of her throat.

"Can you give me a minute to get dressed?" he asked.

Her nod was slow and uncertain, as if agreeing to that change in the scenery wasn't exactly what she wanted. "I'll let the front desk know to have Misty call me when she arrives," she said. "That way she won't wonder where you are."

As she walked out, Nick took a minute to admire her backside—hey, it was only fair—and give his own slow nod of approval. She was easily five-eight in those heels, and the blue cotton dress revealed enough curves to be his kind of woman, and enough toned muscles to be his kind of athlete. A smattering of freckles on a singularly pretty face said her sports were outdoors, and her creamy skin was nature-made.

It's all good, Nicky.

Pulling a pair of cargo shorts and a US Navy T-shirt out of his bag, he mentally high-fived his good luck in getting on the earlier flight. Of course, he'd been planning to work during his spare time, and had hoped he'd have the afternoon to try to get past the latest sticking point, but this new development was too intriguing. Inspiring, even.

And he needed inspiration more than he needed productivity. That's why she'd caught him breaking the rules and listening to Z-Train at way too many decibels for a SEAL on medical leave due to severe hearing loss. So she was *safely* inspiring, which was even better than his favorite music.

As he came around the corner into the living room, he found her perched on the armrest of a chair, phone to one ear. She looked up and met his gaze, long enough for a little zing of...no, too soon for chemistry. Attraction? Definitely, but there was something else about her, too.

Familiarity. That was it. She reminded him of someone. An actress? An ex?

That sense disappeared when she stood, clicked off her call, and put a hand on her hip. No, he wouldn't forget a body that luscious, or a smile that...faltered at the sight of him. He couldn't decide if she was clinging to professionalism because of his relationship to her client, or trying like hell not to give in to mutual attraction.

Didn't matter. He'd get past her defenses if he wanted to. And, damn, he wanted to.

"You look disappointed," he noted, unable to keep the bit of wounded pride from his voice.

"Still getting used to seeing you..." She paused and then added, "Dressed."

He gave a shameless wink. "The opposite is easy enough to arrange."

"Not if it includes bad air-drumming and even worse singing." She was teasing him, but he caught the stiff-arm in her message, and her air of self-protection.

"Come on, we'll tour." She waved him to the door, but he slipped by to open it for her.

"You think my air-drumming is bad, you should hear my air guitar."

She laughed at the joke, stepping into the sunshine that made her hair gleam like wheat stalks blowing in the breeze. "I heard enough."

"Not a Z-Train fan, I take it."

Her foot stumbled on a brick, and he instantly caught her elbow. "Whoa," he said. "Heels might not be the right choice on these bricks."

"You're right." She gave him a quick smile, reaching down to hook her finger in the back of her sandal, taking one off, then the other. The simplest act of disrobing, but man, it kicked him in the southern region. "When in Barefoot Bay…" she said playfully, dangling her shoes from one finger.

"Do as the Barefootians do." He slipped off his own Docksides, and they left both pairs of shoes on the front step. It took everything in him not to reach for her hand. "Where to?"

"You'll get the full resort, spa, restaurant, and destination wedding tour later when Misty's here, so why don't I show you the beach?"

"The beach is why I'm here," he said as they crossed a shady stone pathway too narrow for cars, but just right for golf carts and people.

"I thought you were here to be Misty's man of honor."

"That, too," he said quickly. "But I was hoping a little of the opposite coast might clear my head. I'm a California boy, but I guess your gulf isn't much like the Pacific."

"Mmm." She covered her eyes to shade them from the sun, getting a little ahead of him. "Nothing like the Pacific. The Gulf of Mexico is calm and serene. No surfing here. Just trolling in lots of gentle waves."

"Are you from around here?" he asked, trying to catch up, but she was making it a challenge, walking with purpose. And that purpose seemed to be to avoid eye contact with him.

"Actually, I moved here only a few months ago to start the Barefoot Brides wedding planning business with two friends. We came here for a tour and fell in love."

Damn. No wonder she had her shields up. "Who's the lucky guy?"

She lowered her hand, a frown pulling out her brows and then she smiled with understanding. "No, we fell in love with the *place*. Gussie and Ari—they're my business partners—were on the board of the American Association of Bridal Consultants for a year with me, and during that time, we had to visit about fifteen different resorts."

"Tough call of duty."

She laughed, a sweet sound that lilted up with a musical note, floating on that air of familiarity again. Had he heard that distinctive laugh before? "I know, right? All those free spa treatments and sandy beaches."

"Beats what I did for the last few years," he murmured.

"You were in the military?"

"Am," he corrected. "Navy SEAL."

She gave the impressed look he'd long ago gotten used to seeing on civilians when they heard "Navy SEAL." Over the past decade or so, his arm of the Special Forces had attained celebrity status.

"Are you on leave?" she asked.

"Medical," he confirmed, mentally digging for another topic. "So, at the end of your stint on this board you got to pick one resort to work at?"

"Not quite that simple," she said as they reached a quaint wooden bridge that arched over a thatch of sea oats and led to a wide, pristine beach. "The idea of opening our own firm took hold early in the year, and then we started looking at each resort as a potential new home for our business. We fell in love with Barefoot Bay."

She gestured toward the beach, taking his attention to the view, which pulled a slow whistle of appreciation from him. "I can see why." Before him stretched white sand and turquoise water, all glittering under a powder-blue sky and bathed in balmy sunshine. "Nice place to work."

"It certainly is," she agreed merrily.

"How's business?" he asked. "Did the move work out well for you?

"So far. We all had our own individual wedding consulting businesses, with different areas of expertise, so we've made a good blend. I'm an F&B specialist."

He took a guess. "Food and beverage?"

"Exactly. Ari Chandler handles set design and décor."

"You need a set designer to have a wedding?"

She gave him a playful elbow. The quick tap of skin against skin made him want more. "Have you ever been to a destination wedding?"

"Actually, no. Only the standard church-and-country club kind."

"Well, this is different. It's all about the atmosphere, the resort, the ultimate getaway, and, of course, the bride."

"Not the groom?"

She angled her head. "I honestly don't know Misty's groom's name."

"Steven…something." He'd met the guy exactly once, at a bar in Manhattan, and all he remembered was an expensive suit with a phone to his ear.

"You don't know him?" she asked.

"Like I said, I'm here as a favor for my buddy, Misty's twin brother, Jason. But I get your point. It's all about the bride that day." He threw her a look, unable to resist getting this critical piece of information about her. "Have you had that day yet, personally?"

Her smile was wry as she realized how thinly disguised that fishing expedition really was. "No, I haven't."

He waited for more—like a question about his marital status—but got nothing. After a massively awkward beat, he tried something less personal. "What about your other business partner? What does she handle?"

"Gussie McBain is our stylist, so anything related to fashion and beauty—dresses, makeup, that kind of thing—is her specialty. Barefoot Brides is an all-inclusive service for destination weddings at the Casa Blanca Resort & Spa."

Both their feet hit the sand at the same moment. "And this is our only stipulation," she added. "Bride, groom, wedding party and guests must go barefoot for the ceremony. They can put on their stilettos during the reception."

"Nice." He wiggled his toes in powder-soft sand, so different from the rough grains of Malibu or Santa Monica. "Definitely not the Pacific."

He tried to keep any judgment out of his voice, but he was a six-foot-surf kind of guy, preferably in a Zodiac with an AK-47 in his hands. This place was a lake, and the only surface watercraft nearby was a large pink inner tube.

"No, it's not the Pacific," she agreed. "And I like that."

The comment pulled his attention back to her. "I'm from there. California. Ever been?"

"Of course." She gestured them closer to the shore. "But you have to appreciate what we have here. A billion seashells, pure-white sand, stunning sunsets, and the perfect place to"—she opened her arms with a grand and sweeping gesture of invitation, looking up with a mix of hope and hype and humor in her eyes—"be a barefoot bride."

He laughed, her charm drawing him in and doing a little to erase that nagging sense of familiarity that pinched his gut again. "You don't have to sell me. I'm merely along for the ride. The decision to have a wedding here is Misty's, not mine."

"Just want to be sure you're on our side."

He almost turned his response to that into a flirtatious tease. He'd like to be on her side. *Of the bed.* But he swallowed that because something about the way she was looking at him made that sensation of déjà vu so powerful that he couldn't ignore it.

But how could he forget a woman like this? He looked hard at her, long enough that she took a few steps away, turning to give him a view of her back and all that flaxen long hair. He couldn't get a read on her, damn it. One minute she was protective and professional, the next she was looking at him like...she knew him, too.

"Come and put your feet in the water," she called.

Even her voice sounded...man, *had* he met her before? "I don't suppose you were ever in the military?" he asked, trying to catch up with her as she ran toward the water.

She threw a *not likely* look over her shoulder and marched on like getting to the gulf was the only thing that mattered.

"Where'd you go to college?" Had she been at UCLA? She was probably about his age, nearing thirty, or a little younger. Where else could he have met her?

"Oh my God, look at this shell!" She stopped dead and fell to her knees. "Perfection."

He caught up to her, intrigued by how intently she studied the seashell. He knew a little bit about people and a lot about women. She was dodging his last question, for sure. Maybe she hadn't gone to college. That would be a sore spot, then.

He cut her some slack and crouched next to her, more to get close than to see what she'd found. "Pretty," he said, looking at the way her lashes fanned out atop well-defined cheekbones.

She lifted her gaze and caught him looking. "I meant the shell."

"I meant you."

Her lips parted with a slight inhale, her gaze moving over his face with an expression of awe. Surely she couldn't be surprised at his compliment—she'd probably heard better on a daily basis. Maybe it was the connection crackling between them, real and strong and very nice.

Or maybe they *had* met before.

"This is going to sound like such a stupid line," he ventured, watching her eyes take on the shade of sky behind her. "But do I know you from somewhere?"

She froze, didn't even seem to breathe, staying silent long enough for him to reach for the shell but capture her whole hand instead. "Let me put it a better way. *Can* I know you? Will you have dinner with me tonight?"

"Tonight? I...I...with Misty?"

He laughed softly. "No, with me. From what I observed, Misty doesn't eat."

She frowned and finally managed to get her head to move in the negative, even though something in her expression told him she didn't really want to say no. "I don't know. I have...so much stuff planned."

"Cancel it." He gave her hand a squeeze, and she looked so intently into his eyes, he *knew* he'd met her before. But not her. Someone just like her. Maybe she had a sister? Or he'd dreamed about her? Hell, if he believed in reincarnation, he'd say they'd known each other in another life. "I'm only here for a few days."

"Okay, Nick."

That pang of familiarity hit hard again, frustrating him deep inside, like when he had a word on the tip of his tongue and couldn't quite snag it. "Willow." He heard the hope in his voice. Hope that he'd figure out how he knew her. Hope that she felt the same attraction.

She slowly nodded, as if to say, *Yes, that's me.*

"Don't think I've ever known anyone by that name." Or had he?

"It's unusual." She stood suddenly, leaving him crouched on the sand, staring at the middle of her body. "We better get you back to the villa. Misty will be here, and surely you want to, you know, sing some more."

He came up slowly, using the time to really appreciate her curves and shape, brushing some sand off his knees. "She'll find us. I want to put my feet in the water."

"I better get back to the office. We have so much to prepare for your weekend so we can wow Misty." She gave a quick smile. "I can tell she's going to be an *exacting* bride."

He ignored the comment, too focused on her. One thing he'd learned in training and on the hairy edge of life-and-death, you never swallow, hide, bury, or otherwise ignore your gut feelings or let questions go unasked. Life's too short and information is power.

"What just happened?" he asked directly. "You did say you'd go out with me, right?"

She looked at him hard, searching his face again. "Um, Nick, there's something I have to—"

"There you are! I've been looking all over for you!"

They both turned to see a woman marching over the wooden bridge, her long brown ponytail swinging with purpose, baggy white pants and a see-through tank top hanging off her slender frame. Misty was so different from her twin, Jason. She looked as if a strong breeze could blow her away, while her brother was the size of a boulder and just as strong.

"Didn't you ask to have her call?" Nick asked Willow.

"Yes." She slipped her phone out of her pocket and glanced at it to see if she'd missed a call. "She didn't."

They started toward Misty, and he could have sworn he heard Willow let out a sigh of relief, or maybe she was bracing herself to meet the "exacting" client.

"Hello," Willow called out, her tone much lighter now. "I'm sorry. I took your man of honor on a tour."

Misty didn't move as they hustled closer, staying put on the bridge, as if she preferred not to get sand in her toes.

"Hey there," Nick said as they reached her, bending down to give Misty a quick hug. He didn't know her well— he'd met her only once, on his way home from Afghanistan during a stop in New York City. But he had to remember this was a favor to a guy he owed his life to, so he was always kind, no matter how much the crispy, self-absorbed model rubbed him the wrong way.

Her attention was riveted on Willow. "Are you..."

"Willow Ambrose," she said, holding out her hand. "The front desk was supposed to give you my number to—"

"Oh, they did, but..." She squinted at Willow's face and leaned back, giving her a thorough and complete—and pretty awkward—once-over. "There's no way you're Willie."

22

Willow paled a little. "Willow," she corrected. "Willow Ambrose."

But Misty was having none of it. "Oh my God! You *are* Willie Zatarain."

What? Nick whipped his head to look at Willow. What had Misty said? Willie Zata—

"I'm…" She fought for a word that didn't come, ghost-white now and definitely avoiding his eyes.

"Willie Zatarain?" He choked the name, trying to comprehend what was hitting his brain.

"I've seen pictures of you at your parents' place in New York," Misty said. "You look…different. You're…so…"

"Willie?" The girl he knew in college? Oh…*wow*.

Finally, *finally*, she looked at him, and all that sense of vague familiarity slapped him with unbelievable recognition. But Misty stepped between them, already spewing chatter like sniper fire.

"Your mother is like, well, you know, my mother," Misty babbled, totally unaware of the dynamic of his shock and Willow's—Willie's—attempt to ignore it. "Ona's been a mentor to me ever since I did her first runway show and we got *so* close, like this." She held up two fingers smashed together. "And your dad, oh my God, I love him. But you? You are—"

"Willie Zatarain," Nick said one more time, the question out of his voice. "I know you."

"Well, you know her *father*," Misty said, still clueless. "He's a rock legend. And her mother is Ona Z, the a*ma*zing fashion designer who used to be a supermodel."

"I know." Then the real truth hit him: She'd known who he was from the first minute they met. "We know each other," he said. "We went to UCLA together."

23

Willow merely nodded, finally managing to look at him. "Yeah."

Misty drew back. "Get out! You two know each other?"

"I didn't recognize you," he said. Because, whoa, she was half the girl she was in college and ten times more beautiful. She was the girl who...

Shit. He managed not to cringe, their last conversation coming to his memory with stark relief. No wonder she hadn't come clean. "But you said you're not married. Why the name change?"

"I dropped my family's name and now use my middle name for privacy purposes," she explained.

"Of course you didn't recognize her," Misty said, pointing up and down Willow's body. "She's lost a person or two of weight. Your mother didn't tell me."

Willow ignored Misty and looked at him. "I'm sorry," she whispered softly.

She was sorry? He was the dick who—

"What are you sorry for?" Misty demanded.

"Exactly," Nick said quickly. "I'm the one who should be sorry for..." A clumsy rejection that had left her in tears.

"For asking me out?" Willow asked.

Oh, great. And now she thought he wouldn't have asked her out if he'd have known who she was.

But would he have?

Nick opened his mouth to assure her of the answer, but Misty let out a hoot.

"You asked her out already? Damn, boy. Jason said you were a ladies' man with the well-earned handle of Kiss, but, whoa, that was fast."

"Kiss?" Willow asked.

"It's the last name," he explained. "Hershey."

Misty shielded her eyes. "Can we get out of this horrible sun? Every ray is aging me more."

"And yet she wants a wedding on the beach," Nick murmured as he and Willow waited a beat before following the other woman.

"So, what were you sorry about?" Willow asked.

Was now the time to apologize for how he'd turned her down when she offered him everything she had to give? Or was he just being arrogant to think she even remembered that?

"Nick?" she urged.

He went for easy and casual, putting a light hand on her shoulder to nudge her toward Misty. "Sorry if I, uh, didn't do justice to your dad's song," he muttered.

"Didn't do justice? *Annihilation* is more accurate." Her pretty mouth tipped in an easy smile that he wished reached her eyes. But it didn't. "Don't worry. I'll get you back...*Kiss*."

She slipped out of his touch and followed her client, leaving Nick staring at her and finally comprehending all of the mixed signals he'd been getting. "Hope that's a promise and not a threat," he said, just loud enough for her to hear.

Chapter Three

The next hour was brutal for Willow. She regretted not telling Nick who she was before he asked her out, and now, of course, he was squirming in discomfort. Everything was magnified by Misty Trew's endless verbal diarrhea. Not about her ideas for the wedding, which would have been understandable. Not about the pros and cons of using this resort, which would have been reasonable. But *all* about her "life-altering, mind-blowing, soul-shifting" relationship with Donny and Ona Zatarain.

If Willow heard "They are like surrogate parents to me!" one more time, she actually thought she might throw up.

Because if they really were that close, then wouldn't Misty know that Willow hadn't seen her mother in three years and they barely spoke? Was the bride-to-be getting some wretched satisfaction over flaunting her relationship with Willow's parents when she had to know that Willow had no such relationship with them? At least, not with Ona, and not much of one with Donny.

The minute she could, Willow hauled her guests over to the Barefoot Brides office to introduce them to Gussie and Ari and start the planning meeting. After that, she got out a few pictures, samples, and checklists, and then grabbed an excuse to step away and get some air.

"I have some refreshments prepared," she said, pushing all the materials at Nick and Misty. "Go ahead and start without me."

She didn't make it ten steps into the hallway before Ari caught up with her and grabbed her arm. "Are you leaving the clients alone?"

"They're not alone." Willow didn't want to get into a long explanation, not here in the hall, not now. Later, when she and Ari and Gussie had left the office and gathered at their home on the other end of the island, she'd tell them everything. "You can start without me," Willow said quickly.

"What's the matter with you?" Ari demanded. "This bride contacted you, and that means she's your client. Why are you running off to get food? I'll do it."

"I know she's my client, Ari. I've opened the files and put together the presentation. But I'm also the F&B person, and Chef Ian already made me hors d'oeuvre samples for them. Food is my problem, just like this bride." And her *man* of honor.

"Hey." Ari's sharp gaze softened a little. "I know you think she's a pain, and she talks about your mother like the woman walks on water—"

"Which you know she doesn't."

Ari nodded, a close enough friend to have intimate knowledge of how Willow struggled with her over-controlling mother. "But she's still a client, and one who's in a hurry. We don't have a wedding booked for the weekend she wants, and we need her to..." Her voice faded as Willow shook her head, maybe a little too vehemently. "What is it?" Ari demanded.

Willow looked over her shoulder and gestured for Ari to follow her into the kitchen. "I don't want to talk here."

"Did you hear her say my mother referred her?" Willow asked as they headed down the hall.

"I did, and I think that's awesome, Willow."

She threw Ari a *what the hell?* look.

"Maybe Ona wants to reconcile," Ari suggested.

"Fat chance."

"Pun intended?"

"Probably. But reconciliation would mean my mother knew she'd done something wrong." Ona was far too self-absorbed to get to that point. Had she even realized that she hadn't seen her own daughter in three years, not since Willow had become so adept at using travel as an excuse, aided by her parents' crazy bicoastal lifestyle? She'd even managed to avoid her father, except for the occasional lunch or phone call. She hadn't seen him in, oh, seventy-five pounds.

"She must know," Ari said. "You need to give her some credit."

Willow didn't answer, not wanting to spend one more minute of her energy thinking about her mother. She wasn't the only problem here. Willow bit her lip, thinking about Nick. There was no time to go into the whole college history, even if it could be summed up in a few short sentences.

We lived in the same dorm. He was nicer than most. One night I hit on him. He couldn't get away fast enough.

"But the fact that your mom referred a bride means she obviously cares about your life and success," Ari said, still stuck on the obvious issue of Ona's involvement.

"Doubtful. I guess Misty and my mother are..." *Inseparable* was the word Misty had used, twice—"Business associates. Misty models for the Ona Z line." Which consisted of skinny-girl clothes that Willow had never owned in her life, no matter how much Ona longed for her daughter to be able to wear her designs.

"Well, if you want my opinion," Ari said, "I think this is the universe trying to get you and your mom to have a relationship again."

"Then the universe can suck it."

They entered the kitchen, assaulted by the sharp aromas of sizzling garlic, onions, and basil. Chef Ian must be going Italian today. A flurry of servers and prep cooks zipped around Willow as she headed to a service fridge for the tray of scallop BLTs and mascarpone-and-prosciutto cannoli the chef had prepared.

As she slid out the tray, Ari was right there, reaching for her hands. "Girl, you are vibrating! This is more than some model who wears your mother's clothes."

Did her friend have to be so damn in touch with people's feelings? Nothing got by Ari. Willow closed her eyes, blocking out the clanging of china and the sound of the chef bellowing out orders in a British accent as the Casa Blanca staff geared up for the lunch rush.

"It was a surprise, that's all," she finally said, nodding to the service bar. "Can you hold this while I make some drinks for them?"

Wordlessly, Ari followed with the tray, standing a few steps away as Willow prepared two flutes of cucumber mint lemonade. "Quit looking at me like that," Willow mumbled.

"Like what? How do you know I'm looking at you?"

"I can feel it."

"I'm trying to figure out what's eating you."

"I just told you. Come on, let's go." As they re-entered the hall that led to the business offices, Gussie almost slammed into them, running around the corner.

Willow let out a soft shriek, managing not to spill the drinks.

"You went to college with that guy?" Gussie sputtered.

Oh Lord. That didn't take long. "Yeah, I did."

Once more, she could feel Ari's penetrating gaze. "I knew it wasn't the bridezilla," Ari muttered.

"What wasn't?" Gussie asked. "What's going on?"

Willow tamped down another groan of frustration. "Nothing is going on."

"Except that you're about to jump out of your skin," Ari said. "And I guess now I know it's more than just dear old mom that's got your panties in a bunch."

Willow blew out a puff of resignation. "Yes, I knew Nick Hershey when I was a freshman in college, which was, oh, let's see, eleven years ago. In some freak coincidence, he's a friend of Misty's brother, an Army buddy."

"Navy," Ari corrected. "And there is no such thing as coincidence, freak or otherwise."

"Navy *SEALs,* thank you very much," Gussie added, patting her fluttering heart. "Was he that gah-*orgeous* in college?"

"I never noticed." At their double looks of doubt, she sighed. "Okay, yes. He was a good-looking guy, lived in the same dorm as I did, and we passed in the hall a few times. End of story."

They looked at each other like it was so not the end of the story.

"Were you friends with him?" Ari asked.

"Did you date him?" Gussie one-upped.

"No, Gussie, I did not." They couldn't help it—neither one of these two women, though they were her best friends now—had known her back then. When they met, about a year and a half ago, Willow looked like any other slightly overweight woman who was working her buns off to work her buns off. They'd cheered her on as she lost the last fifty pounds, but hadn't known her when she'd tipped the scales at two sixty.

They knew, empirically, that Willow had been overweight her whole life. She'd shared that with them. But there were no pre-weight-loss pictures of her around since Willow had destroyed any she'd had. They couldn't see Willow Ambrose as she sometimes, all too often, still saw herself: as Willie Zatarain, fat girl.

But that "gah-*orgeous*" Navy SEAL knew exactly who and what she'd been…and had rejected her.

"Still, it's a bizarre coincidence that he's here," Gussie said.

It was Ari's turn to shake her head furiously. "There is absolutely no such thing as coincidence," she announced. "Nothing happens by chance. I firmly believe that the universe has a plan, and you are being carried along in it."

"The only thing being carried along is our business loan, so why don't we get in there and make some money, ladies, before they leave and go to Naples to visit the Ritz." Willow said.

But Ari didn't move. "The universe works in funny ways, my friend. He's here for a reason."

"Yeah, to be in a wedding we are hoping to hold at this resort." Willow tugged the mantle of control over her shoulders, always safer when she had that. "So, let's stop talking about the past, and figure out how to give her a kick-ass wedding, regardless of what baggage she lugs into our lives." She powered past both of them and led the way back to the office.

"Speaking of lugging baggage," Gussie muttered.

Willow almost risked spilling a drink to give her the

finger over her shoulder, but it wasn't worth the risk, or the joke. Gussie was right, and Willow had to leave her bags out here in the hallway and get down to business.

Her relationship with her mother was moot, and her brief, unpleasant history with Nick Hershey was over. *Ever onward!* Clinging to the two words that got her down one pound a week for one hundred and sixty consecutive weeks, Willow swept into the office, where Nick and Misty waited at the small conference table by the window.

Nick had his chair pushed back to balance himself on two legs, arms crossed over his impressive chest. He was listening to Misty, who leaned close, but she stopped whispering the moment Willow walked in.

"Refreshments," Willow said cheerily, gesturing for Ari to put the tray on the table. "I wanted to give you an opportunity to taste-test a few samples of our chef's work while you tell us your vision for the big event."

Misty inched closer, staring. "How much did you lose?"

Nick slammed the front legs of his chair on the floor with a thud. Guess he was interested in that answer, too. Heat crawled up Willow's chest as her friends took seats at the table. "Much," she answered.

"Ona must be thrilled that you can finally wear her clothes."

The warmth moved into her cheeks as she made a show of giving them the plates and linens she'd tucked on the tray.

"This part of the meeting is about you," she said pointedly. "We'll listen while you tell us what we like to call your themes and dreams, your every wedding fantasy." She managed not to even look at Nick at the same time she said the last word. Did he remember she'd told him that he was her fantasy?

Right before he bolted like a scared jackrabbit.

Misty pushed her plate away with that skinny-girl disinterest in food that Willow never understood or trusted. "I think we should build the entire theme around my dress, which is, of course, an Ona Z custom-made original." She gave a sly smile. "Would you like to see the sketches?"

The sketches were possibly the last thing in the world Willow wanted to see. "Of course, but that would be Gussie's department."

Gussie settled into her chair, with Ari next to her. "I'd love to see the sketches," she said, enthusiasm genuine. "I absolutely adore Ona Z designs. But do you want to tell us about the overview for the day first? Afternoon, evening, number of guests, how many bridesmaids, that kind of thing?"

Misty shot a thumb to Nick, who'd just put a cannoli in his mouth. "There's my bridesmaid."

Willow met his gaze across the table, her heart stuttering as he grinned around the sweet, cheesy treat between his teeth. She didn't know which she wanted to eat more—mascarpone or man. Both, she thought, feeling a physical longing churn in her stomach as her desire glands rocketed into overdrive.

That's all she was feeling, she reminded herself sharply. A glandular reaction to sex and food. Nothing more. She'd learned to control one a few years ago, and she certainly could figure out how to control the other. Nick was nothing but six feet of negative impulses, easily kept at bay by her finely tuned willpower.

She would simply treat him like she would a gallon of mint chocolate chip. Ignore, retreat, replace with something more appealing. Like…like…God, nothing was more appealing than that man.

Misty fished through a bag the size of Willow's laundry

sack and pulled out a file, smacking it on the table. "You'll love these," she said to Willow. "Mama O's a genius."

"Mama O?" Holy hell. By the end of this ordeal, she'd be face-first in a gallon of mint chocolate chip.

Misty flipped open the file folder.

Her mother's sketches were so damn...awesome. And unique. And beautiful. And created for a girl who...well, who could carry off the name Willow.

"Holy cow," Gussie exclaimed, turning the paper to face her. "That is absolutely stunning."

Misty smiled, her angular, sharp features stark and clean and beautiful. Willow didn't want to hate her. That emotion was small, and she was above that kind of petty jealousy. Usually. Sometimes. Maybe not right now.

"Now you understand the sand palette," Misty said. "Is that color not to die for?"

Nick leaned forward and picked up his third scallop. "The only palette I understand is the one in my mouth. Did you make these?" he asked Willow.

She shook her head. "Our chef is amazing."

Misty clapped her hands with the satisfaction of a person granted a brilliant idea. "Here's what we'll do," she announced. "I'll go over the setting and fashion with these two"—she pointed to Ari and Gussie—"and, Nick, you and Willie go meet in the kitchen or whatever and figure out the menu."

"Willow," she corrected.

"Good idea," Nick said at exactly the same time.

Misty looked relieved. "Honestly, don't take this personally, but food is the part I'm the least interested in, and you two, well..." She lifted a shoulder. "You have a lot in common. You know each other, and you both love...food."

Willow opened her mouth to protest, but Nick was up in a flash. "Let's go."

For one long second, Willow debated which temptation to give in to—an hour with Nick Hershey, or the need to punch the client in the nose.

Once again, Nick won.

Chapter Four

The kitchen was chaotic, the dining room filling up with the lunch crowd, and all of the Casa Blanca offices were in use. After Willow gathered up a few files of menu selections and price lists, she was forced to take Nick outside and sit at a table near the kidney-shaped resort pool.

She talked too much, fanned herself too often, and did her level best to keep the conversation professional and avoid any rehash of their meager past. To his credit—maybe to his relief—Nick seemed to go along with that.

Until he got through the third sample menu, then pushed it away, leaning back on the two legs of his chair again, a position so natural she imagined he took it at every table. This time, the move inched him out from under the shade of the umbrella, allowing sunshine to pour over his tanned face.

"I don't have a clue why she asked me to do this," he said.

"To be in her wedding?" Willow asked.

"To look at menus. I know why I'm in the wedding." He sounded a little sad, or mad, she couldn't quite tell which, but there was definitely some emotion there.

"Because her brother doesn't have a chance of getting home in time?"

He flipped the menu card around on the table like a pinwheel, drawing her gaze to his strong hands and blunt fingertips. "Slim to none, I'd say."

"It's very nice of you to do this for him."

"Least I could do," he said. "Jason Trew saved my ass—er, life."

And what an ass, er, life, it was. "That's good." She gave a quick smile at how lame that response was. "I mean, obviously."

He came down on the two front legs of the chair, slowly and softly this time, his dark gaze slicing her. "So how have you been for all these years?"

So much for keeping things professional. She silently thanked him for not rubbing in the fact that she'd basically lied to him on the beach. Would he believe her if she said she'd been about to tell him how they knew each other when Misty arrived? Didn't matter now.

"Oh, good, fine," she said, trying to brush off the question. "I can put together a really popular and standard menu for Misty and—"

"You look like a different person."

She'd been in enough Weight Watchers meetings to know that most formerly overweight people loved to bask in the success of their diets, but if Willow could have wiped away the person she'd been from the face of the earth and his memory, she would have. "I am," she said simply.

"Is the, uh, 'new you' the reason you dropped Zatarain?"

"There were many reasons," she admitted. "Now I get the chance to be at the front of the alphabet for a change." The quip sounded hollow, but he seemed to accept it. "So why the military?" she asked quickly, anxious to return the conversation to him. "I do remember that you were in ROTC, but hadn't expected you'd make a lifelong career of it."

"Not sure if it is a lifelong career now," he said, reaching up to tap his ear. "I lost hearing in one ear, so the Navy put me on inactive."

Her eyes widened in surprise. "You lost hearing? In combat?"

He didn't answer right away, his gaze moving over her shoulder toward the water beyond them as he nodded. "Yeah."

"How long does that mean you're on leave?"

"I'm waiting to hear. I had surgery done a few months ago, but the results aren't quite at the level required for active SEAL duty. But I just had another test, and I'm waiting to hear the results, but these things can take forever in the military." He glanced from side to side, as if someone might be listening. "In the meantime..." He lifted his shoulder, almost a little embarrassed.

"You're a man of honor," she supplied. "Don't worry, it's not that unusual anymore."

"No, I..." He cleared his throat and shifted in his seat. "I'm writing a book."

He made the admission so fast, she wasn't quite sure she'd heard him. "A book? What's it about?"

"War," he said simply, humor leaving his eyes. "It's my feeble attempt to rewrite history."

She couldn't resist a sympathetic touch to his arm. "Was it so bad you have to rewrite it?"

"Parts were ghastly, parts were...awesome." He laughed softly. "A lot like my book."

Wow...a book. "It's nothing to be ashamed of, Nick."

"It's not exactly what I went through BUD/S to do," he joked. "But then you're the daughter of a songwriter, so maybe you're more forgiving than most."

"I think it's awesome," she said. "How far along are you?"

"I got stuck in what I guess you'd call act two. The murky middle. Actually, I was hoping to get some creative juices flowing here, and that's why I jumped at the chance to come when Jason suggested it."

She smiled. "A little sea and sunshine to help writer's block?"

"And quiet," he added.

"What has you stuck?" she asked, genuinely interested, and so very happy to have the conversation off her and on him.

"'What doesn't have me stuck?' is a better question." He pushed the chair back again, assuming his favorite precarious position. "I can write the battle scenes and the training stuff like I'm reciting the alphabet, but I know a good story has to have more than military action."

"So, it's fiction?" Somehow she imagined him writing about life in the Navy or recounting battles, not a story.

"Mostly, drawn from real life." He leaned forward, scratching his neck as if unsure how to proceed. "I know it has to have some kind of male-female…thing."

She fought a chuckle, more at the way he said it than what he'd said. "A romance?"

"A relationship. Part of the plot is about this SEAL who's been stuck babysitting this embedded journalist, and some shit gets messed up and…" He paused, the emotion brewing in his eyes. "She died. I mean, she dies. In the story."

Her heart dipped, getting the gut feeling that that wasn't fiction. "Well, I'm no expert, but I'm pretty sure you'll lose the happy-ending fans over that one."

"I don't care about a happy ending. I just want to…" He balled a fist and gave the table a gentle tap.

"Rewrite history," she supplied.

"Exactly."

"Why? What will it accomplish?"

"I'm not sure it accomplish anything, but I'd like to try anyway. Plus..." He laughed again. "When the words flow, it's amazing. Almost as good as..." He winked. "It's good."

"I bet." Safe bet that anything with him was good. "So..." She fought the urge to ask everything about this embedded journalist. Was she real? Did he have a relationship with her? None of her business, though, so she fished around for a less personal question. "Is that how you lost your hearing? When things messed up?"

He shook his head. "It was after, unrelated. Like I said, Trew Blue—that's Misty's brother—really came through, but I still fu...messed up my hearing pretty bad."

She remembered how loud she'd had to yell to get his attention. "And do the doctors recommend you listen to rock music with headphones on?"

He laughed, pointing at her with a teasing grin. "No one was supposed to know about that little infraction. Anyway, I keep the sound off in the left ear. But come on." He put his elbows on the table and leaned closer. "Don't you have a weakness, Willow?"

I might be looking at it. "Many," she acknowledged.

"Then you understand that sometimes I can't resist the music." His eyes lit as he studied her. "But you must know that, being the daughter of a guy who wrote some of the best music ever recorded."

"I don't know if I'd go as far as the best ever recorded, but he's my father, so I've never been quite as enamored with his success. I remember you were a fan."

"Yeah, well, I'm sorry about that."

"For liking my dad's music or for butchering the world's most annoying song while you were committing your 'little infraction'?"

"Most annoying song?" His jaw dropped. "*Will Ya, Will Ya* is a work of art."

"Not the way you sang it."

He let out a hearty laugh. "Well, I'm half-deaf, remember?" His face changed after his laugh faded, dark eyes slicing through her, the smile faltering to an even more handsome, serious expression. "But that's not what I'm sorry for."

She waited, part of her knowing what was next.

"I'm sorry I talked to you only because of your dad. Because I thought you could, you know, arrange a meeting."

Her heart sank a little, an old ache pressing down. "Why didn't you just ask me for backstage passes, then? I would have gotten them for you in a heartbeat."

He lifted one of his mighty, strong shoulders. "First of all, I didn't just want backstage passes. I wanted an open door into the music industry. I had delusions of drummer grandeur. But I chickened out every time it came up, so I never asked you."

"Well, that was crazy, especially in a business where who you know is everything. Heck, I could have had my dad bring you into one of the practice sessions at the studio." Anything. She'd have done anything to be closer to him back then.

He closed his eyes and grunted like she'd slammed his solar plexus with a power-punch. "Shit, I'm an idiot."

"Yep."

"But at least I have integrity."

"No, you were right the first time. Idiocy, not integrity."

His smile faded completely. "I meant I had integrity about…that time. That night…when you…" His voiced drifted off to an embarrassing silence.

She sighed, closing her eyes as she lost any hope of

controlling this conversation and steering it in another direction. "And this would be why I wanted to talk about the menu and not the past."

"Why should we dance around the elephant in the room?"

She snorted softly. "Or the elephant that was in that room. Meaning me."

"Willow!" He reached forward and closed his hand around hers, holding too tightly for her to jerk back. "Listen—"

She managed to free her hand. "Nick, you don't owe me an apology. I understand what happened." *Please don't make me relive it.*

"I wasn't honest that night, and it's important that you know why I did what I did."

She knew why. Because he was grossed out by the idea of sex with a girl who weighed more than he did. "I'd rather not rehash it, Nick. It's ancient—"

"I have to," he said, leaning closer. "Otherwise, it's just going to sit between us and fester."

A festering fat elephant. Did he have any more lovely metaphors as memories? "Look, you had every right to turn me down. I was a little drunk, and you were—"

"Not at all drunk."

She swallowed, certain he didn't realize that just made it worse. Tipping her head to one side, she narrowed her eyes at him. "I weighed"—she took in a ragged breath—"a lot. A whole hell of a lot."

"Do you really think that's all I saw?"

"At eighteen? At UCLA, home of the pencil-thin co-ed? Yeah."

"You're wrong. But that night, when you kissed me, I knew I'd be using you to get to your dad. I felt like shit about it. So I took off and acted like I wasn't interested."

She managed a laugh, despite the sting to her heart. "I guess as excuses go, that's a pretty good one." She kept a smile as she looked at him. He didn't need to know that just sitting here talking about it was like reliving that night in the dorm hallway all over. The distant strains of a Linkin Park song coming out of someone's room, the smell of burned popcorn and beer, the scuffed linoleum floor she stared at after he'd walked—no, damn near run—away. Did it matter why he'd turned her down? Either way, it still hurt like a bitch.

"Then you forgive me?" The hope in his voice told her just how important her absolution was.

Fine. He could have it. Why should he know how lasting an effect that night had? Talk about embarrassing. "I do," she assured him. "It's forgiven and forgotten."

He let out an audible sigh and then quickly added, "Good. Then our date's still on for tonight?"

She drew back in surprise. "You still want to go out with me?"

"And not because I want to meet your dad, I swear." He snagged her hand again and gave a confident squeeze. "I'd really like to get to know you now."

Now that she wasn't two hundred and sixty pounds. She gave a shaky smile and purposely didn't answer. Of course she wanted to go out with this hot and sexy Navy SEAL. But he was also a constant reminder that, under all her muscle tone and dieted-down body, she was still Willie Zatarain. And that scared her in a way she couldn't describe.

"As a rule," she said, "I don't spend time with people who knew me…before."

One brow lifted in surprise. "No one?"

She shook her head.

"Then I have an idea." He took out his phone and tapped it. "Give me your address?"

Something told her he wasn't a man who took no for an answer. But did she want to say no? She told him the address, watching his hands work, imaging those hands...working.

He put the phone down and then threaded her fingers with his, slowly lifting her knuckles to his mouth. She eyed him carefully, aware that he was drawing her whole body closer to his but absolutely unable to back up or stop him until his cheek was touching hers. "Guess what we're going to do together, Willow?"

Goosebumps blossomed up her arms as possibilities danced in her head. But she couldn't. She absolutely couldn't give in to this temptation. Didn't she have any control? Of course, she lived by control. She owned control. Control was her bitch.

"What are we going to do?" she asked softly.

He lightly kissed her cheek. "Rewrite history."

And just like that, control evaporated.

Chapter Five

The vague ringing in Nick's left ear had become so much a part of his life that he didn't even hear it anymore. Especially not when his clumsy index fingers somehow found the right keys and his brain dug up some powerful sentences and his laptop screen slowly went from white to words...words that told a story.

He saw everything in his head, as vivid as a movie, but that didn't make him some kind of great writer. That meant he had a good memory for details. The foul stench of a dusty, vacant stairwell in the north observation post. The jab of rubble and stones in his knees as he positioned himself for a long watch over the tiny village of Koka. The grit of sand in his teeth. The tin taste of anticipation.

He remembered it all. But in the story, something dramatic should happen here. Sighting a Taliban fighter? A grenade in the distance? Something to throw this lieutenant over the edge.

Like the tine of a fork against crystal, the ringing sang in his damaged ear, but he leaned forward, taking an imaginary step in the story. Something dramatic *did* happen in that stairwell, he mused. But this wasn't an autobiography. And that conversation probably wouldn't win any literary awards.

It had been...nice. And nice wasn't the stuff of novels.

Still, he closed his eyes and let himself slip back to that first encounter with Charlotte Blaine, which had happened in a moment much like the one he'd described. On watch, in the desert, on a quiet night in a bunker.

The whole team had been pissed as hell to get a female embed, even for the brief time they were on this particular mission. A journalist among them was a pain in the ass, but a woman? That went against everything, injecting high-quality estrogen into a group that thrived on nothing but nerves, sweat, and testosterone.

But maybe that *was* the action he needed at this point in the story. Maybe he should bring the character of Christina into this scene—yeah. He nodded, picking up his pen to jot a note and think about what he'd written weeks ago, before the block. She and Gannon had already had their run-in at the old airport when she announced how long she'd be there.

So now they could kiss.

He felt his lip curl, and not in empathy with his character. How could he describe a kiss? He knew what it felt like to pull a trigger, to fall out of an airplane and make a low-opening jump, and even how a man's arms could ache from pulling an injured comrade out of the line of fire. He'd internalized those sensations and could make them real on the page.

But a kiss? He didn't think when he had his lips on a woman's mouth. And the times he'd kissed Charlotte? They'd been rare, few, stolen—and he had no memory of anything but his thoughts flatlining from lack of blood to his brain.

He stared at the screen and wrote a few sentences to bring the character onto the page. He tapped out a line of dialogue. A thought. A smile. A touch.

Then, for what felt like an hour, he stared at the screen, his two fingers hovering above the keyboard like a pair of Blackhawks over a bridge about to be bombed.

That damn ringing—crap, it was his cell phone. "Shit!"

He pushed back from the laptop, frustrated as his brain slid down the fast rope of an imaginary moment into the freeze of a real one. Who was—

"Son of a bitch," he murmured, grabbing the phone to see the time. Nine thirty! What the *hell*? He'd lost track of time. He unlocked the screen, a thud of disappointment in his chest when he saw Misty was the caller. What about Willow? Did she think he'd blown her off? *Damn* it.

"Yeah, hey," he said as he answered, digging for composure, swiping back his hair as he stood. "S'up, Misty?"

"Nicky, I'm in Naples."

Italy? He blinked to clear his head and remembered the Florida city across the causeway from this island.

"Having a blast with some friends here." She was louder than usual, although there were club-like sounds behind her. Maybe a little toasted. "Are you okay?" she asked in a singsong voice. "I feel like I ditched you."

"I'm fine, good." Late as hell, but... He squinted at the number in the lower left corner of his laptop screen, doing a quick calculation. Seventeen pages! A record. "I'm great. But don't worry about me. Gonna go have a late dinner with Willow." If she didn't kick him to the curb.

"Really?" Her voice rose so high it made his teeth hurt.

"Yeah, but I'm late, so you take your time and have fun."

"Oh, I am." She dragged out the last word with the hint of a giggle.

"And don't drive," he added.

"No worries. I have a limo, or I'll stay at the Ritz. Ona's taking care of me."

Must be nice. He had a rental, and he hoped to hell the GPS could find the address he had.

The minute he hung up, he tapped in Willow's name, and the number she'd given him—already programmed into his phone—popped up. But before it connected, he ended the call.

He needed to do this in person. He needed to apologize and he needed to...kiss her. For research.

Berries...100
Almonds (17)...150
Oatmeal w/ milk...200
Whole grain roof tile...150

Definitely an A for today, Willow thought with a familiar jolt of satisfaction. Willow stared at her food journal, half of her brain trying to remember how long it had been since she'd had anything but an A, the other half mentally calculating how long it had been since she'd last checked her phone to see what time it was. *Or if anyone had called.*

It had been awhile. A long while.

She set the spiral notebook on the table, leaning back on the porch swing to listen to the water lapping on the shore of Pleasure Pointe Beach across the street. This porch and swing had sealed the deal when they'd found this incredible house with three apartments right on the beach. Ari had the top-floor one-bedroom, Gussie had moved into the middle floor, and Willow lived on the main floor in the largest of the three apartments. So Willow's place had become a central gathering area for them, especially on this porch with the water view.

But her friends were out tonight, and she was…stood up.

How could she call it anything else? She didn't have to look at her phone to know the two most obvious facts: It was *still* about nine thirty, and he *still* hadn't called.

She'd actually given up on her "date" half an hour ago and had gone in to change into running shorts and a tank top, fully intending to hit the sand to jog off the frustration.

But something stopped her.

Hope.

She let out a grunt and pushed up, squinting into the shadows on the porch. How long had she sat out here in the dark…waiting? Waiting for a call or a car or a cancellation, but got…none.

It was too late to join Ari and Gussie, who'd gone out to dinner with a few friends from Casa Blanca. But it wasn't too late to run the beach. She went inside, grabbed a banana, which tasted like mush in her mouth, and drank a little water to hydrate before taking off into the night.

She stretched on the porch, holding on to the railing as she warmed up, kind of hating herself for peering down South Street with that damn hope in her heart.

Face it, he forgot. Or maybe he'd had second thoughts. She'd like to think Misty coerced him into a night on the town, but their BTB specifically told Ari she was hanging out with friends in Naples that evening. Ari said she'd climbed into a limo and disappeared. Who hired a limo for a day of wedding planning, anyway? That was so something her mother would do.

Like mother…like surrogate daughter.

Pushing that thought away, she hit the stairs and then the pavement in a hard trot, one more glance up the street before she crossed, and then she worked her way through the little neighborhood that formed the southern tip of Mimosa Key.

It was cool enough that she could have used a sweatshirt, so she increased her speed and stretched her stride, a comfortable pull on her hams and glutes.

Starting a rhythm of breathing that filled her with fresh oxygen, Willow looked around at the little bungalows and beach homes, waiting for that sense of happiness and contentment she always got from her new life in Florida.

Tonight, they both eluded her. So she looked even harder.

Pleasure Pointe was a true neighborhood, a lovely residential area south of town about a ten-minute drive from Barefoot Bay at the opposite end of the island. Not just *a* neighborhood, but also *her* neighborhood now. Where they knew her—Willow Ambrose—and not a soul would stop her on the street to coo over who her parents were or how much weight she'd lost. Here she was anonymous.

Or she had been before today.

As she worked her way through the narrow streets to get to the eastern shore and start her two-mile route, Willow looked over her shoulder one more time. She wasn't afraid for her safety; a person could run naked down the main drag of Mimosa Key and be safe. Oh, they'd get talked about at the next town council meeting or when they stopped into the Super Min for gas and bad coffee, but there was very little crime here.

No, Willow was checking for headlights going to her house.

Damn hope again. She drummed it out by getting her heart rate up, pumping her arms and puffing out noisy, even breaths. The sounds of the night and the breeze in her ears were almost enough to drown out the sound of Nick

Hershey's flirty invitations that he should have saved for someone who didn't care.

No, no. She meant someone who cared.

Because she didn't care about him. So he was sexy as sin and sweet as pie. She never ate pie, and sin was not generally on her personal menu, either. She certainly didn't want to date a guy who'd known her...*then*. And made it extraordinarily clear what he thought of her.

No, he hadn't insulted her when she'd gotten a little too close that night, put her hand on his leg, and made the most pathetic attempt at flirting in the history of womankind. *I'm a virgin, Nick.* Oh, God, what possessed her to say that? Of course she was a virgin! Anyone could tell that by looking at her.

Then he'd quietly moved her hand, shaken his head, and said...

This is a bad idea, Willie. I can't...you deserve...no, we better say good night.

The sting of that rejection had been enough to keep her from ever making that mistake again. Once bitten, twice...lonely.

She reached the eastern shore, assaulted by the salty air and humidity that hung over this side of the island, away from the gulf breezes. Here, there was no beach, but instead, craggy inlets of saw-grass river water highlighted by the twinkling lights of Naples on the mainland of Florida.

Why had she said yes to that date? Why had he asked?

She hadn't even told Gussie and Ari, only because she didn't want to field a quadrillion questions about their past or listen to Ari obsess about how the universe worked. Maybe her apartment could be dark and quiet when they came back, and they would head right up the side stairs to their own places, no questions asked.

Or not. What else were friends for if not a good man-bashing?

Willow finally reached the end of the beach, the southern-most tip of the island where the land was no more than thirty or forty feet wide, where a person could stand and look left and right and straight ahead and see nothing but water.

Sucking in the cloying scent of a nearby gardenia bush, Willow closed her eyes to listen to the music of the breeze. A distant ping of a sailboat's rigging against a mast matched the rhythm of her well-exercised heart beating against her ribs.

She put her hand over her chest, but not to measure her heart rate as she usually did at this point in her run. No, she wanted to protect that poor organ that had worked overtime today.

"Oh, come on, Willow." Lifting her face to the sky, she let out a grunt, hating her self-pity. She was a world-class *temptation avoider*.

Of course, when temptation failed to show—or call or text or send a freaking smoke signal—then avoiding it just got a whole lot easier.

On that thought, Willow jogged off, clearing her head and focusing on nothing but the satisfying feeling of running and moving and scoring a victory over the body that, for so many years, had beaten her.

Once she hit the sand on the western-facing beach, it was a little more like Barefoot Bay. Real sand, real beach, flat and wide enough that she could haul ass back home.

And haul she did, running at a good clip, a sheen of sweat cooling her, the wind over her ears the only sound she heard. Her mind went stone-cold blank. She didn't think of food or calories or scales or temptations or dates or men nicknamed...*Kiss.* Just muscles and cells and chemicals shooting off to places that could only get better. She ran and ran, away from the past, as always.

By the time she reached the last quarter mile, she was drenched in sweat, every muscle quivering with the effort. She slowed her step, bent over to catch her breath, and closed her eyes against the sting of perspiration.

She walked up the driveway in that position, hands on her hips, taking the steps to the porch two at a time because, damn it, she could. She could do anything. She could run miles. She could get stood up. She could—

"You ate roof tiles for lunch?"

—not breathe. For real.

Please, God, this is not happening. Nick Hershey was not sitting on her porch *reading her food journal.* A cold dribble of sweat meandered down her back.

"Wasa crackers," she croaked between pants. "Same thing." She wiped her brow with the back of her hand, trying to catch a breath that did not want to be caught. "You're late."

"I know. I'm sorry." The simple, plain, and remarkably genuine apology reached her bruised heart, but failed to grab anything.

"Hours late."

He leaned forward, making the swing creak, the street lamp forming half-shadows on his cheeks while the light in the living room behind him added a halo.

Which he so did not deserve.

"I was writing, Willow, *really* writing. I had no idea what time it was, and I'm sorry. Did you eat dinner yet?"

"You should know," she said, still hesitating to go up the stairs into those shadows or near that halo or even one inch closer to that man. "Since you're reading an account of every bite I put in my mouth."

He lifted the journal. "It was open, and I thought you might have left me a note. Sorry."

"You're full of sorry tonight."

He stood, coming around the table to the top of the stairs. "I mean it. I would never have blown you off. Can we still go out?"

"Now?" Was he kidding? Did he think he could just show up hours late, and she'd run to the shower, throw on some makeup, and they could…rewrite history? "No."

He took one of the three steps down so he loomed over her, so tempting he might as well be a waiter offering a tray full of crème brûlée.

"Take a shower." It was an order, delivered with enough edge to make her knees nearly buckle.

"It too late to go out, Nick."

He took one more step.

"Any closer and"—she held up her hand to physically ward him off—"you'll smell me."

He sniffed, and she leaned back, but he did the opposite, coming closer, grinning. "I can cook. Got anything besides"—he lifted her journal—"roof tiles and almonds? Or was that the last seventeen of them in the house?"

She angled her head and gave him a tight smile. "I don't think you actually realize what you're up against."

He reached for her hand. "I realize what I'd *like* to be up against."

She jerked out of his touch.

"Come on, Willow. Let me make you dinner."

"I already ate." A banana, but that counted. "And you seem to be pretty stuffed with crow."

"I am. Sorry, I mean." He managed to snag her hand, inching her closer to the one step that separated them. "I swear, I'm never late, I never miss appointments, I can't even tell you how…how out of step it is for me to do that. My only excuse is that I was writing and got lost."

Looking up at him, she let the sensations wash over her, familiar, even comfortable sensations. The ache to take, the itch to own, the mouthwatering *want* that battered her willpower. She could fight food, but him? Wide shoulders made for a woman to grip and glittering dark eyes as delicious and inviting as a whole box of Godiva Dark Decadence?

She closed her eyes as if that could stop the onslaught of Nick Hershey's heated touch and the smell of the salt air that clung to him.

It would be so…damn…good.

But so would the gallons of ice cream, bags of chips, and too-many-to-count Reubens she'd sacrificed in the name of control. Finally, she looked up at him.

"My answer is no. You're late, I don't want to get dressed, and I can't be sweet-talked when I'm this mad. Good night, Nick."

She brushed by him, grabbing her food journal from the table before she reached for the front door. As she pulled it open, she lost the urge not to look over her shoulder.

"Is that what shell-shocked looks like?" she asked, fighting a satisfied smile at the utter disbelief on his face.

"This is what determination looks like. What's it going to take to change your mind?"

"Tonight? Nothing."

"Tomorrow?"

She just laughed and opened the door. "Is another day."

She slipped inside before he could come after her, latching the door and leaning against it, her food journal in her hand.

Definitely an A for today. But tomorrow was looking shaky.

Chapter Six

Using the thick envelope that had arrived on his doorstep that morning, Nick tapped on the open door of the Barefoot Brides office at noon the next day, determined to win this time.

"Anyone here?" He stepped up to the door, meeting two gazes, but not the Wedgwood blue and pewter gray eyes of the woman he came to see.

"Hello, Nick." Ari, whose desk was closest to the door, stood immediately and flashed a bright smile. With long dark hair and ebony eyes, she was the most exotic looking of the three, with a hint of either Latin or American Indian in her striking appearance. "Of course we're here on a Saturday, although we don't have a wedding this weekend."

He tried not to be obvious as his gaze shifted to the third—and empty—desk in the room, working not to show his disappointment.

"She's in the kitchen," Gussie said, proving that he'd probably failed.

"She's going over some new catering menu items with the chef," Ari said. "I'm not sure if it's the best time to bother her."

He raised his brows. "You think I bother her?"

Gussie winked. "That's why they call it hot and bothered, right?"

"We weren't expecting you or Misty today," Ari said. "You know this is your day to enjoy the resort, but if you have any questions, we're here to help."

"His question is, 'Where's Willow?'" Gussie rose from her desk chair, her pixie-like features fixed in a happy expression framed by pink-tipped platinum hair. Always with the wigs, that one. "Am I right?"

Why lie to her closest friends and business partners? Anyway, there was nothing a soldier needed more in a battle than buddies. Even if they had pink hair. He gave her a slow nod. "You are correct, ma'am."

The two women shared a look and a silent message that he was clueless to decipher. "Any chance I could talk to her?" he asked.

Ari angled her head. "Only if you've come to beg her forgiveness for showing up hours late last night."

So they knew everything. "Even better," he said, holding up the envelope. "I come bearing free spa treatments."

"Why would I want them?"

He spun around at the surprise attack from the back, swearing at his damn pathetic non-working ear. In that nanosecond, she snapped the envelope from his hand, spearing him with a playful and pretty look. "This is all for you, as our guest."

"A hot nautilus shell massage and steam brush facial for men?" He looked skyward. "What Navy SEAL doesn't want to spend his day like that?"

"You're forgetting the men's pedicure." Willow managed to slip by him, slender enough to slide into the office without letting their bodies touch.

He watched her walk to her desk in jeans that showed off

a tight, curved ass to mouthwatering perfection. Damn. How had she gone from the young woman he knew in Sproul Hall to...

Seventeen almonds and a roof tile, that's how. And workouts that no doubt rivaled BUD/S training. Which was almost as much of a turn-on as the way her tight T-shirt tucked into the jeans and showed off her waist.

"Ahem." Gussie gave him an elbow and raised brow. "You're staring."

"Ahem, I'm human. And she's spectacular."

Willow turned as she reached her desk, fighting a smile. "Full-offensive attack today, Lieutenant?"

"With a couple's massage." He fluttered the envelope. "What about it? You. Me. Hot shells and body butter?"

Instantly, Ari swooped up a paper. "Oh, Gussie, we gotta go."

"And miss this?"

"Yes, we do. It's time for that, um, meeting. That important meeting we have that Willow is not invited to."

Willow gave a soft laugh, but Nick shot Ari a look of pure appreciation. "Thanks for having my back."

She shrugged and gave Gussie a prod toward the door. "It's *her* back we're worried about."

"And her front," Gussie added. "No staring."

"Gussie!" Willow chided.

Laughing, the two women disappeared out the door, leaving him alone with the one he wanted. Except she still looked pissed at him.

"So," he said, coming a few steps closer. "Can you play today?"

She relaxed ever so slightly, fighting a smile. "Points for creativity."

"And relentless determination. You can appreciate that,

right?" He gestured toward her body and let his gaze rove over every curve and cut again. "You didn't get this way by being lazy."

The slightest rise of color seeped up her neck. "I didn't get this way from getting couple's massages with our guests."

"So you'd rather hit the gym?"

She shook her head. "I'm leaving in a few minutes, so, sorry."

"Where are you going?" he asked, closing more space.

She escaped the trap, slipping around her desk to make an effort to look like she was organizing papers. "I need to run errands in town."

"Oh, okay." When she looked up, he added, "I'll go with you."

"Why?"

"Because I want to make up my mistake to you. Let's run your errands and have lunch together, and then take a walk by the water and kiss."

Her eyes widened as the last one sank in. "Well, so much for subtlety."

"So overrated, and I need to do some kissing research. You can help."

She gave a quick laugh. "What makes you think I want to?"

"Oh, come on, Willow." He leaned his hands on her desk and got closer.

"I ate already." She slipped into her chair and crossed her arms as if she could create her own bullet-proof vest.

"Roof tiles?" he teased.

"And a spinach smoothie."

He took the guest chair across from her to make her comfortable. "So, is that how you did it? Denial and control?"

"And six billion crunches."

"I bet." He gave her an admiring smile, wishing she'd loosen up those tight arms. "You've probably done more sit-ups than I have in SEAL training."

Suddenly, she pushed back from the desk. "You really want to go with me?"

He stood, too. "Of course."

"First, we're stopping at the florist, then I need to pick something up from a gift shop, and there could be a stop at the fabric store for some tulle. Then one client needs me to choose her toasting crystals, and another has me on a hunt for satin pillows. This is a very girlie errand day. Can you handle that, Lieutenant?"

"If the girlie I'm with is you."

Finally, she let her arms relax, along with her smile. She bent over to get something from under her desk, giving him a direct shot down her V-neck, the sight of a soft, feminine swell firing right through him.

She looked and caught him staring. Hard. "Sorry, you had your shot, Nick."

He closed his eyes, the hit direct. "I have a lot of groveling to do, don't I?"

"It should be epic." She stepped around the desk and softened the tension with a smile.

He led her out, taking his small victory and her hand, unwilling to let go of either one.

A couple's massage couldn't have been much more fun than picking tulle, roses, pillows, or flutes with Nick. At each stop in town, with each joke and casual touch, Willow couldn't help but let her guard slip a little more. By the time they loaded up her car and checked the last thing off her list, all her defenses were down.

Nick closed her hatchback with an air of finality. "Please tell me there's a cold drink at the end of this."

"There could be."

He pointed across Harbor Drive to the frosted windows and the red and white awning of Miss Icey's, a Mimosa Key staple. "What can we get at that place?"

"I've only heard rumors," she joked. "They sell things with names like praline pecan and vanilla fudge ripple."

"Ice cream?" His eyes popped like a six-year-old boy's. "Don't deny me."

"Knock yourself out. I can't be in the same room with the stuff."

He took her hand. "When's the last time you had ice cream?" he asked.

Willow knew exactly when that was. She could probably give him the date. She'd been on her way back to her house in Canyon Country after spending the day in Pacific Palisades with her parents, about three and a half years ago. Ona had been in rare form that day, and Willow had left feeling like a human punching bag. Only fatter.

That night, she'd chosen Premium Churned Reduced Fat No Sugar Added Caramel Turtle Truffle. The next day, she was up two pounds. But she'd made a decision to limit her exposure to her mother to...nothing. Which was freakishly easy. That was the week that Willow launched a complete transformation of her life and self. Which was also freakishly easy, at least in retrospect.

"I haven't had ice cream for years," she finally admitted.

For a long time, he looked at her, considering that answer. "Don't you ever just lose control, Willow?"

"Not if I can help it."

"I don't think that's healthy."

She launched a brow north. "My scale would say differently, and so would your lusty looks."

He smiled. "You're fun to look at, I won't lie, but don't you ever want to cheat or just, you know, eat ice cream?"

How much fun would it be to eat ice cream with Nick? To share a cone and...a kiss. All kinds of physical desires fluttered around in her. "I'm afraid of it," she whispered, surprising herself with the honest answer.

"Then it owns you," he said quickly. "I learned that in training. When you're scared of something, you need to face it, even experience it, regularly. Then it loses all its power over you."

She looked up at him, feeling a little like she might if she were staring into the Rocky Road bin. This could feel so good...but the consequences would not.

"You're thinking about it," he said, taking her hands and easing her closer.

"I'm thinking about you."

"Even better." And closer. "We could skip the ice cream and go make out."

"In broad daylight?"

"The better to see you."

She laughed, shaking her head, tamping down those feminine nerve cells that were dancing around like little prisoners who heard the guard rattling the keys. "I choose ice cream," she said. "It's the lesser of two evils."

Chapter Seven

Defenses down, Rocky Road in hand, Willow tried to remind herself to be careful. A total loss of control could lead to…well, not in broad daylight. Not here. But eventually?

He was the one who mentioned a kiss. How could she not think about it?

"So, am I completely forgiven yet for almost standing you up last night?" he asked, pulling her out of the reverie.

"Mmm." She closed her eyes to enjoy the cold, sweet richness on her tongue and the ping to her heart because he seemed to care so much. "You think all it takes is a little makeup ice cream and we're good?"

"Not to mention I spent my afternoon buying pink mosquito netting."

"Tulle," she corrected, nudging him. "I guess I'll forgive you, if you tell me about what you wrote that kept you so engrossed you forgot about me."

He slid her a look. "That won't happen again," he said softly. "And what I wrote was…pretty good, I think. Maybe. Oh, hell, it could have sucked bear balls for all I know."

"Is writing a book something you've always wanted to do?"

"Not particularly, though I've always dug reading."

"I know," she said, letting him guide her across the street. "The first time I saw you was in the dorm lounge at three in the morning, your nose in a John Steinbeck novel."

He smiled. "I remember. You walked past me three times in one hour."

She felt the embarrassed burn of a busted stalker. "So what made you decide to try writing?" she asked quickly.

"For one thing, I'm bored as hell." They paused at the intersection and then wordlessly agreed to walk toward the small park along the water's edge. "I miss active duty."

"When can you go back?"

He didn't answer right away, eating some ice cream. "Not sure I will."

"What's the deciding factor?"

He tapped his left ear. "When the surgery works. I'm treating my ear with corticosteroids and time. If I passed the test I took last week, I can go back in for training and deployment. But, truth be told, SEAL standards are high, and I may never see deployment again."

She could hear a world of hurt in that admission, but didn't want to ruin the moment by dwelling on it. "Well, it's good you have the writing to keep your mind off it." She added a teasing elbow. "And other things, like dinner dates."

He laughed. "The best part about last night was how caught up in the story I got. I didn't have as much of that stuck feeling that's been killing me for the past few weeks. I wrote and wrote and wrote. I wish I knew what happened, so I could bottle and drink it every day. Something broke the dam."

"Salt air?"

"Nah, I'm living a stone's throw from the Pacific Ocean, and there's plenty of salt air there."

"Time change?"

"Obviously not looking at the clock." At an empty bench, they sat down, facing the wide body of water that separated the island from the mainland, dotted with a dozen pleasure craft and jet skiers on this sunny April afternoon.

They didn't talk for a moment, taking in the view, the treat, the companionship. Then Willow felt his gaze on her and not the cobalt water.

"What?"

"I was just thinking that I know who you reminded me of yesterday on the beach."

"I reminded you of *me*," she said. "And if anyone should be throwing around apologies, it's me for not being straight from the moment I recognized you."

"That's true," he agreed heartily. "We're definitely even. When did you recognize me, exactly?"

"As soon as I saw your face."

"Which took a long while, as I recall."

She laughed at the tease. "Your singing—and other things—rendered me, um, speechless."

He leaned into her. "I'll buy that excuse for when I wasn't dressed. But what about after, when you knew I hadn't recognized you? Why not say something then?"

She opened her mouth to make a quip, change the topic, or brush off the truth. But something about the question in his eyes stopped her. "I told you, Willie Zatarain no longer exists. I really didn't want to go through the whole 'oh, wow, you're so different' business. And, for what it's worth, I was about to tell you when Misty showed up."

"I would have figured it out, though. Especially when I realized how much you look like your mother."

She almost choked on her sugar cone. "I do not," she corrected him. "I favor my father, without the long hair, tattoos, and road-worn face."

He regarded her for a moment, the scrutiny making her uncomfortable. "You have prominent cheekbones, that little cleft in your chin, and eyes that never stay the same color for five minutes. I think you look more like the woman on the magazine covers than the man on the album covers."

She had to change the subject. "So, what do you think of this sweet little island I've adopted as my home?"

"It's pretty." He nodded to the water. "Not too touristy, considering the location."

"That is changing with the resort up in Barefoot Bay and a new minor league baseball stadium coming in next year. Still, I love it. When Gussie and Ari and I arrived here to preview Casa Blanca as a destination wedding resort, we couldn't believe there was anything like Mimosa Key left on Florida's west coast. No high-rises, no restaurant chains, no real tourist traffic."

"You like that?" He sounded amazed. "After growing up in Los Angeles?"

"I *love* that after growing up in Los Angeles. And so do the brides that are looking for a completely unique destination for their weddings, which is one of the reasons we chose to locate our business here."

"What were the other reasons?" he asked, resting his arm across the back of the bench, nearly around her. She had to fight the desire to curl closer.

"Obviously, there are a lot of factors when three people make a move that big," she said. "We were all coming from different parts of the country, and the location appealed to all of us."

"From different parts of the country? I'm surprised, because you seem like you've been friends forever."

"Feels that way," she agreed, thinking about how quickly the three of them had evolved from professional colleagues to best friends. "I told you we traveled together for one solid year to visit resorts, and we clicked. And I was totally ready for friends again…"

She realized how that sounded the minute it came out.

"I mean, friends and a new business and a change," she said quickly. "We bonded instantly and knew that we could be a powerhouse operation as a threesome rather than struggling individually."

"What do you mean you were ready for friends again?"

Of course he was too smart to let that slip by. She attempted a casual shrug. "Oh, I mean friends that are in the same business."

She wasn't going to keep letting him take her back there, damn it.

"Don't you ever miss Los Angeles?" he asked, and she sensed it was just another way of asking how and when and why she'd shunned her friends and family.

She had prepared answers for those questions. She'd been asked this before. "I didn't really live in LA, per se. I moved way out to Canyon Country years ago, and that turned out to be an inconvenient place to have a business. I was living on the freeway to meet clients and review sites. This"—she made a sweeping gesture toward the water and boats, the sweeping arc of the causeway that led to the mainland—"is like paradise compared to Southern California."

He didn't answer, studying the view with a hesitation just long enough to make her think he didn't agree.

"Do *you* miss California?" she countered. She knew he'd grown up outside of San Francisco and assumed he lived up there.

"Not how I'm living now. While I'm on this leave, I'm staying with my younger brother in Manhattan Beach, which is not conducive to writing—or sleeping or thinking—since he's got a lot of friends and they are in and out constantly. I had an apartment down in San Diego when I first entered the SEALs, but when I was deployed the first time, I let the place go."

"Where would you live if you ended up leaving the SEALs?"

He closed his eyes and very slowly shook his head. "I don't want to even think about it, Willow."

"So if you're not deployed, would you quit the service?"

"I'm not big on quitting, really. But...I didn't train like a beast to push papers in some building." He gave his head a little shake, like the thought actually hurt him, but then he turned to her.

"You must get back to LA to see your parents, right?" he asked. "Or is it New York where Misty said she sees your mother?"

She laughed softly.

"Why is that funny?" he asked.

"It's like we're doing a perfectly choreographed dance of subjects neither one of us wants to talk about."

He brushed his fingers on her shoulder. "Your mother?"

All right, she'd be honest. "I don't talk to my mother that often."

"Is that by choice?" he asked.

Her lips formed a tight smile as she nodded, her focus on a boat headed south on the navy water. "Yep. Mine."

He waited a beat, then, "Can I ask why?"

A hundred responses floated through her brain, so she chose the one that would resonate with a man who missed dangerous battles. "Consider it a survival technique," she said. "Surely a Navy SEAL would understand that."

For a long moment, he looked at her, his eyes registering that, on some level, he understood.

"We're not...what's the word? *Estranged*," she added. Just the opposite, in fact. They knew each other far too well. "And we do talk sometimes." Briefly, rarely, and only by phone. "But mostly, I can't stand her manipulative personality. Constantly trying to get me to be or do things that she wants with no regard for what I want."

"That would suck. What about your dad?"

"He loves to be manipulated by her, that's why they're still so in love. But my dad..." She felt a slow smile growing. "My dad's okay. She's his weakness, and I forgive him for that."

"Do you see him?"

"Once in a while. They both have insane schedules. He's still on the road a lot, and my mother runs a monstrously successful design business. They're rarely on this continent, let alone at home. But, yeah, I see him if we can work it out." Except she hadn't seen him in...eighty pounds. Which was the way Willow measured time over the last few years.

To lighten the conversation, she leaned a little closer, letting their shoulders touch. "Betcha I could get you an autograph. If you promise never, ever to sing *Will Ya, Will Ya* again."

He laughed, closing the rest of the space between them by dipping close to her ear. "Gotta know if it's real, gotta know it's forevah," he sang softly.

She closed her eyes and gave a soft grunt. "Oh, that stupid song."

He dropped back, his jaw hanging open. "Stupid! Not only is that one of the most important songs in the history of 1980s rock music, it's also one of my personal favorites in the history of all music."

She couldn't help laughing. "God, your bar is low."

"Your father *wrote* it." He practically sputtered.

"Not only that, he proposed to my mom by singing that at

a concert in front of fifty thousand people."

"I read that somewhere. They all sang, 'Will ya marry me?' instead of 'Be my girl.'"

"You *are* a hard-core fan. So, here's something even the biggest Z-Train fans don't know." She dipped her head close to his to whisper. "I was conceived to that song."

He slapped his hand over his heart as if it had cracked into pieces in his chest. "Oh, man, I think I just fell in love with you."

And *her* heart skipped, rolled, dropped, and landed somewhere in the vicinity of her belly. "Well, that didn't take much."

Turning to her, he reached for her hand. "You know this means I'll never listen to *Will Ya, Will Ya* again and not think of you."

Imagining how many times that would have him thinking of her, everything in her melted like the last bits of ice cream in the bottom of her cone.

"Now, Willow. Let's stay on this subject of things you want to avoid."

She gave him a pleading look. "Come on, Nick. I ate ice cream. I told you about my mother. I confessed I am the result of a hit song. Now what line do you want me to cross?"

He just smiled and inched closer. "I told you, I'm researching kissing."

His eyes were so dark, they pulled her into him, making her want to get closer, deeper, *inside* those eyes. Something that felt very much like what she now thought of as "empty-hunger" engulfed her. That need to be filled, to be satisfied, to be comforted, even though nothing was really empty or dissatisfied or uncomfortable. Empty-hunger was what got her into trouble with food, and empty-lust was about to get her into trouble with Nick.

Except it didn't feel empty, like the desire for a piece of cheesecake. It felt real. Like the longing for a sweet taste of his mouth. "I thought writers had great imaginations. Can't you wing it?"

"Then my kiss will read like some idiot wrote it."

She grinned.

"Some other idiot," he corrected. "Like when I read a battle scene and they get the weapons wrong, it pisses me off. What if I get it wrong?"

"Lips are the only weapons involved. You can't mess that up."

"There's so much more to a kiss, Willow."

Really? She wanted to know. She might have inched closer, but at that moment, she wasn't really in control of every movement. He lifted their joined hands and brought them close to his lips. "Why do you seem so dead set against a little, tiny, simple, inconsequential kiss?"

"Because one loss of control leads to the next, and what if I can't stop?"

"I'm okay with that."

She laughed, reaching up to put a hand on his shoulder to push him back but, oh, man, that was a nice shoulder. Hard, thick, powerful. A shoulder to lean on. A shoulder...to ride.

"Your eyes are turning gray."

She widened them. "What does that mean?"

"I think this is what happens right before you give in. They turned gray when I asked you to get ice cream."

"It's the color of fear," she whispered.

"You know what I taught you about fears." He closed almost all the space between their mouths, still holding her gaze. "You face them, you live them, you beat them. Fear of losing control will be gone."

But she wasn't really afraid of losing control. This was

Nick Hershey. She'd kissed him once before, and he'd been so turned off, she had practically tasted the aversion to her on his lips.

That was her fear, and it wasn't even deep-seated. It was right on the surface, clawing at her heart.

Ancient insecurities and a lifetime of self-hatred welled up like a bubbling fountain, pulling her back.

"This is not research," she said. "Where's your notebook?"

"Right here." He pulled out his phone. "This is absolutely for research purposes only. In fact, we can stop and take notes after each kiss."

"How many will there be?"

"How many can I have?"

She had to laugh. "How many do you want?"

He lifted their joined hands to his lips, a smile breaking behind his knuckles. "Let's start with one and see what happens."

What could one hurt, right?

She closed her eyes and gave a simple nod. Nick remained perfectly still for a long beat. Too long. Long enough that the ache inside her turned cold.

She opened her eyes, and he was staring at...his phone. She peered down to see him typing in a note-taking app. His fingers glided over the screen as he typed *Willow*.

"How many research partners do you have?"

"Just one."

Then, he placed one hand on her jaw, cupping it with strong fingers and a warm palm. It took everything in her not to nuzzle him like an affection-deprived dog, practically itching for his hand to slip deeper into her hair and cradle her whole head as he kissed her.

But he still didn't do it. In fact, he dragged his hand from her face and picked up the freaking phone again.

"Now what?"

"I want to write what I'm feeling." He tapped the screen. "I think it's important that I remember exactly what it feels like before the actual kiss."

Was he serious? Or looking for a way out...

"For God's sake, Nick, just kiss me."

"I thought you'd never ask." He dipped his head and brushed her lips with his, making her shudder at the touch before she slowly lifted her arms.

Her hands settled on his upper arms, her grip tightening as each amazing sensation rolled through her. The tangy, rich taste of chocolate and mint, the warm pressure of his lips on hers, the scent of ice cream and aftershave, and the gentle caress of his hand on her jaw. His fingers slipped deeper into her hair, hot and strong, holding her as if she were precious.

She couldn't help the softest whimper, which made him angle his head and intensify the kiss. She leaned closer so he could slide his hand through her hair and pull her into him to kiss her cheek, her jaw, her hair, her ear. She heard him laugh and felt him sigh.

"I like kissing you, Willow," he whispered.

"For research."

"You fell for that?" He chuckled and leaned in for another kiss. "Not for research, for real." He kissed her again, opening his lips to tease her teeth with his tongue, sending a thousand fluttering butterflies roaring through her stomach.

No, not for real. This couldn't feel real. It was too soon, too close, too wrapped up in the past. She inched back, breaking the kiss with a bit of insistence.

"Then you better take notes and get home and write that book."

His smile faltered as the words hit him. "What's going on?"

"What's going on? We're kissing in the middle of the day in a park like...like..."

"Like people who are attracted to each other and spending the day together in a way that is perfectly acceptable."

Was he attracted to her? He hadn't been before. She tried to cling to that, however irrational it felt out here in the sunshine, a new woman living her new life.

"But..." The word bubbled on her lips.

"But what?"

"But we should go." She started to stand, but he still had one of her hands and brought her right back down.

"Whoa, just a minute there, darling."

"Darling?"

"It's a term of endearment." He squeezed her hand. "I find you endearing, so therefore, I use it. I find you..."

"Repulsive."

He choked, eyes wide. "*What?*"

"I mean, you did, long ago. And I—"

"I told you what happened, Willow, and I apologized and I meant it. You have to let go of the past or—"

"I did. I have. I know I have to let go, in fact, I have made an art form of letting go of the past, and it's working out really well for me, and you, frankly, are the embodiment of all I hated about myself in the past, so let's just leave this at res—"

"Hush." He put his hand on her mouth, narrowing his eyes. "You're a runner, Willow."

She frowned. "I like to jog. I hardly call myself a runner."

"No, you run. I noticed that about you. When things get sticky, or interesting, depending on your point of view, you take off."

She leaned back, freeing her hand so she could cross her arms.

"Or you do that." He gestured toward her protective position. "You wrap yourself up and won't let anyone in."

"That's pretty amazing analysis considering you've known me for two days."

"And eleven years. But it doesn't take a shrink to see what you're doing or why." He stroked her arm, tempting her to let down that shield and wrap him in another hug.

But that would be...stupid.

"You can't always detach yourself from someone who wants to be attached to you," he said.

"I don't." He gave her a *get real* look, and she shrugged. "Okay, sometimes. But I don't understand what difference it makes to you."

He looked perplexed by the statement. "I like you," he said simply. "And I'm frustrated that you don't like me back."

She couldn't help smiling. "Is life always that simple for you, Nick?"

"Rarely, but when it is, I grab the moment."

She finally stood, remembering that "moments" were all they had, because he'd be gone tomorrow, and she'd see him once for a wedding after that, then never again. So...he was a bad candidate for what she wanted.

Except that until that kiss, she hadn't known what she wanted. And now she wanted...more.

"Let's get you back to your villa so you can write all this up and have it make sense."

He laughed as he got up. "This shit never makes sense, Willow."

Chapter Eight

Sunday morning, Willow slipped out of her apartment early to grab some coffee and hit the office for some quiet time. There, she plugged in her headset to get lost in a Mozart concerto and skim through a fairly light email in-box.

She powered through messages and typed with flying fingers, ignoring the questions.

She never even heard her business partners arrive in the office until Gussie slid her backside onto Willow's desk, draped over, and yanked out one of her earbuds. "We missed you for Sunday breakfast. No one was home in your apartment, and Ari and I had to eat in town."

"I needed to work." Willow made a face at Gussie's choice of a jet-black wig with bangs and rhinestone cat-eye glasses. Willow gestured to the eyewear. "Over-the-top, even for you."

Gussie ignored the comment and stuck the earbud in her own ear. "So's this music. Still rebelling against your rock 'n' roll upbringing, I see."

She rolled her eyes. "I can't get away from it, I'm afraid." She unhooked her other earbud and pushed back from the desk. "I didn't think you guys would be in for a while."

"You're avoiding us," Gussie accused.

"Not at all. But since you're here now, we better get focused on Misty. She's coming in later with her decision on whether or not to have the wedding here. I'm sure Nick's coming with her, too."

Ari came up behind Gussie, and they shared a look. "Less than ten seconds," Ari said, holding out her hand to Gussie. "Pay up."

Gussie mumbled and reached into her pocket, pulling out a black and yellow-wrapped candy. "Do you know how hard it is to find Black Cows? I had to go to Fort Myers for these."

Candy-obsessed, both of them.

"A bet is a bet."

Neither one of them seemed to notice Willow's unlocked jaw. "You two are gambling on...us?" Not that she and Nick were an "us" or that she should be surprised, considering how these two went to war over rare candies.

"On how long it would take you to mention his name," Gussie said, reaching to grab Ari's hand. "Do not unwrap that. I still might get it back." Then, to Willow, "Did you kiss him?"

"I...I..."

Gussie grinned with sheer satisfaction and flipped her palm upward to Ari. "Give 'er back. I told you."

Ari held tight to the candy. "Not so fast. Are you going to see him again or not?" She squeezed Gussie's fingers. "Remember, another date wins me a bag of Squirrel Nut Zippers, which could require an online order. You can't find those anywhere."

Willow shut her eyes, not sure if she should laugh or be disgusted. "Another date? There wasn't a first one, not technically. I'm going to see him in a few minutes, if he even comes to the meeting with Misty. After that? He's going back to California and may be deployed again, depending on what his last hearing test said."

One of Gussie's brows shot up behind the sparkly glasses. "Know an awful lot about his life, don't you?"

"Well, we were together for hours, and we talked. Did you bet on whether or not we had a conversation? Because we did."

"Didn't bet on that," Gussie admitted, taking the candy. "With no second date, this is mine, Ari."

"Put it on the table," Ari said. "There's still this afternoon."

Willow pushed back from the desk as the other women headed to their own workstations. "He's leaving this afternoon, thank God."

They both whipped around to look at Willow. "Thank God?" they asked in unison.

"Why?" Ari demanded.

"He's hot and awesome," Gussie added. "Not to state the obvious or anything."

Willow rolled the cords of her earbuds in a neat circle around her iPod, giving a half-assed shrug.

"Willow?" Gussie prompted.

"Tell us what's going on," Ari insisted.

How could she when she didn't understand why she felt how she felt? Hell, she didn't even know how she felt, so she used the excuse she gave Nick. "He's so much a piece of a past I'd really like to forget."

Gussie squirreled up her pretty features into a mix of disbelief and disgust. "Seriously, Willow? That was a zillion years ago."

"Eleven years and a lot of..." She gave a wry smile. "Pounds."

"Exactly!" Gussie said, coming closer so fast her neon-green maxi dress swooshed. "And look at you. You're perfect."

"Hardly." But she only battled the same ten pounds that many women went to war with, and she knew it.

Ari got next to Gussie in a show of solidarity. "Willow, you *are* your past. I'm sorry, but you can't disconnect from it even if you really want to, any more than you can disconnect from the earth under your feet or every thought you have during a day. It's part of the tapestry of you."

Gussie nodded. "She's right. You didn't emerge from the sea, fully formed as this new person. I think it's kind of wonderful that he knew you before. I wish we knew you before. Don't roll your eyes, Willow. I've never even seen a picture of you when you weighed more."

Nor would they. "You're not missing anything."

"Don't say that." Ari's eyes sparked. "I mean it when I say your past is everything about you. History and time and events all fold together into one spirit—"

Willow sliced the air with her hand. "Please, Ari. Can the woo-woo. If my past is everything, then I am nothing."

They both stared at her, slack-jawed, making her realize just how harsh and wrong and stupid that sounded. But they didn't understand what it was like to hate—truly, deeply, madly *hate*—yourself for most of your life. They didn't understand what it was like to use food to escape the manipulation of a woman who lived to manipulate.

Willow had finally let go of that hate and had grown into tolerance, even like, for herself. Nick Hershey brought all the self-loathing back to the forefront. Everything would be easier if she could get away from Nick, the human embodiment of one of the Worst Days of her life. The only person who might send her reeling even further back would be her mother, and Misty certainly brought that possibility to the forefront.

"Much as you'd like to make it out to be more, this guy's nothing. He's not an issue. He's leaving today, and if Misty chooses Casa Blanca, he'll be back in a month for a weekend wedding, and then this will have been nothing but one afternoon of shopping and ice cream."

"Ice cream?" Gussie gasped.

"He got you to eat ice cream?" Ari asked on a choke of disbelief.

Willow gestured toward the candy. "Should have bet on that."

Gussie shook her head, hands on hips. "Neither one of us is dumb enough to bet on you and ice cream."

"I can't believe you ate ice cream," Ari teased. "Next, you'll be breaking the pact."

"What pact?" Lacey Walker, owner of the Casa Blanca resort, tapped on the frame of the open door to announce herself.

Brown eyes twinkling and her reddish-blond curls tumbling, Lacey was an unlikely resort owner. But her status as a lifelong resident of Barefoot Bay and a survivor of a hurricane that had made way for Casa Blanca gave her tremendous street cred. Plus, she was a damn nice lady who'd given them an office and welcomed an on-site wedding planning firm with open arms.

"I don't know about a pact," she reiterated after they'd waved her in with a warm greeting.

"Should we tell her?" Gussie asked.

Willow and Ari shrugged and nodded. "It's not a secret," Ari said. "The three of us decided we'd stick with planning and never actually have weddings of our own."

Lacey looked surprised. "You never want to get married?

Not one of you is over thirty yet. You don't know what can happen."

"Oh, we might get married," Ari explained as she pulled out her chair to settle in. "But we don't want weddings."

"We've seen one too many bridezillas," Willow explained. "They're all fraught with anxiety and stress. Wasn't your wedding stressful?"

Lacey laughed. "My wedding? Well, I thought I was attending the Casa Blanca groundbreaking ceremony when the mayor appeared, Clay proposed, and we said 'I do' in the same two minutes."

Ari pumped her fist in the air. "That's the way to do it, baby."

"Well, I wouldn't go making pacts you might not be able to keep," Lacey warned.

"We'll keep it," Willow assured her. "We are the anti-wedding wedding planners, but please, don't tell the clients."

"I won't," Lacey said. "And speaking of clients, how can I thank you?"

They all looked perplexed. "For what?" Ari asked.

"For the one-month rental of Artemisia." Lacey opened the file in her hands and flattened it on the conference table. "This is especially nice for us in the spring when we don't always book every villa."

"Misty is staying for a month?" Willow asked.

"No, she already took off in her limo and asked that we let you know the wedding's a go, and she'll handle everything by phone or conference call or—"

"Then who is it?" Willow asked, hating that her voice sounded so tense.

"Her man of honor. That hot Navy SEAL that has every female head in the resort getting whiplash when he runs the beach."

Willow could feel Ari and Gussie grinning. She didn't even have to look. "He's…staying for a month?"

"Misty said Nick Hershey could handle the little details that need to be done in person." Lacey slid the file forward. "I guess he's a writer or something. Did you guys know that?"

Willow kept her eyes on Lacey, refusing to meet her friends' eyes. "Yes, I did know that," she said.

"Apparently, there's something in the air in Barefoot Bay," Lacey said with a laugh.

"Something." Ari spoke under her breath, but Willow heard her.

"He's had a creative breakthrough."

"Is that what they call it now?" Gussie whispered.

"So he doesn't want to leave," Lacey continued with a huge smile. "We *love* long-term bookings, so thank you. You guys are such an awesome addition to Casa Blanca."

While the others turned the moment into a little love fest of mutual appreciation, Willow nodded, still not sure of her voice.

He was staying for a month? No one, not the strongest woman on earth, could avoid temptation that long.

Then maybe she shouldn't.

Lacey wasn't five feet down the hall when Ari made a dive for the candy on the desk. "I won that bet! There will so be a second date."

"Double or nothing on a third," Gussie said.

"You guys." Willow nearly stomped her foot. "Stop and let me deal."

"What's to deal?" Gussie asked. "He's staying to write his book. Whatever happened yesterday must have *really* inspired him."

Willow fought a smile, the idea of Nick staying for a month settling slowly on her heart. Would it be *that* bad?

Ari looked positively satisfied as she opened the candy. "The universe is speaking. It is *demanding* that you come to terms with your past and give this guy a shot."

Without responding, Willow gathered Lacey's file and flipped it open, reading the information.

Nicholas S. Hershey

Gussie leaned over her shoulders. "S for Smokin'."

No, Spencer. But she didn't tell them she knew that many details about him. That would just fuel their gambling habit. "I think I'll go talk to him," she said.

"Does that count for date number two?" Gussie asked Ari, but Willow didn't stick around for the answer. She was out the door before they made the next wager.

Chapter Nine

The pounding sounded like gunfire. Nick dug deeper into sleep, unwilling to let the sounds of distant firefights steal the shut-eye he so desperately needed. He'd been up all night, fighting.

They'd gone to a farmhouse, backing up Marines who'd been pinned by enemy sniper fire.

Hadn't they? Or did he dream that? The *rat-a-tat* got louder. An AK? They'd seen action in the village, and Charlotte had insisted on taking pictures. He'd yelled at her. She'd smiled at him.

"Don't make me use the master key again!"

What did she say? He grunted in his sleep, his face flat in the pillow, the material…way too mushy for a vacant house in the middle of Afghanistan. Too silky. Too soft. Too…much like a woman in his arms.

The voice invaded his dreams. A woman. Charlotte wasn't here. They'd made her leave when—

"Nicholas Spencer Hershey, I'm coming in!"

Not Lieutenant. Not Nick. Not *Kiss*. His whole name. Like an eagle's talons were dragging his lids up, he managed to open his eyes, then instantly closed them again when daylight assaulted. Instinctively, he flipped the pillow over his head, smashing it hard to block everything. It smelled like flowers or mint or the purple soap his mother put out for guests. On a pillow?

A pillow? There was no such thing in combat.

Instantly, he threw the puffy mass off his head and sat up, blinking and rising to consciousness, a punch of relief followed by the hot splash of an adrenaline dump. He'd been dreaming.

A door latch snapped. "I'm in, and you better be dressed this time."

Willow. The resort. The book. Reality crashed like a six-foot wave at Redondo, rushing over him with a sweet and satisfying pressure. This was so, so much better than a bunker and a battle.

"I am," he called, his voice rough from deep sleep. "Sort of," he added in a whisper he knew she couldn't hear.

The click of heels on hardwood echoed through the villa. *His* villa. For a whole month. He had his own writing oasis, and here came his—

"You're staying?"

His inspiration. He squinted at her, still not used to the outrageous sunlight because he'd forgotten to close his blinds at dawn. Maybe it was the light, but she was a study in hues of lemon yellow, a tall blonde in a buttery dress, a beautiful Willow.

"Man, your parents gave you the right name."

Her eyes flashed a hundred different emotions, none of them very...nice. "You're staying for a month?" she asked again, with not too much joy in the question.

"Yeah." He dragged the word out and gave a sleepy smile, sitting up on the bed, suddenly aware of how big that bed was. And how much he wanted to throw back the sheet and fill it with Willow. "Is that not the shitz?"

She frowned but didn't answer.

He gestured toward the laptop still open on a small desk. "It *works* here, Willow. My writing just works. I don't know why, but it's good."

Her brows furrowed some more, and she lost a fight not to let her gaze slip to his bare chest. "That's...great."

"It is," he insisted, even though it was obvious she didn't agree. "It's so huge." He pushed the sheet back and threw his legs out, seeing her eyes widen at his naked body, which was the only way he slept when not deployed.

"Yes...it...is..." She pursed her lips and tried valiantly to look anywhere but at his dick. "Huge."

As she flushed, he felt an erection stir, probably from waking up. Maybe from being this close to her. Grabbing sweats he'd dropped on the floor, he stepped into them, still smiling at her. "And you can help me."

"Help you?" Her voice cracked as she finally found his face. "With planning the wedding?"

He laughed. "With writing."

"How?"

Judging by how gray and stormy her eyes looked, that prospect didn't exactly thrill her. So he took a few steps closer, eyeing her since she refused to look right at him. "I was on fire last night, Willow."

Her gaze dropped over his bare chest, eyes widening. "Really."

"The book is..." He shook his head, not wanting to jinx it with bragging. He didn't know if what he'd written was good or not, only that the words and story felt so damn right.

Would it all be different this morning?

Turning to the laptop, he tapped the keyboard, firing up the screen to the last scene. He scrolled through the pages, getting another head rush at how much progress he'd made.

Last night, for the first time, he'd believed he could finish this book and it could be good.

"You want to read the kiss scene? I know we joked, but that kiss, our kiss, it really did help. I want you to be the first reader."

"I don't..." When her voice trailed off, he looked over his shoulder at her.

"Sure, you do. It doesn't suck. Well, if it does, you can tell me. We can talk about it while we do all those wedding errands together and—"

"Nick." She crossed her arms, and he could practically hear those heels digging into the wood. "You can't just decide I'm going to read your book and help you run wedding errands and...and...*be* here for you."

He flinched at the tone. "You're right, that was presumptuous. I'll...pay you?" It came out as a question, and her raised eyebrow was all the answer he needed.

"I already have a job, Nick."

"Okay, bad idea. But I'm excited and..." He wanted her to be, too. "What's wrong?"

She arched an eyebrow and looked pointedly at his chest. "Put a shirt on."

He obliged, snagging a T-shirt off the back of the nearest chair and yanking it over his head. She didn't look any happier when he popped out. "You don't want me to stay," he said, stating the über-obvious.

"I don't want you to..." She held up her hands as if she could physically stave him off. "I don't want you to take charge of me."

"We don't have to kiss again." Except they would. And often. Soon, even, if he had anything to say about it. "Or eat ice cream," he added, hoping for some levity.

"We won't...we can't...I can't." She swiped some hair

off her face in frustration. "Not that I don't want to."

There. Now they were talking. "Then, good. We're good. I'll work when you're working, and when we're free, we'll"—*do everything*—"take care of that wedding sh...stuff." As if he could prove that was true, he glanced around, looking for the paper Misty said she'd leave. "Hang on, let me find her list."

He didn't see it and vaguely recalled her saying it would be in the living area, so he held up a hand as if that would freeze Willow in place. "Wait here. Don't move."

"You're big on giving orders."

"Military training."

"I thought you *took* orders in the military."

He smiled. "If I have to. Hang on." He slipped by her and went into the living room looking for Misty's list or folder. He hardly remembered what he'd agreed to the night before. At that point, he was up four thousand words and on a roll like he'd never been on before.

Telling the story—retelling it, actually, and changing the facts so they mirrored what he'd *wanted* to happen—was an absolute high. He spied a piece of paper folded in half on the kitchen pass-through counter and snagged it, opening it to read the list.

Leaving the F&B entirely up to you. RD & CP (go crazy, it's on Steven), WP brunch, hd's & recpt. dinner. Cake. DA brunch. All themed, whatever you and W work out. Will call you and be back soon w/ mf!! xo

Huh? The only thing he understood was "cake." Thank God for Willow. Heading back to the room, he glanced at the paper, looking up when he reached the doorway. He opened his mouth to joke about how weddings had more acronyms than the military, but froze at the sight of her reading his laptop.

She was leaning over to get closer to the screen, bracing her hands on the desk, and he was torn between the minor thrill of watching someone actually read what he'd written and the major thrill of checking out her backside in a very sexy pose.

Her hips were round, her legs crossed as she tapped one shoe on the floor. Even the slope of her back and the way her hair tumbled over her shoulders turned him on. Whatever magic, denial, or deal she'd made with the devil to get in shape had worked.

She had to see how awesome this month could be. But he didn't want to interrupt her reading, so he stepped back, and instantly, she turned.

He'd almost forgotten what it was like to hear someone behind you that easily. The thought kicked him a little, but he pushed it away, trying to read her expression and hide his own lusty thoughts.

"You want to read more?" he asked hopefully.

"I have to—"

"Good." When she laughed, he winked. "I'll make some coffee. And bagels. Or…fruit. There's tons of fruit. Would you like that?"

"Fruit's perfect."

He held out both hands. "Sit down and read. Enjoy. Will you?"

She laughed again. "I get the impression this is really important to you."

"It is." Why lie?

"Okay. Fruit and coffee. And quit staring at me."

"A and B I can do. C? Not so sure." He grinned. "You got a nice back view, Willie."

Her jaw tightened. "Don't call me that. Ever."

He didn't want to push his luck or lose her, so he backed

up, nodding, letting her go. "You can scroll up to the top of the document and start from the beginning."

"I already did."

His heart slammed with affection. Smiling, he made coffee and cut up fruit from the basket she'd hand delivered, and only checked on her progress three times. The last time, when he asked how she took her coffee, her answer was curt enough that his hope soared. She didn't want to be interrupted.

He took her raspberries and bananas with a cup of black coffee, then backed away to give her some space to read the pages he'd written so far—eighty-five by computer count—unfold in front of her. He drank his own coffee on the patio, but the minute he was done, he stepped back into the bedroom.

She looked up, narrowing her eyes at him. "Are you going to watch me read?"

Yeah. "No. I'm going to…run. The beach. What page are you on?"

"Thirty-two."

"What scene?"

"He's arguing with that moron Mitchell guy about the farmhouse."

Just the fact that she got Mitchell was a moron did something insane to his insides. "Did you like when—"

She pointed to the door. "Out."

"Out?"

"To the beach. The garden. The moon. Let me read."

He felt the smile overtake his face. "You like it?"

"O-U-T."

"That's a yes."

She laughed softly and shook her head. "I would never have taken you for so insecure."

"I'm not," he denied hotly, straightening up. "I want you to like the book."

"Then let me read it."

"Okay, fair enough." He scooped up a pair of sneakers from the floor, opting for the dirty socks stuffed inside rather than taking a minute of her reading time to find clean ones. "I'm out."

"Thank you." She returned her attention to the screen, and he froze mid-step, drinking her in.

"No, thank *you*."

She nodded, riveted on the words on the screen. His words. On an impulse, he slammed his hands on the armrests of her chair, earning a gasp from her as she jerked back.

"What?"

"I said thank you," he murmured.

"You're welcome." Plenty of sarcasm in that, but he smiled and leaned over the laptop, right into her mouth, for a quick kiss. Too quick. The second it was over, he wanted more.

But he resisted, standing straight, kind of enjoying the look on her face, then heading out without another word, hitting the sand with the same fury and speed he had in training, eating up the beach at Barefoot Bay like it was a second breakfast and he was starving.

He *was* starving. For feedback. And encouragement. And someone he respected to tell him he wasn't wasting his time and life. That he could tell a story.

Then he could change history, erase his mistakes, and turn them into something good, at least on paper.

He ran up and down the beach, past the exit to the property, along the road that led into town, then all the way back, coming back to the Arte-whatever villa drenched in sweat. When he opened the front door, he half-expected her to be standing there with champagne and a smile, ready to toast his story. He'd been gone well over an hour, long enough to read what he'd written so far.

But the living room was empty, so he went back to where he'd left her. That was empty, too.

"Willow?" he called.

"Out here."

He went to the French doors and stepped out onto the back patio that led to a screened-in pool, finding her sitting on the ground, feet in the water, her yellow dress pulled up to her thighs.

"Well?" He blamed his racing, slamming, unstoppable heart on the run, but after the kind of training he did, he knew this pulse rate was due to nerves and anticipation.

"Yeah, well."

He blinked at her. What the hell did that mean? "Yeah, well, what?"

"It's…" She gave him a tight smile, her eyes turning deep blue now. An apologetic, pitiful blue. "It's good, Nick."

Just good. And not a really enthusiastic good, either. More like a…*meh* kind of good. "Not great?"

She didn't answer right away, but looked like she was searching for words. Words that wouldn't sting. Shit.

"It has so much potential. You have so much potential."

He stared at her. Screw potential. That's not what he wanted to hear.

"You know what you have to do, right?"

Curse? Punch a wall? Quit? "Start over?"

"No, you have to tell the truth."

"It's fiction, Willow."

"Okay, then tell your truth."

He closed his eyes, the shot a direct hit.

Chapter Ten

"I could have lied," Willow said. And maybe she should have, because Nick's gutted expression made her remember how she felt when something she said, did, wanted, or wore didn't stand up to her mother's rigorous expectations. "But that book's too good to lie."

"You just said it sucked."

"No, no." She shook her head vehemently. "I did not. I said it could be even better. Would I be out here cooling myself off if that make-out scene didn't...affect me?" And by affect, she meant turn her entire lower half into a pool of liquid lust. His language was evocative and tantalizing, the imagery completely sexy without being corny.

"It affected you?" A spark of hope lit his eyes, but she didn't get to enjoy it, because he snagged the bottom of his T-shirt and ripped it over his head. Speaking of evocative and tantalizing...

His abs were so defined, there were shadows in between the muscle cuts. His chest, damp with sweat, heaved with a deep breath, drawing her gaze to the blue ink near his left shoulder, the semicircle that represented the earth and single star high above it. This wasn't the first time she'd seen a fan with the Zenith album graphic tattooed on him, but it was definitely the first time she'd had the urge to…lick it.

He toed off his sneakers and tipped his head toward the water. "I'm hot."

No kidding.

"I'm going in."

"Suit yourself."

"Actually…" He pulled at the waistband of his sweats. "Unsuit myself is more appropriate."

Her jaw unhinged. "You're going in naked?"

"You've seen it before."

"Doesn't mean I want to see it again." *Liar, liar.* But, still, after reading that kiss, she wasn't sure her libido could stand the pressure.

"I hate clothes."

Just her luck. She leaned back on her palms, squinting up at him. "Sadly, our society requires them."

He thumbed his sweats lower, revealing more skin and muscle. "If it offends you, look away. I'll be in the pool in a second."

"I don't think the word is 'offend.'"

She waited for his grin or quip, but his expression was still dark. He inched the sweats down, following that sweet strip of dark hair, sliding over those narrow hips, across the ripped muscles that led right to…

She really ought to close her eyes. Or turn her head. *Or peel off her dress and join him.*

"You're killing me, Nick," she admitted.

"Punishment for hating my book."

"Oh, yeah, looking at you bare-ass naked is absolute torture."

Finally, he smiled. "As bad as the book?"

"Would you stop? I didn't hate it. I think it's amazing and could be even more amazing."

He didn't answer, but in one smooth move, he dove into the deep end in a way that gave her a perfect view of his ass. Which, even upside-down, made her mouth go bone dry.

She watched him swim, his perfect form distorted enough by the water that it wasn't completely obscene, just…wonderful. He moved like he'd been born in the water, shooting from one side of the pool to the other in long, powerful, silent strokes.

As he neared her end, she leaned forward to really get a good look and, whoosh, he turned with the grace of a trained swimmer and pushed himself back to the other side.

She expected him to pop up, but he came back again, then returned, then back again.

How long could he hold his breath? He had to have been under there forty-five seconds already.

But he gave an easy kick and shot across the bottom again, back and forth until she lost count. Finally, he surfaced about six inches away from her, not a bit winded.

"Damn," he muttered. "I didn't even make two minutes." He smacked the water.

"How long did you want to stay under?"

He shook his hands in the air. "Unbound and in seventy-five-degree water? Two minutes sucks. Shit." He snorted some water. "I suck today."

"Okay, pity party's over." She splashed some water with her feet. "Can we talk about the book now? Because I loved so much of it."

He swiped his hair off his face and stood in five feet of water in front of her, his shoulders and head glistening in the sun, the dark nest of hair and man below the water line, everything visible enough to torment the hell out of her.

He took a step closer, and she fought not to look down. Didn't most men shy away from water for fear of shrinkage?

Of course, if that thing shrank, it would be nearing normal. His eyes were mesmerizing enough to hold her gaze, water droplets on the lashes almost like tears.

"Tell me what you loved."

She flipped her feet and made waves around his chest, enjoying the hint of vulnerability on a man who looked anything but right now. "I got a little misty-eyed when he left his sister."

"You cried?"

"It felt, you know, real."

He grunted softly and dropped underwater. *What the hell?*

But before she could figure out what had just happened, he surfaced, shaking water off his head before saying, "It was real."

"So the book is autobiographical?"

His head went under. Damn it! She kicked water so hard her toe touched his forehead, and she instantly snatched it back, but not before his hand clamped around her ankle. She shrieked as he tugged.

He emerged slowly, gripping her ankle firmly, his large hand easily spanning the diameter. "You wanna play water games with a SEAL?" He grinned. "'Cause you'll lose."

Tugging a little more, he inched her closer to the edge. She'd be in and soaking wet in seconds. The thought of being in the water with him sent something unholy right down to the toes that practically curled in his hand. He'd peel off her dress, strip her down to nothing, and—

"No," he said, the word ripping her from Fantasy Land.

"What?"

"No, it's not autobiographical."

She eyed him. "Lieutenant *Spencer* Gannon is a SEAL from Northern California who played every sport ever invented, went to UCLA, and was deployed in Afghanistan. You're telling me he's not based on Lieutenant Nicholas *Spencer* Hershey with the same bio?"

He narrowed his eyes and cocked his head. "How do you know my middle name?"

Because she'd licked up crumbs of information about Nick Hershey like a starving puppy cleaning the kitchen floor. "I'm smart like that. Am I right? That Gannon character is you, through and through."

He didn't answer right away, probably because denial would have been a lie. "They say write what you know," he finally said.

As he spoke, he reached for her other ankle, and she didn't bother to fight that. The pleasure of it was instant and real, like taking a thumbnail-size piece of a chocolate-chip cookie. So easy to rationalize the quick flash of deliciousness, so small it didn't count.

But then she should have inched away, wrested free, or demanded he let go.

She didn't. That was the second bite. She waited for the twist of guilt, but the only thing she felt was much lower and sharper and more primal. After all, a gorgeous man was stark naked and holding on to her ankles, and she was in a dress with enough flowy material in the skirt that he could easily…spread her legs.

So she didn't fight or move or, really, breathe. She simply reveled in the sensation of his hands on her skin.

"Tell me the truth: Am I wasting my time?" he asked quietly. "Is this a pipe dream?"

"Trying to get me in the water with you? Yes."

He gave her a look. "You know what I mean. The book. Is it a complete clusterfuck that should be deleted?"

"Nick, I'm not a professional who knows anything about

books. You could ask a literary agent or a publisher or someone who reads military memoirs."

"I will, but it's not a memoir." He squeezed a little harder. "It's fiction. It's an action thriller set in the theater of war."

Not to her. "I think it's more of a romance."

His lip curled in pure disdain. "Like hell it is."

"Well, Gannon likes that reporter, Charlotte."

His eyes flashed in shock. "That's not her name. It's Christina."

"Yeah, I noticed you switched back and forth. It was Christina in the beginning, but the stuff you wrote toward the end, you called her Charlotte. I made a note of that for you."

He grimaced. "I was power writing at that point. Fast."

"So, maybe that tells you something about this character."

A whisper of fear flickered over his face, as fleeting as a moving shadow. "Like what?"

"Like I said, I'm no expert, but maybe the fact that you don't have her name straight is a sign she's not completely clear in your head."

"No, she's clear." Suddenly, he let go of her ankles and disappeared again, launching into another lengthy underwater session.

Willow let the water lap against her legs, though it did little to cool her off while she watched his naked form glide from end to end. She inhaled a whiff of summer-scented air, suddenly getting another clear insight into Nick. He was like an ostrich—only his hiding place was water, not sand.

And Charlotte/Christina was real. She knew that like she knew her own name.

He finally popped up.

"I now understand why you became a SEAL."

"The classic response to that is so I can blow shit up, as you've probably heard."

"Not you," she said, fluttering her feet in the water. "You go underwater when you want to avoid something."

He considered that, blinking water out of his eyes. "And you run. We all have our avoidance techniques."

"You don't want to avoid my comments, do you?"

"If you tell me I'm writing a romance novel, I do. Because it's a military—"

"Action thriller. Got it. Do they all have so much kissing, touching and, whoa, tender scenes outside of the village?"

"Tender?" He sounded wounded. "I was going for 'rip your guts out' with that gunfire in the background."

"Reminded me of his heartbeat."

He shook his head. "And how he washed out her injury? Dude's capable."

"And romantic."

"Shit." He slapped the water, eyeing it like the escape called to him. She sneaked a good long look at what was below the water line, not quite clear enough to make out the details, but sufficiently visible to make her whole body sweat and tingle and knot with need.

"It's not a freaking romance novel," he murmured, ducking back to wet his hair and swipe it straight off his face. Even with the Dracula look, he was handsome.

"Does she live or die?" Willow asked.

He stared at her, silent. Maybe speechless.

"Because that will dictate what kind of book you're writing," she explained. "I don't know about the business of writing a book, but I read a lot. And my guess is that if she dies, you have a better shot at the military-action-thriller reader, but if she lives, you're going to get the happy-ending people. I've never read a romance that didn't have a happy ending, and someone dies in every military thriller."

"Lots of books have happy endings." Frustration and emotion made his voice gruff. "I don't understand why that matters where the hell they stick it in a bookstore."

"All I know is that if she dies, you're safe. It's not a romance."

A storm brewed in his eyes. "Well, she's going to live," he said softly. "She *has* to live." That last sentence was spoken even more softly, but still she could hear one thing in his voice. This mattered to him.

"Will that feel real?"

"Real? I don't care if it feels real. It's better than real." Down he went under the water again.

Had he loved this Charlotte/Christina? Or just lost her? Whatever, Willow had no doubt the woman was real, and he wanted her to live...at least in fiction, and probably in his memory.

When he shot up, he shook his head like a wet dog, and she waited for him to look at her again.

"Don't." Willow pointed at him.

He froze, his expression dark. "Don't what? Don't let her live? I have to. That's the whole point of the book. If she dies, then...then. No, I won't even listen to that. It's not up for consideration."

Definitely still alive in his memory. "I was going to say, 'Don't go underwater again.'"

"Oh." He stepped closer, humor gone from his eyes as they narrowed and locked on her.

She sighed, giving a little kick. "Hey, listen to me. That book *doesn't* suck. You should really, really write your heart out and..." *Heal whatever's hurting you.* "Get this off your chest."

"I don't have anything on my chest," he said.

Only a tattoo of her dad's biggest-selling album and some pretty well-developed muscles. Not to mention some memories that were apparently weighing him down.

"Why don't you just tell me the book is great and I should have at it?"

Good question. Because, deep inside—hell, right on the surface—she cared about him and wanted to help him. Well, get out the Stupid file and stick *that* thought in there. "Because the book is so good I didn't want to stop reading. That's not something just anyone can do, you know. As soon as I finished one scene, I wanted to gobble up another."

He took a few steps closer. "Thanks, Willow."

"Thanks for letting me read it."

He toyed with her ankles again. "You care if that dress stays dry or not?"

She laughed. "Yes, I care if it stays dry."

"Really? 'Cause I was thinking about…more water games."

"More subject avoidance, I'd say."

He quirked a brow and fought a smile. "Semantics. Come on in." He tugged at her legs.

"No."

"If your dress gets soaked, you'll have to take it off. Remember the regs. Full frontal gets full frontal."

She kicked some water at him. "I think it's more like 'honest critique gets dunked.'"

Without answering, he clutched her ankles firmly, very slowly moving them side to side over the top of the water.

"Don't even think about it," she warned.

"Too late for that. I'm thinking. *Hard.*"

The emphasis on the last word hit her like a little bullet way down low in the part of her that was burning enough to need to be in that water. This was desire. She might not know a lot about…this, but she knew desire when it lit up her ladybits with sparks.

She was definitely playing with fire, in spite of all the water around.

"I have a conference call scheduled in a few minutes, and I'm not sure what my partners would say if I arrived in a soaking-wet dress," she finally said. In other words, *I gotta run*.

"Misty left some clothes in the closet that she didn't feel like packing." He tugged her legs a little harder, moving her rear end over the warm stones by the pool. Temptation nearly drowned her as if she were already under.

"As if that pencil's clothes would fit me."

He winced, a look she knew all too well. Shame or discomfort or flat-out not knowing if it's proper to mention a woman's weight—even her former, dieted-off weight—or not.

"Then take off your dress and keep it dry."

She gave in to a smile. "I'm not going swimming with you."

"But you're thinking about it."

"Am not."

"Of course you are. I can tell by"—very slowly, he spread her legs, her swing skirt easily accommodating the move—"your eyes." He stepped right between her legs, his waist at the side of the pool. She had to look down at him. She had to put her hands on his wet, strong shoulders because…she *had* to.

"What about my eyes?" she asked, spreading her palms over the warm, hard skin.

"They go full-on slate gray." He closed the space and then slowly lifted his face toward hers. "When you're thinking about sexy things."

Then they must be positively silver around him. "There is a naked man standing between my legs, his face two inches from my boobs. Yes, it is possible I'm thinking sexy things."

That made him grin. He leaned a little closer, enough so that she could feel his breath on her cleavage, exposed in a scoop-necked top. "Then come in the water, Willow."

She pushed his shoulders back. "On one condition."

He looked to the sky. "I hate conditions."

"One."

His gaze dropped to her breasts, his expression hungry enough to make the very nipples he was so close to pop like little buds. "All right," he conceded. "What's the one condition?"

"Tell that story how it really happened."

Even in the blazing sunshine, he paled. "No."

She shrugged, and in one fast, sharp, lightning move, she escaped his touch and stood up. Or maybe he let go. She couldn't tell. "Then your book won't be as wonderful as it could be. I have to go."

"Willow, come on. Don't leave."

"I have work to do. And so do you." She stepped away from the side of the pool and blew him a kiss. "Or you could hide underwater."

He waited exactly three heartbeats before he did precisely that. Willow left before he emerged and tempted her to stay.

Chapter Eleven

"Hey, you're here." Gussie pushed Willow's kitchen door open, wearing a baseball cap and beach cover-up, her skin glowing from an afternoon in the sun. A few strands of her rarely seen natural golden brown hair slipped out from under one side, and her unmade-up eyes looked almost eerily clear after seeing them under pounds of makeup all week. "You never came back to the office, so we figured you were still with Nick."

"God, no, I left him this afternoon and had a bunch of other stuff to do. I figured with Misty gone, we didn't have that much pending at work today."

"We didn't. Ari and I went to the beach. She just went upstairs to change, and I was on my way when I saw you in the window. I guess you don't want to go out to dinner." She gestured toward the giant salad bowl and the carrot and knife in Willow's hand.

"No, I'll eat in tonight. How was the beach?"

"Hot. How was Nick?"

"The same." She eased into a smile. "He swam naked."

"Get out of town!"

"I wish he was, but he's not."

"Damn, I should have put big candy on that one."

Willow laughed and handed her a carrot. "Here. Eat nature's candy."

Gussie's face said exactly what she thought of that, but she took the carrot. "Were you naked, too?"

"Nope. That never seems to stop him, though."

She crunched a bite, eyeing Willow from under her baseball cap. "Can I ask why not?"

"As if you wouldn't ask even if I said no to that question."

Gussie shrugged. "True that. So, what's going on with you two?"

Willow didn't answer right away, wiping her cutting board clean and choosing a pepper to cut up next. "Nothing, actually. No, that's a lie because there's definitely something, but I don't think it's anything."

She got a good guffaw in response to that. "So, nothing, something, or anything. Take your pick."

It was as convoluted as it sounded. "Well, he asked me to read what he's written of his novel, and I did, but I don't think he loved what I had to say."

"It's not good?"

"It's very good, but it could be even better. He's holding back and not really being honest." She looked up, knife in mid-cut. "He seems to want my opinion but not want it, you know? Plus, who am I to tell him what to write? I read books, not write them. But I really wanted to be honest, because it's good enough to be amazing if he works on it."

"The fact that you'd tell him that makes you the perfect person to give him an opinion. Plus, he probably figures next time you will get naked with him."

Willow shook her head. "He just likes to get naked."

"And the problem with that…"

"I…I…" *Am not going to talk about this.* "It's too soon and too late."

Gussie laughed again. "You're a walking contradiction today, Willow."

"Because I'm confused," she admitted, setting down the knife. "This is not my first time around Nick, as you know."

"But everything is different now, especially you."

Not everything was different now. There were some things that no diet, discipline, or distance would ever change. And the truth of that was starting to weigh heavily on her.

"Right, Willow?"

Willow smiled at her friend. A dear friend, a trusted friend, and a friend who wouldn't mock her for choices she'd made or hadn't made in the past, right? "Right," she agreed, her voice tight. Then, on a sigh, she added, "I guess."

"What does that mean?"

"It means that…" She toyed with the pepper stem, twirling it in her hand and thinking how Gussie would react if she knew everything about Willow. It wouldn't change how Gussie felt about Willow, but—

"Trouble, you guys." Ari pushed open the kitchen door, holding her phone out. "I just got a text from Jill Peyton."

Willow sighed with relief at the reprieve. "Uh oh," she said. "The bride who put the cray in crazy."

"No kidding," Ari said, also still dressed in a beach cover-up, her amber-gold skin glistening from sunscreen. "Her last red-flag email was an order that only a specific pattern of Waterford crystal be on the tables and, of course, it's only available from the manufacturer. In Ireland. With a six-month wait."

"But you brilliantly found it all on Ebay, so whatever she wants, we shall solve. I hope." Gussie was always so optimistic.

Ari waved the phone. "Unless I can find twins on Ebay,

we're out of luck. She wants us to provide a 'matching' ring bearer and flower girl."

"What about her cousin's kids?" Gussie asked. "We already found that four-year-old girl a persimmon and peach dress and matching boy's tux that shipped to us last Wednesday and will be here tomorrow."

"Jill had a falling out with her cousin, and now she needs replacement kids," Ari said. "And we have exactly ten days to supply them, and they have to match, and they have to fit in the clothes that have been ordered."

"She's wack!" Gussie exclaimed. "We don't supply the wedding party. The bride and groom do."

"Ahem," Willow fake-cleared. "Barefoot Brides? Kick off your shoes and let us plan."

Ari nodded. "Okay, then what about Tessa and Chef Ian's twins?" she suggested, referring to the nearly five-year-old tow-headed children of the resort's chef.

"Great idea," Willow agreed. "We can talk to Tessa to see if she'll agree. But this reminds me of something I got from Nick today."

"An eyeful?" Gussie teased. "You'll have to tell Ari how he skinny-dipped for your viewing pleasure."

"If she can decipher this." Willow pulled out the note that Misty had written for Nick, letting them both read the brief and unintelligible message.

Leaving the F&B entirely up to you. RD & CP (go crazy, it's on Steven), WP brunch, hd's & recpt. dinner. Cake. DA brunch. All themed, whatever you and W work out. Will call you and be back soon w/ mf!! xo

"F&B is food and bev," Gussie said. "RD is rehearsal dinner. CP?" She squished up her nose. "I don't know, but let's charge a lot if it's on Steven."

"Cocktail party?" Ari suggested.

"WP is wedding party brunch," Gussie said. "And hd's? Hot dogs? Happy dates? Huge dic—"

"Hors d'oeuvres," Willow interjected. "Get your mind out of the gutter, will you?"

"Says the woman who's seen his hammer twice."

"Cake means cake," Ari said.

"You're a genius." Gussie gave her an elbow. "And DA would be…"

"Day-after brunch."

"But what's this mean?" Willow tapped the page. "I'll get back to you soon with mf?"

"My fiancé," Ari said with a smug smile. "See? I do speak Misty."

"Apparently, you do." Willow stepped back to her vegetables, picking up the pepper, but seeing that cryptic note in her mind's eye. "Why would she leave so many critical details and sparse directions to a guy she barely knows? It's weird."

"She's a busy model," Gussie said. "He's here, and we're here, she's back in New York."

"Really," Ari agreed. "Don't question a gift! The universe could be stingy next time."

Willow rolled her eyes. "I've never seen any bride less interested in the planning of a wedding, not to mention one that has no mother, maid of honor, sister, or best friend to nudge her along. It's like the only thing she got excited about was the dress."

"I just said, she's a model," Gussie repeated, as though that explained it.

Willow wasn't buying it. "Have you ever, in your career, met a bride willing to let a guy handle the *cake*? The reception menu? Anything more important than buying the groomsmen some gifts?"

Ari crossed her arms and leaned her hip against the counter. "I have to agree, it's strange."

"It's like she doesn't even care about this wedding," Willow said. "It's like an afterthought to her." She sliced the pepper carefully.

"I guess that means you'll have to be very involved," Ari said. "And spending a lot of time with Nick."

Willow slowly put the pepper slices on top of her salad, considering just what that would mean. "If I do, he's going to want me to help him with this book, I just know it."

"She's his muse," Gussie explained to Ari.

"Do you want that job?" Ari asked.

Willow gnawed at her lip, thinking about it. "I'd love to help him, and he obviously has some stuff from the war he needs to get over, but should I?" She looked at her friends, wishing they had the answer…except they both didn't know the extent of the question.

"Because you're scared you'll get hurt again?" Gussie asked.

Yes and no. "I guess I'm afraid that if I help him face his past, he's going to make me face my own."

Ari gave a slow smile. "Oh, I love when the universe does its magical things." She reached into the salad bowl and stole a fresh pepper, biting it with a gleam in her eyes. "You can't do anything but sit back and enjoy the ride."

After he ran, Nick did a hundred push-ups, three hundred crunches, and held a plank for as long as it took to listen to Z-Train's live version of *My Sweet Ambrosia*. And he still had energy to burn. After writing until two A.M., he wasn't sure what kind of juice he was running on, but it felt good.

Creative juice. That's what it was. Ever since Willow left yesterday, he'd been swimming in the stuff. He'd written until his fingers felt like they were going to fall off—well, he'd rewritten, more accurately.

It hadn't been easy at first. He had to stew about her advice for a while, stare at the pages and rationalize why she was wrong, but then…he went back over some of the scenes where he'd introduced the character of Christina.

Two things happened. He wrote fast and furious, and when he went to sleep, instead of dreaming about a sultry brunette with a risky streak, his mind was on a willowy blonde with a wry smile and the inability to look away when he stripped.

So maybe she was right. And kind of an inspiration, because when he woke up, all he wanted to do was write more…and have Willow read it.

On his bed, his cell buzzed, making him hope it was her. But when he looked at the screen, a different kind of happiness hit. Damn, he needed this call, too.

"Trew Blue," he said, forgoing a standard greeting for his closest friend, Lieutenant Jason Trew. "How's it hanging, bro?"

"Low and long, my man." Jason Trew's voice echoed with his signature sense of joy, an unwavering belief that all the shit in the world didn't matter as long as you had friends who had your back.

Trew had sure had Nick's back when that IED blew. If it hadn't been for Trew's reflexes and willingness to take a chance, Nick would have lost a lot more than his hearing. Most likely a limb…or his life.

"Where are you?" Nick asked, closing his eyes to imagine where his platoon could be now. No way of knowing. He was out of the loop.

"Some fucking hellhole near water."

Nick snorted, getting a lot from that non-answer. First, Trew wasn't at liberty to say, even to another SEAL teammate. Second, it was not land-locked. Third, it was somewhere hot. Hot for action or hot in the air, but hot. He didn't need to know much more.

"Staying out of trouble?" Nick asked, knowing that despite the casual nature of the question, Trew would know it was quite serious.

"We could use you, Nicky. Your sub is kind of a dick. How the hell's your ear?"

Nick lifted his left hand to touch the ear, a sickening drop in his stomach. "No change as far as I can tell."

"Damn it, really? When are you coming back?"

His whole body literally ached with the desire to answer that question with "soon." But that would have been a lie, and he knew it.

"Not cleared yet." Because he was still deaf in one ear. "Doc wants to give it more time."

He heard Trew's exhale of frustration. "Ah, that blows."

"No shit. But I'm alive, man."

Trew barely grunted. "Anybody talking about the next move for you?"

"Not yet." But it was only a matter of time until the Navy made a decision about what to do with him. He hadn't had enough combat experience to do much training, but he might work at the SEAL prep school or some other desk job. Until he could hear the enemy sneaking up on him, he wasn't going back into action, that was for sure. And he missed it. A lot.

"In the meantime, I'm here doing your dirty work, my man." Nick went for light, but it might not have come out that way.

"It doesn't suck, right?"

"Hell, no, it doesn't suck."

"You don't hate it there, do you?" Jason sounded anxious to be reassured about the MOH stand-in duty and, hell, that was the least Nick could do.

"On the contrary," Nick assured him. "And, look, don't think I don't know why you cooked up this whole 'my sister needs a companion' deal. I know why you did it."

"You *know*?"

Nick laughed softly that Trew could be so naive. "Of course I know." Medical leaves brought bad, bad mind-sets, that much was common knowledge. When a SEAL was less than two years out of BUD/S training and finally deployed and making a difference, a medical leave was a huge setback, and Trew knew it was no different in Nick's case. A lot of guys never really got out of the hospital bed, at least not figuratively. Some of them stayed so wasted that they couldn't get up.

There was a long silence, then Trew asked, "And you're not pissed? 'Cause I really thought you'd beat the shit out of me when you found out why I asked you to go there."

Beat the shit out of him? Why? "For sending me to a first-class resort on the beach?" He snorted softly. "First of all, I do appreciate the concern, though you had nothing to worry about with me. But I am trying to get...something accomplished. And this place..." He glanced around the room that had somehow become a cocoon of creativity for him, to the window that faced the heartbreaking view of the bay.

"What about it?"

"It's good, man," Nick said in a masterstroke of understatement. "It's working. In fact, I decided to stay for a month."

"Get out! That's awesome, except I'd rather you were here."

"Me, too, man, but this is"—different, if not better—"fine." He couldn't resist adding the truth. "Place is crawling with tail, Blue."

"Excellent. Anything in particular?"

"One." He closed his eyes and pictured Willow. "Blond, blue-eyed, hot."

"Different for you."

They both knew he meant Charlotte. Jason Trew was the only SEAL on the team who knew about Nick's budding relationship with the embedded journalist. And even he didn't know the real truth about Charlotte's death, but he knew what it had done to Nick.

"She is different," Nick mused, his brain firmly on the present and not the past. "And I knew her in college."

"Seriously? In California? How the hell did that happen?"

"Someone up there loves me, I guess." He grinned and paced the room. "And I'm not complaining."

"Is she a guest?"

"No, no, she's the wedding planner working for your sister."

"*What*?" The word came sharp through the phone, a jab of shock.

Nick laughed. "Is that against the wedding rules or something?"

"Nick, you can't tell her. Holy shit, you can*not* tell her. Misty will fucking kill me."

What the hell was he talking about? "Tell her what? That I'm your stand-in? Too late, man. I told her everything. She knows you were supposed to be here, but I'm here instead. Misty explained that you and she had this planned since you were kids."

All he heard was a light choke of disbelief.

"Why the hell can't she know that?"

"Not *that*," Trew said. "The whole reason why you're there."

Nick stopped pacing, dropping onto the bed to process what his friend was saying. And it still didn't make sense. "Which would be...what?"

Trew swore softly.

"What?" Nick demanded again.

"Man, I gotta talk to Misty. Is she there?"

"No, she left. I think she went back to New York. Why do you have to talk to her?"

Jason Trew, normally a talkative bastard, was dead silent. In the background, all Nick could hear was the ambient sounds of the mess hall.

"What the hell is going on, Blue?"

"I'll, um, I'll tell you after I talk to Misty. Did you tell her you know this wedding planner chick? Does she realize that?"

"Yeah. What difference does it make?"

"Oh, none, I guess. I gotta book. They're haulin' us out of here, and I didn't get any chow. We'll talk soon."

He thought about pushing for an explanation, but whatever was gnawing at Trew's ass didn't matter. God only knew when they'd talk again, but when they did, his friend would probably tell him it was some stupid thing about catching the bouquet that he thought would piss Nick off. "You stay in one piece out there, Blue."

When he hung up, he forgot about the weird conversation as soon as he turned on his laptop. Instead, he let the familiar clatter of the mess hall work as background music in his head while he wrote for three solid hours. He was on fire.

Chapter Twelve

Willow was about to hit send on the email to Jill Peyton, sending pictures of Chef Ian and Tessa's "matched set" of twins they'd successfully recruited for the wedding party, when her email dinged with a new message. Tempted to ignore it, she glanced at the window that didn't quite offer a beachfront view, but the soft golden light told her that it was sunset on Barefoot Bay, and she wanted to get out to enjoy it if at all possible.

Maybe a certain resort guest would be out there watching that same sunset on the beach. She hadn't seen Nick since she'd left his villa yesterday, and her whole body hummed with a need to change that, pronto. She might not have seen him, but she sure as heck thought about him a lot.

She sent the email and clicked over to her in-box, a tightening in her belly at the name. Misty Trew. And the subject line. NEED HELP ASAP!

Willow took a sniff of the air. Trouble, trouble, trouble. She opened the note, her eyes shuttering at the sheer length of it, not to mention the ridiculous overuse of exclamation points! After every sentence! Which were not so much sentences as commands!

The very last bullet point was a note that the preliminary

guest list was attached and that they should immediately start assigning rooms and villas for the guests with stars next to their names.

Willow's heart did a roller-coaster dip. From the moment Misty had revealed that she knew Willow's mother, this seemed inevitable. Would her mother be here for the wedding? A hot burst of fear mixed with dread and topped with a great big dollop of anything-but-Ona splashed in Willow's stomach at the thought.

She looked at the attachment, but didn't actually open it. How long did she think she could actually avoid her mother?

Long. She'd managed to do so for three years, a feat that had been remarkably easy. Ona was always busy, always traveling, always late, always surrounded by important, beautiful, powerful, *skinny* people who did exactly as she wanted.

Like Misty.

Oh, boy. Willow dropped back against her chair, that hot feeling of dread melting into something even uglier. Wasn't she above being jealous at this point in her life? Not that she envied Misty her reed-thin body, cover girl looks, or her job in front of the camera. But...weren't those the very things that caused Willow's constant sense that she was a disappointment to her mother? Willow with the body that embarrassed Ona. And Willow with the looks that favored her father and not her magazine-cover mother. And Willow who was openly disdainful of modeling as a career choice.

Obviously, Misty and Ona would have all those common bonds where Willow and Ona had nothing but...arguments and anger and the inability to ever see things through the other person's eyes.

Misty probably agreed with everything that control freak demanded. Hell, they had the same personality. Was *that* what was eating at her with this client? Because it really felt a lot like the green monster was chewing at her insides.

Her finger lingered over the mouse button, ready to click. What if Ona and Donny Zatarain's names *were* on the guest list? What would that mean, other than Willow would have to see her parents in a month?

She opened the list, not really surprised at how tight her throat was, but kind of shocked by how short the list was. Fewer than fifteen names. Misty had said a small wedding, but even by "intimate" Barefoot Bay wedding standards, this was tiny. Still, her gaze went straight to the bottom. Yardley was the last name. No Z's. No Zatarains.

A slow exhale of pure relief escaped as she stared at the space under the last name.

"You're so intense when you work."

Her head shot up at the words, making her turn to the door with a soft inhale of surprise. And delight. Forget the sunset. The sight of Nick Hershey filling her office doorway was as glorious as anything nature could provide.

"I like it." He didn't move, leaning against the jamb with his arms folded, his dark eyes searing her, his expression softly humorous.

"I'm just reading an email from Misty," she said, happy the words didn't come out as a rasp despite her dry throat.

"How is she?"

"Demanding."

His mouth twisted in a curve, punctuated by a shrug of one mighty shoulder. "She appears to be a woman who likes to get her way."

"I know the type," Willow agreed. "I was raised by one." Why did she admit that? Because Ona was on her brain? Or because something about him made her want to share? Both.

"Can I come in?"

"Of course." She turned her chair to face him, unable to resist a quick—okay, maybe not *that* quick—scan of his whole body, nicely on display in a simple white T-shirt and baggy cargo shorts. "Wow, clothes. What's the occasion?"

He grinned and propped his hip against her desk, looking down at her. "New pages, that's the occasion. About twenty-two of them."

She met his happy expression with a genuine one of her own. "Really? Did you take my advice?"

"Like the bitter pill it was, but yes, I did. And as much as I seemed resistant to your comments, I have to say thank you." He reached into his pocket and pulled out a tiny jump drive, holding it out to her. "And please tell me what you think of what I've written."

She coughed softly, not sure how to react.

He took her hand and put the jump drive in her palm, closing his fingers around hers. "Please."

Electricity zinged through her at the touch. Oh, she'd missed him, all right. Him and his touch and smile and penchant for nudity. And he was handing her an excuse to spend as much time as possible basking in all of those. Still, she didn't want to appear *too* easy.

"I really didn't think you liked what I had to say."

He slid around the desk without letting go of her hand, eliminating the barrier as he came into her personal space. "I didn't, but I came around and realized you have a gift."

He closed the space between them, looming over her now, all muscle and man with his hips dangerously close to her face. She either had to stare at his crotch, or crane her neck to look up at his face. Using good judgment, she went with his face.

"A gift?"

"You inspire me." Smiling, he slowly dropped down to

accommodate the difference in their height, taking one knee and still holding her hand. "I need you to do this, and in return, I'll do anything you want."

For a moment, she couldn't speak, but had to drink up the deliriously wonderful sight of Nick Hershey on one knee, holding her hand, a plea in his voice and a promise in his eyes. "Anything?"

"I'll get Misty off your back. I'll never sing off-key. I'll teach you how to hold your breath underwater for two minutes. I'll never get naked again."

"Don't go crazy."

His eyes widened as he picked up that cue. "Or I'll get naked all the time," he amended. "Whatever you want."

"What I want is…" *You.*

The word kicked her heart, shaking her a little, making her whole body shiver with how clear and strong and real that desire was.

"Name it," he whispered. "Whatever you want."

She lost the fight, leaned forward, and put her mouth on his.

"Oh," he murmured into the kiss.

Willow instantly tried to back away, but Nick got his hand behind her head to keep her where she was and angle them both for the optimal amount of mouth-to-mouth. Warm and sweet, soft and tender, his lips played against hers with the perfect amount of hunger and vulnerability and trepidation.

The last one was on her end, and it finally knocked some sense into her, so she ended the contact, no matter how much she didn't want to.

"Sex?" he asked.

She let out a quick laugh. "Are you asking for it or about it?"

"I'm interpreting your answer to the question of how I can repay you for reading all the shitty drafts of my book and helping me get it right."

"With sex." She should have made it a question, but was too stunned at the suggestion to do that.

"Okay."

"No, no." She shook her head, pressing on his broad, strong shoulders but not exactly pushing him away. "That's not what I…" She couldn't even deny it. It was exactly what she wanted. "That's not why I kissed you."

"Then why did you?"

"I guess because I wanted to."

"I can tell. I can see it in your eyes."

She rolled those very eyes. "Yes, I know. Blue means happy. Green means mad."

"And that gray the color of an impending storm? Lust."

She had to laugh, and not just because he was serious and charming and funny and…right.

"It's nothing to be ashamed of," he added. "I feel the same way about you, but my eyes don't change color."

She searched the depths of those dark eyes, mentally grabbing the first half of that statement but forcing herself to think about the second. "No, they don't change color," she agreed. "And I'm not ashamed. I'm not…"

"Ready? Interested? Willing?"

Emotions swamped her. She was quite ready, more than interested, and totally willing. Except…how could she tell him?

"Come on, Willie."

Willie. Well, that killed the moment. "Honestly, Nick," she said, pushing him back with a little too much force. "Do you really think I need sex that badly that I'd read your book for it?"

He choked a laugh. "There are so many insults in that question, I don't know where to begin."

"I don't mean to insult you, but..." She didn't know any other way of getting out of this.

Slowly, he stood, ending the bliss of Nick on one knee. Too bad. She'd have to conjure up that image on lonely nights.

Taking the jump drive out of her hand, he placed it on the desk and took a step backward. "It's your call, Willow." He rounded the desk and walked to the door, sliding one last look over his shoulder. "You know where to find me."

She managed a shrug of sheer indifference. "Of course. Naked and underwater."

He grinned and left her alone, the sound of his footsteps in the empty hall outside like a tap on her heart.

Why didn't she say yes? Nick Hershey had been her first choice years ago, and here he was, basically offering the same thing she'd always wanted. Why the hell wouldn't she take it?

She picked up the drive and stuck it in the nearest USB port on her computer, the soft ring like a fighter's bell. Round two. TKO dead ahead.

Really, this was long overdue.

Chapter Thirteen

Ona Zatarain thumbed the pictures on Misty's iPhone, tamping down a little frustration when image after image denied her what she wanted more than life itself. "I still don't see her," she sighed.

"Keep going." Misty leaned over and tried to wrest the phone. "I can find the ones with her."

Ona refused to give up the device, physically turning away to cling to this tiny, merciless, unsatisfying connection with her daughter. "I know how to work the phone," she said, angling the screen at the next shot, which showed a wide, white beach speckled with sunny yellow umbrellas. In the distance, a blond woman stood near the water.

"There she is," Misty said, her whole body leaning over so she could see the screen. "That's her."

Pushing up from the plush sofa to cross the room, Ona clutched the tiny phone and peered at the screen, then flicked it to zoom in. "Oh my Lord, look at her. Donny!" She spun around, shifting her focus from the screen to the expanse of the Ritz-Carlton suite, zeroing in on her husband who didn't lift his head from the putter and practice green, his attention riveted on lining up his shot.

"If you take a picture of me with that thing, Ona, I'm filing for divorce."

Heh. It was tempting to threaten him with a picture of a nearly sixty-year-old man golfing that would wreck his well-cultivated bad-boy rocker image, but her need to share this moment trumped amusement. "Just look at her, honey."

"One second." He drew the putter back, glancing at the hole not far from where Ona stood. "I will." He let go and swung softly.

"She looks happy."

The ball rolled and missed the hole by a good three inches, making Donny swear softly. "She *is* happy, Ona. The last time I talked to her, she sounded downright chipper."

Envy stung, the way it had these past few months when her husband mentioned a conversation or email or text with Willie. They were rare, of course, but when he had contact with her, old demons came out to torture Ona. But then she remembered that something bigger and better had crushed those demons and given her a second chance.

A second chance at life, and a second chance at motherhood. She was taking them both with every bit of energy and determination she could muster. And for Ona, that was *a lot*.

As Donny walked to the hole, he paused to glance at the phone she held out. Wordlessly, he peered at the screen, then he nodded.

"Well?" she demanded.

He barely lifted a shoulder.

Ona spun around to the young woman she'd left lounging on her couch. "I hope your future husband is more communicative than my *current* one," she said. "I know I'll choose more wisely next time."

Misty looked surprised at the comment, but behind Ona,

Donny snorted. And grabbed her ass as he carried his ball back to putt again. "He better have balls of steel, woman, since you love nothing more than breaking them."

She slipped out of his touch, sharing a look that they both knew meant two things: Neither of them took the other's threats seriously, and there'd be some action when Misty left.

"I'm serious about this," she told him, returning to the phone to flip through the pictures.

"Obviously," Donny shot back, lining up his next put. "Or you wouldn't have put us all through this total insanity, including poor Misty, who just wants to get married in peace and not be part of the scheme of the century."

"Oh, no, you're wrong, Mr. Z." Misty leaped up from the sofa, her long ponytail swinging. "I love this scheme of the century."

"It's not a scheme!" Ona insisted. "And Misty *is* going to get married in peace, a year from now, in the massive wedding she wants. We, on the other hand, are going to have our vows renewed on the beach in a gorgeous ceremony exactly as I want it, which means our daughter will not only be there, we—I—will be reconciled with her. I know this is going to happen."

With the last sentence, Donny gave her a look she knew all too well. A little pity, a little confusion, a little plea in his hazel eyes. "You could try asking her instead of your usual master manipulation."

"I'm not manipulating what I know will happen." What she had seen and knew *would* eventually happen was what she meant, but Donny had little patience for that. He was a pragmatist, and this situation could use a little of that, too. "And you know as well as I that the answer would be no," she added. "She'd claim she's busy or traveling or whatever.

She's managed to avoid seeing me face-to-face for three years, and if I don't do something to change that, it'll be thirty years I'm in maternal prison."

Not that Ona didn't deserve every one of those years. But a new day had dawned, and she was going to right every wrong with her daughter, and it would be done face-to-face.

She'd gone...somewhere. She didn't claim to understand where, but while there, she'd been given her marching orders, and they were to march right into Willie's arms. Her heart swelled at the thought. It had been so, so long since she'd seen her daughter.

"Are there any more pictures of her, Misty?"

"I think I have one more." She took the phone and swiped through the shots with the confidence of youth raised on touch screens, then nodded, handing it back to Ona. "Here. She's talking to Nick, my brother's stand-in."

"So sweet of him to go with you, Misty. I hope he doesn't mind when the truth comes out. I never expected your brother to force that issue."

Misty shook her head. "You're doing Jason a favor, believe me. When I told him about this whole plan, he jumped on the idea of sending Nick, who Jason thinks is having a hard time being on a medical leave. It's so like Jason to worry about his friend," she said, her eyes bright with sisterly pride. "I hope Jase really can make the wedding when it happens."

"I hope so, too," Ona agreed, peering at the picture on the phone. "Oh, this young man looks very handsome. And..." She frowned and squinted at the phone, cursing her need for reading glasses that she was too vain to wear. Was it her eyes or did this picture of the couple standing near the deep-blue water look like something she'd...dreamed?

They weren't dreams, Ona.

"So the weirdest thing is Willow knows him from UCLA," Misty continued. "They lived in the same dorm or something."

"Really?" Ona's eyes widened.

"I know, right? Freaky coincidence."

Ona resisted a quick look skyward, knowing that there weren't any such things in this life. "What did you say his name was again?" she asked, attempting to sound casual.

Donny already thought she'd lost her marbles, and Misty was going to cut her only so much slack. Ona couldn't tell them *everything* she'd seen that hour she spent on the other side.

"Nick Hershey," Misty said. "And I guess Jason was right about him needing a vacation, since he decided to stay for a month and work on some writing project he's doing."

"Oh, Lord, he knows Willie?" The impact of that truly hit her. "What if he tells her?"

"I thought of that," Misty said. "I was going to tell him when I got there before we even talked to anyone, but by the time I showed up, they were all chummy and walking on the beach and he'd already asked her out to dinner."

"He had?" Ona's voice rose with interest.

"Ona…" Donny warned harshly. "Don't even go there."

"I'm not going anywhere. But if he feels some sort of loyalty to her, he's going to tell her what we're doing."

"I know!" Misty agreed. "So I decided not to tell him. I'm hoping that he's having such a good time being there that when there's no wedding, he's cool about it."

"And he asked her to go to dinner?" For some reason, that gave Ona a little shiver of satisfaction. Nothing could make her happier than for Willie to find the kind of love that Ona had enjoyed her whole life.

Donny was next to her in a second. "You're pulling enough puppet strings, love."

She narrowed her eyes at him. "I'm doing nothing of the sort." She gave Misty a nudge, wanting very much to hear more about this Nick Hershey. "Why don't we go downstairs and sit by the pool and you can tell me every single detail?"

"Don't." Donny's hand landed on Ona's shoulder, surprising her not just with the power of his touch, but the pressure he added. "I want to hear, too."

She gave him a slow smile over her shoulder. "I'm not going to scheme."

"And the sun won't come up tomorrow."

With a wry smile, she leaned into him. "You never know, Donny Z. That's why you have to do what's right on the days it does come up."

"Don't leave," he said after a second.

She knew that tone so well since she'd heard it many times since her accident. Ona's incredibly close brush with death had not only changed her priorities and plans, the incident had struck pure terror in the heart of her husband. He might play the part of a caustic, hardened, sex-charged— if weathered—rock star on stage. But Donny Zatarain, secret golfer and faithful husband, lived in abject fear that the next time, Ona wouldn't come back from her astonishing trip to the other side.

"I can't, anyway, Ona," Misty said. "Steven's plane lands in an hour, and I want to meet him at the airport." She gathered up her large bag and gave Ona a smile. "I can tell you this much about your daughter. She has no idea you are behind any of this."

Ona fought a twinge of guilt and shame, but quickly brushed both away. If she'd learned anything from that hour she'd spent in the most glorious, beautiful, peaceful place imaginable, it was that guilt and shame were a waste of time.

What mattered in this fleeting, temporal life was

forgiveness and love, and Ona was determined to get one and give the other.

She air-kissed Misty and walked her to the door, adding a long hug of gratitude. "You're wonderful to do this for me."

Misty's narrow shoulders shook with a light laugh. "For you? You're paying for my entire wedding at the Ritz-Carlton, Ona! Pretending to plan one at some little resort out in the gulf is no skin off my back." She frowned, searching Ona's face. "I just hope you know what you're doing."

"Hush. You sound like Donny now. You know what happened to me. I nearly died that day in the ocean." She closed her eyes, the swirling, black, terrifying sensation so easy to recall. It was always right at the surface. "But it changed me right down to the soul."

Misty gave her a smile and a kiss, then headed down the hall, while Ona stood in the doorway and watched her disappear, still thinking about those waters that had nearly consumed her the day she'd gone for a swim at their Malibu house. Just one wave, one undertow, one moment she was alive, and the next...

She had no recollection of being pulled from the sea or having her chest slammed and strange paramedics hovering over her. She had no memory of the trip to the hospital. She had no remembrance of being declared dead...only of the light and the beauty and the clear message that had been given to her on the other side.

Undo the damage you've done, Ona Zatarain.

And the whole time, the power that held her there kept her hovering over constantly changing images of her daughter. Willie as a child. Willie as a miserable teenager. Willie as a young woman, fighting to find herself. Willie...as a bride.

It was the last one that made her wake up, for some

reason. That last image of Willow in a wedding gown, with a man tilting her back for a kiss. A man who looked freakishly like that picture on Misty's phone.

Then she'd awakened, and Donny cried like a two-year-old, and the doctors mumbled about how stunned they were, and all the nurses proclaimed it a miracle. Ona didn't know about any of that. All she knew was that she had to find her way back to her daughter.

And if she'd learned anything from her experience, it could be summed up in three words that had become her mantra.

Nothing is impossible.

Not even this.

Chapter Fourteen

Willow clicked off her tablet and pushed off her bed, restless. The imagery that had been painted in her brain remained vivid, even after the words disappeared from the screen.

Her body hummed from the sights and sounds…and emotions. She could see the vast and desolate desert, and smell the harsh scents of war. She could hear the rapid punch of mortar, the scream of a missile through the night air, freakishly loud even though a fireworks display was the closest she'd ever been to anything like that. She could feel her eyes burn with "moon dust" that covered Afghanistan, her throat on fire like—how had he described it? Like someone had snapped a lighter in her mouth. Body parts, debris, and bombed-out Humvees. Vomit and blood and death.

Had Nick experienced all of that firsthand? Of course he had. How could she be so naive as to think he could make that up without living through it? A powerful punch of sympathy slammed her chest.

He almost hadn't. No, no, that was Lieutenant Spencer Gannon who'd narrowly escaped death. Or was it?

God, she needed air. It was all but dark now, nearly eight o'clock, so she grabbed a water bottle and made her way out to the front porch just as Gussie and Ari walked up the driveway.

"Hey, we went for a walk down by the water," Ari said. "We knocked, but you didn't answer."

Too engrossed in the book. "Sorry, I didn't hear you." Her head had been in Afghanistan, and her heart was in pieces. Or at least in the hands of a very talented writer.

"What did you do for dinner?" Gussie asked as she came up the stairs.

"I skipped."

Her friend raised her eyebrows in surprise. "I don't think I've ever known you to do that."

"True enough." She might have lost a lot of weight over the past few years, but she never missed dinner. That only led to dangerous temptations at midnight. "What about you?"

"We're going to grab a bite on the mainland," Ari told her. "Want to come? There's a new restaurant in Fort Myers."

"And your favorite candy store that's open until midnight," Willow teased. "I'll pass on that stop."

"You okay?" Gussie asked, sitting on the swing next to her. "You look kind of dazed."

"It was Nick's book," she said. "It hit me. Here." She thudded her chest.

"Ah, the man of dishonor." Ari dropped onto a wicker chair.

"Why would you call him that?" Willow asked, defensiveness rising.

"Not me, the staff. The restaurant workers. The brides I had out on tour this afternoon when we saw him. Females in general. They all want to do something dishonorable with him."

Get in line, Willow thought. "Well, the man of dishonor

131

can write a book."

"I thought you were struggling with what to tell him about it," Ari said.

"I thought I was, too, but he really hit his stride. It's so authentic and powerful now." She couldn't resist a sly smile. "He says I inspire him."

"Is that what they're calling it now?" Gussie teased.

"Well, don't let us keep you from reading," Ari added.

"I don't have any more to read," she replied sadly. "I'm caught up. I've read every word he's written. All I can do is wait for more." Or go and talk to him about what she'd read.

Speaking of dangerous temptations at midnight.

"So come out to dinner with us and tell us about it," Ari suggested.

She didn't answer, not wanting to turn down the invitation but not exactly interested in accepting it, either. She took another look at the clock. "Is eight o'clock early enough that it doesn't seem like a booty call to turn up at a guy's villa?"

They both stared at her, but Gussie could barely keep a straight face.

"Well, is it?"

"No." Gussie made a little shriek sound.

"Did you two bet on this?" Willow demanded.

"No, we didn't. I'm just...happy for you. I'm excited about this."

"You're excited about it?" Willow teased. "I'm"—she looked from one to the other—"not really sure how much to tell you guys."

"What?" they asked in perfect unison.

"You tell us everything," Ari said.

"Or we'll bet on what it is."

"I don't think either one of you is going to bet on this.

But if you did, the odds would be in your favor."

Again, they both just looked hard at her.

"Um, okay." She looked down and plucked at a button on the seat cushion. "Just don't judge, okay?"

"We won't," Ari assured her.

"No promises," Gussie added.

Willow laughed nervously as they leaned in closer, riveted.

"You know that when I was in college I knew Nick and I, you know, sort of asked him to relieve me of my virginity because, like, who wants to be a nineteen-year-old virgin, right? And he was so hot and sweet and kind to me, but...but..."

"He said no," Gussie supplied. "And he told you why, which was pretty legit, in my opinion. We know, and we understand why that might make you a little nervous about taking the next natural step with this guy, but—"

"It's not natural to—"

"Yes, it is!" Ari insisted.

"—be a virgin at twenty-nine," she finished.

Two speechless, stunned faces looked back at her.

"Holy shit," Gussie finally whispered. "Really?"

Very slowly, she nodded. "Really."

"No one? Ever?" Ari asked.

"After Nick, I just couldn't bear to even think about trying again. I don't want to put all the blame on him, but that rejection hurt like a son of a bitch. I blamed my weight, of course, which made me angry and frustrated and hungrier than ever."

"But all these years..." Gussie was still in shock. "And you never told us."

"I know, and I'm sorry. It's just become such a horrible burden of weirdness. I mean, they make movies about freaks like me."

"Willow!" Ari said. "That's not true. There are plenty of celibate people our age. It's nothing to be ashamed of. On the contrary, it's kind of cool."

"Not anymore. For years, I used my weight as an excuse, then I lost weight, and I have dated a few guys, one I really liked, but..." She just couldn't do it. "I didn't like him enough."

"But you like Nick enough," Gussie said, no question in her voice.

"I do, but...you know. The irony might be too much if he says no again. Not to mention the embarrassment, agony, and regret."

"He is not going to say no," Ari said. "A blind man could see how bad he has it for you."

Willow hugged herself, as if Ari's very words could wrap around her. "I think you're right," she admitted. "And I think I'm ready."

"Then what are you doing here?" Ari asked.

"Well, I'm not going over to his villa to screw his brains out tonight."

"May I ask why not?" Gussie teased.

"Because I...I need to see how he feels about it."

They looked at each other, fighting a laugh.

"Okay, he'll be down for it, you're right," she agreed. "But when he finds out I'm a virgin, how do you think he'll feel?"

"Honored," Ari said.

"Horny...er," Gussie replied. "In all seriousness, Willow, it isn't going to happen unless you set the wheels in motion. You should go over there and...take those walls down. And clothes off."

Willow looked at Ari, usually more of a voice of reason.

But Ari was nodding.

"I agree, Willow. I also think there's no irony at all in him being your first, since he was your first choice. Maybe you've been waiting for him to come back into your life all along."

"Yeah," Gussie said. "He was meant to be your cherry-picker."

Willow laughed softly, but deep inside, she couldn't argue that. The disappointment that Nick Hershey hadn't been her first had been real and long lasting. So long lasting that she'd damn near made it to thirty as a virgin.

Willow pushed back the swing and stood up. "I'm going out, girls."

"Are you naked?"

For a second, Nick wasn't sure if the question came from one of the characters living in his head or not. A loud knock on the villa door followed, giving him the answer. The answer, in fact, that he wanted most.

Willow.

"Define naked," he called, pushing himself up from the sofa and glancing at his faded boxer shorts.

"That would be man parts visible."

"Hang on." He glanced around, spying the worn camo pants he'd had on earlier, so he stepped into them and added a black T-shirt. There, fully dressed.

He put his hand on the door and imagined what he'd see when he opened it. "Are *you* naked?" he asked hopefully.

When she didn't answer, he turned the knob and slowly opened, feigning—sort of—disappointment at the sight of her fully clothed in jeans and a tank top.

She held out the jump drive like a lifeline.

"Did you read it?" he asked, closing his hand over hers, the softness of her skin sending a surprising skitter of anticipation and warmth through him.

"Every word."

He opened the door a little wider and eased her in, unwilling to let go of her hand. "Perfect timing. I'm writing now."

She glanced at the coffee table, taking in the open laptop, the messy notebook, and the bottle of Bud. "What happens next?"

"I don't know." He stroked her knuckles. "I'm throwing things at the wall, but nothing is sticking." He inched her closer, fighting the urge to pull her all the way in and enjoying the mix of panic and desire on her face as they got closer. "But here is my muse."

She smiled. "I don't know if I can help with what happens next, but I can tell you that I loved what you wrote."

"That's music to my ears. Even the one that doesn't work." He leaned down and let his lips brush her soft, sweet-smelling hair. "You could curl up next to me and help me think things through."

He could have sworn she shivered. She didn't answer right away, but gave him a long look, her eyes smoky and gray in the dim light. "All right. And I'll live completely dangerously and ask if you have another beer."

"Absolutely. This place is fully stocked." He took a few steps toward the kitchen, then paused, reaching for her again. "Come on."

"You worried I'll read what you're working on while you're gone?"

"I'm worried you might leave while I'm gone."

"I'm not going anywhere, Nick." Unless he was brain-dead and his woman radar was non-functional, the message came across crystal clear.

"Must have really dug those chapters," he teased, bringing her all the way into the kitchen.

"I did," she told him, leaning against the counter. "Although they scared me."

He gave a questioning glance over his shoulder from the fridge.

"War scares me," she explained.

No shit. "It should. Did you eat dinner yet?"

"I grabbed something before I left."

He imagined her finishing his chapters, snagging one of her roof tiles, and rushing over here. The idea did crazy stupid things to him.

Because she wanted to talk about the book? Or because she wanted to talk to him?

He twisted the top off the cold Bud and handed it to her, letting their fingers brush again. "I skipped dinner, so I should be starved," he said. "But I lost track of time again."

Lifting the bottle, she toasted him. "I was glad you let McManus live. I was really worried he wasn't going to pull through."

Nick felt the blood drain from his face, exactly the way it had drained from McAllister's body that day. But they'd saved him. Pulled "Preacher" out of a wrecked Humvee and got him on the dustoff with the medics. "He almost didn't," he said gruffly.

"I thought it wasn't autobiographical," she said.

Shrugging, he ushered her back to the living room sofa, where they sat down together. "Parts of it are, of course," he admitted.

"The good parts." She tipped the bottle to her mouth,

sliding a sharp look to the side. After she swallowed, she put down the bottle and kicked off her sandals, turning to him. "The parts I like the most, I'm guessing."

He took a swig of his own beer, not wanting to talk about the book for a change. Instead, he wanted to brush her corn-silk hair off her face and let his fingers graze her smooth skin. He wanted to lean in and make out and drink up this sexy woman who showed up at his door like a surprise angel.

"Then you aren't going to like what I'm working on now," he said instead.

She inched toward the laptop, turning the screen so she could read. "What's happening now?"

"Debriefing and a strategy session about what to do with Char—Christina."

She sipped again, nodding and glancing at his words, making him wonder what she thought as she read.

"Gannon knows what he wants to do with her," she said wryly. "Why don't you let them get to it?"

"Screwing the embedded journalist a SEAL saved while taking her to safety is generally frowned upon in the Navy."

She inhaled slowly and then put the beer down. "Did you?"

He felt himself flinch and heat rise to his neck. "This isn't autobiographical, Willow." The words ground out through gritted teeth. "But, no, we did not break any—too many—regs."

She took another long drink of beer, then asked, "Were you in love with her?"

He turned to stare at the computer. No, he hadn't been in love with Charlotte. But maybe he could have been...if she'd lived long enough. "I was not," he said definitively. He cared for her, absolutely. She amused and amazed him, but she would never have been right for him. That didn't mean he didn't regret the hell out of what happened with her, though.

"Was she in love with you?"

Lust, not love. She'd said so herself. Swallowing, he stayed silent on her second question, too, as a guilty man in an interrogation. Maybe if one of them had been in love, the story ending wouldn't have been so dismal. It would have been...tragic, in the sense that it somehow made sense. Instead, it was just a shitty decision.

Made by him.

"Nick? If you don't tell me, I'm going to imagine the worst."

"Imagine it. She's dead." He closed his eyes and leaned back. "That's not the story I'm telling, Willow."

"But that's the one I want to hear."

He puffed another slow breath through rounded lips, long and noisy. "No, really, it's not...that interesting. It's not..."

"Happy? I realize that, Nick. But I still want to know what happened."

"I've never told anyone the...truth."

"Really?" She barely whispered the question. "You mean you've lied about what happened to her?"

"Oh, no, that's not what I mean." Everyone knew what happened to her. They just didn't know his role. "If you knew the story, you'd see there's no reason to lie, but no reason to tell every person I meet."

"Nick." She took his hand. "I'm not every person you'll meet."

He looked at her, the truth of that weirdly comforting.

She added a squeeze to her touch, increasing the comfort level. "Deep, dark secrets always hurt to share. That's why we keep them in the deep dark."

He regarded her for another minute, taking some time to

appreciate each pretty feature, but getting lost in her eyes, as usual. There was something there...something hidden that he very much wanted to uncover.

"Do you have a secret down in the deep, dark basement, Willow?"

For a flash, he saw her think of it, a millisecond of an expression, before she looked away, and he knew the answer.

"Hey, Willow." He dipped his head a little so she was forced to look at him. "If you tell me your deep, dark secret, I'll tell you mine."

She laughed. "Sorry, my secret is not deep or dark. It's ordinary, and inconsequential."

"Then you wouldn't keep it a secret." When she didn't answer, he touched her chin and turned her face back to him. "Come on. Let's share. It'll be intimate."

She closed her eyes when he whispered that word. "God, you're good."

"So you promise?"

"Only if you don't..."

"I won't tell anyone," he assured her. "I won't throw it back in your face. I won't make you sorry you told me. And I know you'd promise the same thing to me."

She smiled. "None of those are what I was going to say, but that'll work." She slid her bare feet up on his lap while she settled back into the cushions on the armrest. Resting the beer bottle on her stomach, she eyed him from under her lashes. "You first, Lieutenant."

Shit. Now he had to tell her.

But deep inside he knew he'd wanted to tell her everything.

Maybe she knew, too.

Chapter Fifteen

Nick leaned his head back and closed his eyes, looking relaxed and at ease. But there was nothing relaxed about his grip on Willow's ankles. His fingers were strong, sure, and tight enough to let her know he was bracing for his confession, whatever it might be. From her vantage point against the armrest, she watched him, slowly moving her beer bottle to the coffee table so nothing could disrupt her view of his profile.

Had she ever noticed that his nose was not quite perfect? Or that his jawline slanted ever so slightly downward? Had she ever noticed his temple had the tiniest blue vein, one that pulsed lightly right now? Did that mean his blood was stirred?

By the touch of her skin or…the memory of another woman…or the pain of his past?

Maybe she'd come over here hoping for a different kind of intimacy, but right at that moment, she was as deeply invested in this relationship as if they were making out and stripping off clothes. Sinking deeper into the sofa cushions, she studied the shadow of his whiskers, the thick cords of his neck, and an Adam's apple that rose and fell with a strained swallow. And waited, a little breathlessly, for his secret.

"She should never have been there once, let alone twice," he finally said. "But Charlotte Blaine did not understand the meaning of the word 'can't.'"

Charlotte Blaine. She had a full name now. Willow mulled it over for a second while Nick took a long pull on his beer. She sounded smart. Adventurous. Razor-thin, of course. A woman who blazed into war zones probably didn't go to battle with German chocolate cake on a regular basis.

Don't hate her, Willow. She's dead, and you're on the sofa with Nick.

"On her first trip, she got embedded with an Army unit, some boots on the ground in Kandahar. We had to come in and do some backup in a pretty bad situation with some well-armed fighters. It wasn't until we got them out of the thick of it that we found out the Army unit had an embed." He glanced at her. "Embedded journalist."

She nodded. "I'm picking up the slang and shorthand while I read."

"Too much of it?" he asked.

She smiled, always touched when that hint of vulnerability shadowed his eyes. "Just right." She wiggled her foot. "Keep going."

Another swig, then he dropped his head back and looked to the ceiling, remembering. "She became my problem from the very beginning."

"Just like in the book."

He nodded. "I can't say I hated it, because she was easy on the eyes and...droll."

So that hadn't changed from real life to the book, either. The character of Christina had a dry wit and...what had he written? Eyes "the color of aged whiskey"? A color that had inebriated him.

"But she didn't like to follow orders and..." He closed his eyes. "She liked me. A lot."

A hot little ball of *jealous* rolled around in her stomach. "What's not to like?" she teased, hoping her voice came off lighter than she felt.

It must have, since the tiniest smile lifted the corner of his mouth. "You manage to find things."

"Keep talking. So, did you kiss in the observation post like they did in the book?"

"Yeah." He turned and narrowed his eyes. "Didn't go quite as far as things did in the book."

"And the whole village thing happened?"

"Pretty much as written," he acknowledged.

So, there'd been a heavy make-out session. "And then she left? She had to go back to the States?"

"Yep. Back to New York."

That's where "Christina" had gone in the last chapter, after some blazing-hot kisses, and not-so-empty promises to someday see each other again.

"But she comes back," he said softly.

The present tense threw her. "In the story or..."

He turned to her. "She came back in real life, and...I haven't decided yet, in the story. It complicates the whole Taliban-spy plot, which, I'm here to tell you, did *not* happen in real life, but I like the idea of it for the book."

"Ahh." She smiled and finally sat up to sip her beer. "So not everything is autobiographical."

"I told you, Willow, it's fiction. There's some stuff that is taken from my experience, but it's a novel, not a memoir. I swear."

The beer was cold and a little bitter in her throat, which was surprisingly dry. She took a second sip, then put it down on the table and fell back on the cushions. "Okay, let's forget the fiction for a minute. Let's go totally IRL."

He frowned. "Not a military acronym."

"In Real Life."

"Isn't a muse supposed to stay focused on fiction?" he asked.

"I don't know, I've never had the job before, but if you don't tell me what happened with this woman, I'm going to scream."

He gave in to a slight smile. "Are you jealous?"

"Indescribably," she shot back. "You never did tell me if you were in love with her or not."

His eyebrows lifted in surprise. "I thought you were being facetious. You *are* jealous."

"Were you?"

"No." The straightforward, simple honesty of the syllable was as cooling as the drink of Bud. "I liked her. I was fascinated and frustrated by her. I admired her. I was even a little in awe of her, but it wasn't love."

"Well, it sure sounds"—what would it be like to be fascinating, frustrating, awe-inspiring to a man?—"like more than a casual fling."

"Obviously that works for a book, but IRL, as you say, it wasn't even a fling. I would never risk my military career by being that stupid. She was completely my responsibility, and that would have been a gross misuse of my position. So, no. No *flinging*."

She smiled at the euphemism, which she was pretty sure was not in the Navy SEAL slang handbook.

"But we had feelings for each other. That much was real."

"So what happened, Nick?" She leaned up, her own feelings of attraction fading as she imagined this admirable, adventurous woman with a gorgeous, protective SEAL lost in the dust bowl of Afghanistan. He was right about one thing. It made for a compelling story.

"We were headed into a blind mess that came up out of nowhere. Sniper fire trapped some Marines searching for weapons caches in a farmhouse, and they called in for SEAL help. Trust me, that doesn't happen unless shit is getting real."

He shifted in his seat, his grip tightening. Willow's whole body grew cold at what she imagined she might hear next.

"We had to go in, and all hell was breaking loose. They needed every one of us, which meant leaving Charlotte at the COP, the combat outpost, we were using. As we were scrambling to get out of there, we got another report that another band of fighters, including suicide bombers, were coming up from the south, planning to cause some damage to the outpost while it was undermanned." His voice got very soft, and then trailed off completely as he stared ahead.

For a long, painful minute, he didn't talk.

Very slowly, Willow sat up, waiting.

He swallowed, forced to let go of her ankles as she repositioned. "I made a bad decision."

It wasn't what she was expecting. "What do you mean?"

"She could have gone on one of three helicopters out of there. I picked the last one, stealing those additional few minutes with her. She wanted me to, but I'm not blaming her. I took a chance to have more time to say good-bye." He turned to her, his eyes misted. "She was certain I was going to get killed. For some reason, she was just sure of that, and she didn't want to leave until the last possible minute. So we put her on the last bird, and…"

In the silence, all Willow could hear was the thumping of her own pulse.

"It got shot down." He whispered the words. "I saw the fireball in the sky. I saw it. The other two helicopters made it out in one piece. If only I'd put her on one of those."

She reached for him. "That wasn't your mistake. It was bad luck."

He closed his eyes. "I kept her longer than I should have. I...I..." He dropped his head forward, letting it thump into his upturned palms. "I should have put her on the first one."

"Other people made the same decision and got on that helicopter," she said.

"But I made it for selfish reasons. And I rationalized it because I thought that's what she wanted. One decision. One choice. One...woman's life, over." Clearly, the decision still haunted him.

She reached out to comfort him by placing a hand on his arm. "Anyone could have made that decision."

He whipped around to face her. "But *I* made that decision, and *I* was charged with protecting her, and *I* fucked up."

"Any of those helicopters could have been shot down."

"I know." He pressed the heels of his hands against his brow. "And that's why I want to rewrite history."

"You think that's going to free you from this guilt?"

He didn't reply, his head still down.

"It might," he finally said.

"But it might not."

After a second, he pushed up to stand. Without a word, he strode out of the room toward the French doors and disappeared out onto the patio.

Willow didn't move, stunned by his sudden exit, and still humming from the details of his story. She stared at his open laptop, the screen dark now, and imagined the woman who made him feel all that pain.

The woman or the decision? She wasn't sure where the source of his misery lay, but all she wanted to do was help him get rid of it.

Damn it. *Damn it!* Nick marched out into the night air, sucking in a lungful and eyeing the pool, looking for a place to hide. Why did he tell Willow that? Not only did he sound like a man who second-guessed himself—which he was, and he hated it—but now she'd want to make him put the truth in his story, and he wasn't going to do that.

He turned away from the dark hole of the pool to face the west, looking out to the Gulf of Mexico, nearly black now, but for the white streak of moonlight down the middle. That's where he wanted to swim, not this bathtub. He wanted to go deep and dark and stay under until he couldn't stand the pain in his lungs.

That always got rid of the pain in his heart.

"I know a little about changing history." The sound of Willow's voice pulled him back to the moment, making him turn to see her silhouetted in the doorway. "My approach is to try to delete it completely rather than rewrite it."

"And that's working for you?"

"More or less. It's a shaky strategy, though. Especially when"—she took a few steps onto the patio—"someone from said deleted history shows up and makes you remember that the past is never really gone. Some memory is always lurking right around the corner."

He had to get off his secrets and on to hers. "So, your turn."

She laughed, shaking her head. "Mine will really kill your mood."

"Precisely. I'd like this mood killed."

She took a few steps closer. "I think that writing it out is really smart and will help you. You need to see that you didn't do anything wrong. It's no different than if you take an extra ten minutes to say good-bye and then get into a car accident. Would it have happened if you hadn't taken that time? It's just…what happened. You need to let go of your guilt and, honestly, I really think in the process of telling this story, you're going to realize that."

Was he? He didn't know yet, but he wanted to think Willow was right. Standing there in the moonlight, her eyes soft, her heart full of compassion, her words soothed him. "Thanks," he said. "For not judging me too harshly." He reached for her hands and pulled her closer. "Now, won't you let me return the favor?"

She thought about it for a second, then slowly shook her head. "Tonight's probably not the best time."

He eased her closer. "It's the very best time. Plus, you promised."

Lifting a shoulder, she let out a laugh that was supposed to be casual, but he knew better. "Nah, my secret is so…mundane."

"Because no one died?"

"Yeah. No one died." She gave his hands a squeeze. "Thanks for the beer and secrets, Lieutenant. I appreciate both." She tried to drop his hands, but he clasped tighter.

"No, you don't."

"Yes, I do. You need to write. You know exactly how to fix your problem now. You can tell the truth, and the story will be that much stronger. A total tearjerker. My muse advice is always going to be the same: Tell the truth."

He shoved the advice away and pulled her closer. "You promised me a secret."

"My secret won't help you." She gave a soft, wry laugh. "Just the opposite, I'm afraid."

Curiosity burned. "I have to know," he admitted, releasing his hands to let his fingers walk up her arms and settle on her shoulders, already knowing there was another place he could hide from the pain. In Willow's arms. "And you're going to tell me."

She bit her lip and gave her head a little shake, and that only made him want to know more.

He tunneled his fingers into her hair. "You are breaking a promise."

"I didn't swear to tell you." She shrugged into his touch, laughing as he got her closer. "And you can't kiss it out of me, either."

He angled his head one way, then the other, planning the kiss. "I can try." He didn't wait for her to respond, taking the kiss easily. At first, she stiffened, but after a few seconds, he felt her whole body soften into his.

"Tell me your secret, Willow," he murmured into her ear.

"Mmm." She let her head fall back enough to entice him to her throat, peppering her silky skin with light kisses. "No."

He laughed lightly and worked his way back up to her mouth. After a long, sweet, wet kiss, he lifted his head and looked into her eyes. "Okay, you don't want to tell me. I get that. But will you tell me why? Even after I promised you I'd never tell anyone or tease or ever, ever use your secret against you?"

"Oh, I know you won't ever tell anyone or tease me, and you'd never use it against me because..." She nibbled that lip again, this time like she was trying to keep the words trapped in her mouth.

"Because why?"

"Because you happen to be the reason I have this secret."

He froze for a moment, his mind blank. "What? How is that possible? I haven't seen you in more than ten years."

She stared at him, one eyebrow slightly raised, the message clear: He should know. He forced himself back to the past to figure out *what* he should know. They'd been casual acquaintances who lived in the same dorm, he remembered. They had a few conversations, mostly about her father. And then she'd kissed him one night and asked him to…

"You're figuring it out, aren't you?"

Not even close. "I don't know how I could cause you to do anything or…"

"Or *not*."

He frowned, still blanking out. "Willow, what…"

"Or *not do anything*," she said slowly, as if trying to give him a really obvious hint.

Not a clue yet. "Just tell me."

"I can't say it out loud."

"What?" Her secret that *he'd* caused was so bad she couldn't say it out loud? "What did I do? I didn't touch you, Willow."

Again, he got a raised eyebrow that would only be directed at an idiot, which he no doubt completely deserved. "That's your secret? That I…" He didn't want to say it. He'd already explained and apologized. "I turned you down?"

She sighed into a soft laugh. "Yeah, that's my secret. I never tell anyone that horrible story."

"Which means it is *not* a secret from me." He wrapped his arms all the way around her. "So there must be something else, right?"

"Let's forget it, okay?" She tried to step away, but he still had her in his arms and moved with her like they were dancing. "You should write. You do your best work at night."

"Do you really think there's any possibility of my writing a single word while I'm trying to figure out what your secret is?"

She tried another step, this one taking them closer to the edge of the pool. "You have to." She moved again, and he came with her. "You have a month here and you're going to finish"—one more step for both of them—"your book."

He glanced at the pool, now less than a foot away.

She immediately read his mind. "You wouldn't."

"I might."

"Oh, no, you don't!" She jerked away, but he was too fast, scooping her right off her feet to cradle her in his arms.

"Nick!" she shrieked with a laugh and a powerful kick. "Don't!"

He easily subdued her, taking the last step right to the deep end. "Tell or swim."

"Nick!" She dropped her head back, laughter caught in her chest. "Don't you dare!"

He leaned over her and peeked at the water. "You have a cell phone?"

"It's in my purse, but Nick…" She tried to wiggle out of his hold, laughing too hard to have any strength, clinging to his neck.

"Wearing a watch?"

"No, but I swear to God, Nick, if I go in, you go in."

That made him laugh. "Have you met me? I've been dying to get wet with you for days."

"But…I…"

He quieted her protest with a kiss. The angle was awkward, and his balance was precarious, but she tasted good. Their tongues touched and grazed, and she lifted her whole body higher to get more of him.

"I might fall into the water if we kiss any more," he warned.

She let out a soft whimper, her eyes still closed. "I guess that would be okay."

"To go in the water?"

"To kiss some more."

He obliged, longer, deeper, harder...and leaning closer and closer to the edge. It would be so easy to take one step, and they'd be in the pool. Clothes would come off, skin would melt together, and he'd be inside her before they could stop to think. One step. One little step.

"Nick," she whispered into the kiss. "Remember that night? In the lounge?"

He lifted his head to look at her. "Yeah."

"I told you that I wanted you to be my first."

He nodded, still shamed at the honor of the request and how shitty he handled it. "I remember, Willow. And I'm—"

"I'm asking again. The same thing. Be my first."

The words sank into his brain with a thud. "*What*?"

"I never did unload that pesky virginity of mine."

He couldn't even think of an answer, he was so stunned. He did the only thing he could do and walked right into the pool with Willow still in his arms.

Chapter Sixteen

Willow stayed under long enough to hopefully let the shock of her admission wear off. Before that could possibly have happened, Nick dragged her to the surface.

"You need to take your jeans off," he ordered.

She sputtered out some water. "Well, that didn't take long."

"Or we can go in the shallow end, because they are going to get very heavy, and I don't want to have to save your life."

"Nick, we're in a backyard swimming pool." She tried to kick away, but she could barely move. "Oh, you're right."

"Want me to help you?" To make his point, he hoisted up soaked camo pants and flung them to the side of the pool, where they landed with a thunk.

She glanced down at the dark water separating them. "I'd put my money on commando, right?"

"What difference does it make?" He gave a sly smile. "Of course it all came off at once."

Laughing, she managed to kick away, but the weight of wet jeans was too awful. "I can't believe you did that."

"I can't believe..." He stroked the water, staying a few

feet away in the deep end. "I can't believe what you told me."

"Well, believe it, and don't make me feel like a freak."

"You're not a freak, Willow. You're...you're..."

"A virgin. At twenty-"—she battled her way to the shallower end until her toes finally touched the pool bottom—"nine." Oh, God, these jeans! She fumbled with the button, but it wouldn't go through the hole. "Damn it, how did you do that?"

He didn't move. "How did *you*?"

"It was remarkably easy." The jeans practically pulled her under. "I can't get the zipper, either. I'm getting out." She turned and tried to take a step, but she might as well have been in quicksand. Cursing softly, she used all her strength to move her leg.

Behind her, all she could hear was his soft laugh, a splash, and then Nick popped out of the water a foot from her face. "Don't leave."

"I can't..." His hair was wet, leaving rivulets down his face, the water glistening in the moonlight. He looked so hot and sexy and wet and dreamy. His gaze burned on her, staying on her face before he slowly, slowly dropped it to her very clingy tank top.

Heat coiled through her and squeezed, and every single cell in her body did a little dance of desire.

"I can't"—*resist you.* She yanked the stiff zipper—"manage this."

"Let me help." He floated closer and got his hands on the button, releasing it with a single move and then thumbed the zipper. The whole time his face was inches from hers, his gaze locked on her eyes. "I think I..."

His words caught in his throat as if he was speechless.

"I'll get out."

"No." He gripped the waistband of her jeans and yanked her closer. "Stay. Just get"—he worked the zipper all the way down—"safe."

Safe? There was nothing safe about this. Nothing safe about a man with a body that could bring a woman to tears standing in three feet of water five inches away wearing nothing but a soaking-wet T-shirt that stuck to him like a second skin.

He pushed the jeans down, and somehow she found the wherewithal to float back a foot and fight the jeans over her hips. She dragged them down her thighs, vaguely aware that her panties came, too.

They were both naked from the waist down.

"How'd you do that?" she asked.

"I'm a professional."

"I bet you are." She managed to lug the wet jeans from the water and threw them at his face. Of course he caught them, smiling. But not a predatory, this is it, we are naked in the water, baby, kind of smile. Not a smug, I finally got your jeans off smile. This was more of a...*shit*. A pity smile.

"And you're a virgin," he repeated, as if the hard, cold facts couldn't be stated enough times.

"As we've established." Already, her lower half tingled and tightened. Her heart rate was way past normal. And each breath got a little harder to take.

"But that could change." Her statement came out as a whisper, not much louder than the soft splash of water lapping against the tiles. She wasn't sure he'd heard her. Hell, she wasn't sure she'd spoken out loud.

He stared at her as a trickle of water dripped from a lock of hair and snaked down his cheek. "It's my fault, isn't it?"

The initial chill of the pool disappeared as she got used to the temperature. Or maybe that was her own spike in internal heat warming things up.

She knew what he wanted to hear her say. *No, it wasn't your fault.* He wanted a litany of issues—her weight, her broken relationship with her mother, her own insecurities after she lost the weight—that would let him off the twenty-nine-year-old-virgin hook.

But part of her needed him to know. "After what happened with you," she said, choosing each word carefully, "I was pretty scared to take that risk again." *Until now.*

"Shit, another bad decision with long-term recriminations."

"I don't think you can compare the two things."

"You're right," he agreed instantly. "But I'm so—"

"No, don't. Please." She ventured closer, forgetting their lower halves were bare and wet and so dangerously attracted to each other. "Don't apologize again, and please believe me when I say I'm not blaming you, Nick. I'm the one who held myself back from…life."

"From sex," he corrected. "Weren't you curious?"

"No past tense, Hershey. I'm curious as hell. And I have dated guys. I'm not completely a nun."

"But you are a virgin."

She smiled, because it was a little like he couldn't stop saying the word. "I try not to let it define me."

He didn't answer for a moment, studying her again, almost as if he saw her differently. Damn it. She didn't want that.

"How is it possible you haven't met some guy that you couldn't resist?"

She wet her lower lip, suddenly aware that her throat was parched and her pulse hammered steady and hard in her chest.

"I have met someone I can't resist," she said, taking a chance to lift her hand and place it lightly on his shoulder. His broad, hard, sexy shoulder. "And if he suddenly disappears underwater to hold his breath and come up to dole out more excuses, I will"—*Cry. Die. Eat a fracking pound cake*—"not be happy."

He was fighting the urge to do just that, based on the battle waged on his handsome features, his dark brows drawn, his strong jaw clenched. Even his shoulder tensed, as if his body was preparing to escape.

"Willow, that's quite a..." He hesitated for a second. "Quite an honor."

"Well, you are the man of honor."

He laughed and shook his head. "Dishonor, according to my history with you."

"Nick." She took a step closer. "You didn't dishonor me. If you'd taken me up on my offer and then ignored me or slut-shamed me or scribbled 'for a good time, call Willie Z' on the dorm bathroom wall, then, yeah. That would have been a dishonor. But in a weird, twisted way, you respected me."

"Yeah, I respected you right into a life of abstinence."

"I did that to myself." She rubbed her thumb over the hard, smooth muscle under his soaked T-shirt. Biting her lower lip, she came closer. "And I'm ready to lose this particular albatross, Nick. So..."

She saw his chest rise and fall with a slow exhale and his Adam's apple do the same against a throat she imagined was as desert dry as hers.

"You have no idea," he said slowly, "how much I would like to make love to you."

She fought a smile, inwardly thanking him for choosing that sweet expression over all the other options he had.

"But..."

Her smile disappeared. Son of a bitch, he was going to turn her down again.

He swiped some wet hair off his face, forcing her to endure the hard, serious stare. "I'm scared," he admitted.

"Of what?"

"Of not being..."

"Please don't say good, big, experienced, or sexy enough." She took a step closer. "'Cause I'll shove you under water and hold you down for three minutes if you do."

He reached out and touched her face with that knuckle caress she was starting to get way too fond of.

"Are you sure this is what you want?"

She let her hand slide off his shoulder, down his chest, where his heart was beating as fast and furiously as hers. But she didn't linger over that confirmation, her fingers traveling south, sliding over one ab muscle. Then another. Then...holy hell. With each cut and dip and rock-hard muscle, she knew she was completely sure. "Yes."

His hand closed over her wrist before she reached her destination, his fingers strong and forceful. Then he leaned closer, and she braced for a kiss, letting her head tilt to the perfect angle. But he kissed her forehead.

"The first time is too important to be in a pool with half your clothes on," he said.

"Then we'll go inside and take off the rest."

He chuckled into her hair, the low, sexy sound vibrating his chest. "We should have a proper date and get to know each other."

"You took me out for ice cream, and I already know you." Who cared if she sounded desperate? He smelled good and felt better, and she was inches away from...paradise.

He finally let go of her wrist, putting both his hands on her shoulders, forcing her to look at him. "You're making this impossible. I'm trying to be a gentleman and respect you and—"

She cut him off with a kiss, pressing hard against his chest, sucking in a shocked breath when his erection slammed against her stomach, wet skin to wet skin. She nearly bit his tongue, it felt so good.

And he made it worse by sliding one hand into her hair and holding her head while he crushed the kiss right back.

If he'd lift her up, she could wrap her legs around him and...

He broke the kiss first, but she held on for stability.

"You're stopping." It wasn't a question.

"I'm thinking."

She slapped both hands on his chest. "You're not supposed to think at times like this."

"Let's make a deal."

She didn't like the sound of that. At all. "What kind of deal?"

"We'll take it in stages and see how you like it."

Was he kidding? "What's not to like?"

"You have a point, but..." He threaded her hair, scanning her face with his gaze, looking at her like...like she was precious. "If I'm going to be your first, it's going to be memorable."

Like she'd forget him.

"And slow." He thumbed her cheekbone tenderly. "And sweet."

"Fast and dirty's okay, too."

He laughed, looking skyward as if he needed help. "Woman, you are killing me. I'm trying to do this right."

"Okay. What do you propose? Dinner dates, long walks on the beach, rose petals on the bed, and a hundred flickering candles?"

He thought about that, nodding. "Exactly."

But that would take *forever*. And she wanted *now*.

"I have an idea," he said. "I need you as my muse. And you need me as your…"

"Virginity destroyer."

He laughed. "Okay, for every five chapters I write, we can take this one step further."

"That'll take so long."

"Not if I'm inspired."

She rocked her hips enough to press into one very excited man. "You feel inspired."

Smiling, he pulled away, his eyes dark, but his expression set. "Look, I really messed up last time. I'm not going to do that again. I'm going to make it up to you with the best, most mind-blowing, most amazing loss of virginity any twenty-nine-year-old woman ever experienced. Let me do it right."

How could she possibly say no to that? It was downright heroic. Frustrating as hell, but damn if it didn't make her like him more.

"Okay. Deal." She stepped back, nodding. Very slowly, she walked to the side of the pool to the three steps that would take her to solid ground, away from Nick.

One foot in front of the other, Willow did something she'd never done in her whole life. She walked away from a man and let him see every inch of her bare ass. As she walked up the steps, she looked over her shoulder.

He was staring, his jaw loose, his eyes wide.

"Write fast, Nick."

Chapter Seventeen

After what could be technically classified as a sleepless night—since even when she did drift off, her dreams were full of Nick Hershey—Willow rose early for a run she hoped would burn off some of the...energy.

If that's what she could call the achy, hollow, needy feeling mixed with spurts of adrenaline and anticipation. On her way to the kitchen to whip up a breakfast smoothie she didn't really think she could drink, she heard a knock on the back door and was certain she knew who it was.

Ari was still in her pajamas, coffee in hand. "Dying to know how it went."

Laughing, Willow opened the door wider to let her in. "Where's Gussie?"

"I just stopped at her apartment, and she was getting out of the shower and starting her makeup. I can't wait that long."

Willow gestured her to the island counter and pulled out her blender. "How are the bets running?"

"I bet you told him. Gussie said you chickened out."

"What obscure candy did you wager with?"

"Jujubes."

Willow made a face. "Better make an appointment with the dentist, Ari, because you won."

Her eyes widened. "Wait a sec." She pulled out her phone and touched the screen. "I'm texting her."

It took Gussie less than a minute to appear at the door, wrapped in a teal robe with giant orange polka dots, a pink wig already in place, and one eye totally made up. The other was bare naked, giving her the look of living, breathing before-and-after pictures. "That's not the only thing we bet on," she said, pointing an eyeliner pencil at Willow. "I put good candy on you doing everything but."

"My money was on all the way," Ari admitted.

Willow rolled her eyes. "Give her back the Jujubes, Ari."

"No, we bet the Jujubes on telling him. For the deed itself? Nik-L-Nips. Do you have any idea what they are worth?"

Wax bottles full of sugar water? "Those are so gross. Why don't you two eat Hershey Kisses like normal women?"

"Ahem, speaking of *Hershey* kisses." Gussie wiggled her one carefully applied brow. "We saw you."

"What?"

"Coming in at one," Ari said. "I was up and happened to look out my window when you pulled in. You did not go over there in a turquoise minidress. I texted Gussie."

"Shit," Willow murmured, fighting a laugh. "It's like living with the FBI."

"Gory details, please." Gussie tapped her eyeliner on the counter. "Not one thing left out."

She puffed a sigh but couldn't really act put-upon. For one thing, she'd do the same if the tables were turned, and for another...she was dying to share everything. "He thinks we need to build up to a...a perfect deflowering."

"Ahhh," Ari sighed.

"It's sweet, yeah," Willow said. "But come on. I've waited twenty-nine and a half years. I'm built up already."

"But maybe he's right," Gussie countered. "You might think you're ready, but are you ready in every way?"

"Mentally, emotionally, physically, and every otherly. I am ready."

But Gussie shook her head.

"You mean, do I, like, have birth control or something?" Willow asked.

"Actually, I was worried about this last night, but didn't want to kill your mojo." She reached to drag the neckline of Willow's old running shirt to the side "Just as I thought. A disgusting bra."

"I'm not going to do the deed in my sports bra."

"But do you have gorgeous underwear?" Gussie demanded. "Are you properly groomed in your nether regions?"

Willow snorted, not even sure she wanted to answer that.

"And maybe you have some pertinent questions," Ari said. "Gussie's right, and honestly, so is Nick. This is a big deal, and his willingness to draw it out and make it awesome is not just romantic, it's practical. You can be as ready as one of our brides."

"Agree!" Gussie exclaimed. "Do you know what's on our schedule today, Ari?"

"Of course. I just checked the master calendar, and we have no meetings except a phone conference with Deanna Bartlett at eleven."

"Nice bride," Gussie said. "And she'll understand if we push that back a few hours."

"Don't forget the Peyton-Orinson wedding party starts to arrive tomorrow morning," Willow reminded them. "With Jill Peyton in the lead."

"Not-nice bride," Gussie sighed. "So this is our last day with some relative freedom. If we leave now, we can hit Silk for some serious shopping and maybe a spa visit with a nice lunch before we get back to work."

"What is Silk?" Willow asked.

"An absolutely to-die-for lingerie boutique. They have one up in Boston where I used to send my brides all the time, and I found out they opened one in Naples. We are going there this morning."

"She's right," Ari agreed. "A deflowering occurs only once. Let's make it beautiful for you."

Willow looked skyward again, but she couldn't help smiling for how much she adored these two women. "Spoken like a true wedding consultant."

An hour later, they were inhaling the powdery, irresistible satins and laces of exquisite undergarments. They giggled like a bridal party all the way back to the oversized dressing rooms with soft lighting and rooms for privacy or showing off. Silk was glorious, and so was the lingerie sold in the elegant boutique.

In her dressing room, Willow admired the array of breathtaking bras and camisoles spread over lavender, tufted sofas, listening to Gussie and Ari's chatter outside the door. Willow slipped into a new bra—smaller cup size than her last, hooray! But that wasn't why she couldn't wipe the smile off her face. Right at that moment, she loved her life and her friends, and...*now she had to turn to the mirror.*

This was the part she hated most—at least for the vast majority of her life. This was why she didn't go underwear shopping with friends. This was why she was still a virgin at twenty-nine. This was why she avoided three-way mirrors.

Slowly, she turned and...oh.

She gave into a small shudder of delight.

"How's that one fit?" Ari asked.

"They have it in..." Gussie's voice faded, but maybe that was because the blood in Willow's head pounded so hard as she stared in the mirror. Nick was going to see this.

Outside, she heard some voices, the attendant asking a question and some other footsteps, but it all simply faded to white noise as Willow stared in the mirror.

Well, look at you, girl. She'd studied her body in the mirror plenty over the last three years, but never while wearing a baby-blue lace bra that made her breasts look young and perky. Every run, every sit-up, every uneaten cookie, every damn spinach leaf had been worth this moment. Chills rose over her skin and tears welled up as she looked at herself...as Nick would see her.

"He's going to love this," she whispered, loud enough for the girls to hear. But they didn't answer. "Ari? Gussie?" She unlatched the door and tried to inch it open, but one of them was pressed against it, holding it closed tight. "Hey, what's going on?"

"Um...stay in there for a...*what should I do?*" Willow could tell the last question was fired at Ari with a minor note of panic.

"Gussie, what is going on?" Willow demanded, giving the door a little nudge.

Gussie tugged it open, her bottle-brush lashes wide with something unspoken.

"What is it?" Willow asked.

"Let me in," Gussie whispered.

Confused, Willow opened the door, but Gussie slipped in and closed it instantly behind her, staring at Willow. "You're not going to believe who's out there."

And then she knew, her chills turning to something more heated and excited. It had to be Nick. This was something he'd do. Her mind whirring, she tried to figure out how. He'd probably asked Misty, who'd been given the name of the place from Gussie.

And he was here buying something to make her first time amazing.

"I don't want to see him," she whispered.

"Him?" Gussie's brows furrowed under her pink bangs. "There's no him. Just her."

"Her?" Disappointment spiraled, but that didn't matter. "One of our brides?"

She shook her head, gnawing on her lower lip.

"Who is it?" Willow demanded.

"Didn't you hear what the attendant said?"

"No."

Ari tapped on the door. "She's gone," she whispered.

What the hell? Willow inched Gussie out of the way and pulled the door open. "Who's gone?"

"Shhh!" Ari said, finger to her lips. "Unless you want to talk to her, in which case, have at it."

She stepped to the side, and Willow peeked around her, seeing no one else in the plush gathering area of the dressing rooms. "Who is it?"

Ari and Gussie looked at each other, a thousand words silently exchanged, but Willow didn't catch a single one. "Who is it?" she demanded, her voice rising.

"Oh, you left one in the dressing room!" The attendant's voice preceded the woman who sailed into the room. "It's right here, Mrs. Zatarain."

Willow's world tilted a little.

"She's in the store," Ari said softly.

Willow tried to swallow, but her throat was bone dry, every muscle tense and frozen.

The attendant scooped up a burgundy silk robe hanging

over a chair, catching the look from all three women as they stared at her.

"Did you see her?" the woman asked breathlessly. "Ona Z herself is shopping here! Can you believe it?"

No, Willow almost said. She didn't believe it. But, then, Ona was a world traveler, and this boutique catered to wealthy women.

Ari turned, her face ghost-white. "This is not a coincidence," she whispered, her words barely puffs of air. "The universe has put her in your path for a reason, Willow. Why else would she be here?"

To ruin her day? To steal the simple moment of joy she'd been embracing? To send her back to a life of criticism and judgment and disappointment? What universe would *do* that to her?

"A trunk show, a TV interview, a meeting with models," Willow explained, knowing exactly how her mother lived and worked. "Lots of things could get her to a place like Naples, where the wealthy congregate."

"Do you want to talk to her?" Gussie asked.

When Willow didn't answer, Ari's look made it clear what she thought was the right thing to do. "Paths don't cross for no reason," she said.

Willow could feel herself slowly shaking her head.

"Willow," Gussie said, giving her a slight nudge. "You could show her how you look. Show her the gorgeous woman you've become. Maybe you could—"

"No." They both recoiled at the force of the word, making Willow gesture a quick apology. "I mean, not now."

But she meant *not ever*.

"Are you sure?" Ari asked softly. "You may never get another moment like this one."

"We can only hope."

"Willow," Gussie said, her voice uncharacteristically soft. "She *is* your mother. Are you sure you don't want to show her how far you've come? It might be good for you."

Willow swallowed the retort, not expecting someone who'd never met Ona Zatarain to understand what it was like to be raised by her. It *wouldn't* be good for her—it would be like throwing ice-cold water over this lovely day of excitement and anticipation.

She could just imagine the reaction. *Hmmm. Not quite there yet, Willow, but maybe someday you will be the girl I wanted you to be.*

Except that she wouldn't ever be that girl. Not for her and maybe…not for Nick.

Well, thank you very much, Ona Z. You've managed to suck my joy once again.

"No," she replied, backing into the dressing room. "I don't want to talk to her. Let me know when she's gone."

Chapter Eighteen

As much as he wanted to put the headphones on and blast his ears, Nick chose the sensible option and plugged his iPhone into the sound system built into the villa, and let Z-Train's *Garden of Evil* rock the house and patio instead.

Not quite the same, but it did the job, which was to celebrate the end of a chapter...the fifth since he'd seen Willow Ambrose three nights ago. That was about to change. Grabbing an icy bottle of water, he stepped out into the afternoon sunshine and flopped on a chaise next to the pool.

From this spot, almost the entire beach was visible to him. Normally, his gaze glossed over the lemon-yellow umbrellas and relaxed vacationers and focused on the horizon where navy met baby blue to the ends of the earth. In a few hours, those colors would change to a palette of peach and purple and a pool of setting sun.

But today, his attention was on the sands of Barefoot Bay, not the postcard view beyond it. Small groups of people gathered and talked, Casa Blanca staff set up, then moved some tables and chairs. A canopy of white silk was erected, then disassembled and moved down the beach.

At the middle of it, one young woman seemed to be causing the chaos.

This must be the high-maintenance bride Willow had mentioned in her very brief response to his last text. In her defense, his communication hadn't exactly been highly respondable.

First, he'd sent her a 1, then a 2. She'd sent back a smile on the first and a winky-face on the second. Then a 3 and a 4. She'd written that she was busy with a high-maintenance bride, but...

But they were both counting chapters.

He looked at the cell phone he'd set on the table next to him, already eager to send her one more digit...5.

Low in his belly, way too low to be anything but raw, unfettered lust, everything stirred and hardened. His body was deep into battle with his brain, and he knew which side Willow was on.

Which meant...tonight?

In the background, Donny Zatarain's nimble fingers slid through a heartstopping solo riff in the middle of one of his favorite songs, the weeping high notes followed by a line that left little room for nuance.

Baby, let's be dirty, let's be sinful, let's be so damn bad in the garden of evil.

How was it that the daughter of a man who made a career promoting sex had managed to stay a virgin until she was damn near thirty? Was it only because some douchebag turned her down when he was eighteen and stupid? Or was her purity also a rebellion against her dad?

He wanted to know. In fact, he wanted to know everything about her. As he reached for the phone, he spied three women walking across the beach barefoot but in street clothes, one on the phone, one with a clipboard, and one—

the one with orange hair—carrying a long swatch of fabric.

Willow had the clipboard, and as they moved north on the beach, he could get a better look at her. She wore a pale-blue sundress, about the color of the sky behind her—and her eyes right after he kissed her. She had her hair up in a knot, but even from here, he could see that a few stray locks fell in waves around her face and neck.

And even from here, he caught her turning and looking right at his villa.

He gave it a few more minutes while the troupe moved closer and he could see Willow better. A soft breeze fluttered the loose skirt she favored, giving him a nice view of her legs.

He closed his eyes and remembered the whole package climbing out of the pool.

That did it. He tapped his phone to life, touched the text message box and typed one single digit.

5

He hit send and kept his vision locked on her like she was a moving target he couldn't and wouldn't miss. Almost instantly, she reached into the pocket of her skirt and pulled out her phone to read the text.

He stayed right where he was, in full view of anyone who knew exactly where the Artemisia patio was tucked into the foliage, his heartbeat surprisingly strong as he wondered what her reaction would be.

Was she smiling? He couldn't tell. She leaned closer to one of the women, Ari, and showed her the text. Ari lifted her hands as if to say, *Why not?*

Why not?

Willow still didn't look his way, but only because the woman he assumed was the bride was calling something out, and all three of the wedding planners marched toward her, then gathered in deep conversation.

C'mon, Willow. Turn around. Give me a sign. Tell me you—

She broke away from the group, still carrying her clipboard, and strode across the sand, taking out the phone to dial.

Okay, then. Woman means business. He turned his phone over and stared at the black screen, imagining what she might say.

Right now?

I'm ready.

Or…nothing else came to mind or, for that matter, to his phone. He could see her talking on the phone now, so obviously she hadn't been dialing him. Frustrated, he leaned over the balustrade and watched her reach the path, slide on some shoes, then disappear, but not until his tracking skills verified which direction she was walking.

This way.

Nothing was on this side of the resort except the villas and, at the far end, the small farm that serviced the resort. Everything she would need—her office, the restaurants, the spas, and the main hotel building—was in the other direction.

So she had to be coming to see him.

Donny hit a high note and ended *Garden of Evil*, sliding right into the next track, *Rock Hard*. The opening drum solo reached into Nick's soul and tore a little piece out with the perfection of the rhythm.

Automatically, he raised his right hand and matched the beat.

Was she coming to his villa? he wondered as he air-drummed. Or passing by?

She couldn't just pass by. Not if the music was loud enough to lure her in. He walked to the sound system in the living room and hit the volume, shaking the walls when Donny Z screamed out his opening line.

Now is the hour. Now is the time.

You've got the power. Give me a sign.

Oh, yes, she did have the power and he needed a sign.

So he opened the front door that led out to the pathway, so she couldn't miss the message to underscore the text…that she hadn't yet responded to.

He waited a few minutes, then stepped out on the stone patio. No one could walk past here and miss that music. In fact, any minute security would probably come by and ask him to turn it down.

Still, he walked to the wrought iron gate that closed off the villa property, sticking his head out to the road.

In time to catch a flash of blue. He walked out to the path and waited for her as she rounded a curve, her step faltering ever so slightly as she saw him.

He continued toward her, unable to stop how much he wanted to greet her with a touch and a kiss.

"I love that you're replying in person."

"Replying to what?" she asked.

He reached her and paused to drink in how pretty she looked. "I knew your eyes would match that dress."

Brows drawing together in a frown, she shook her head. "You saw this dress?"

"I was watching you on the beach."

"Really."

"And I texted you."

"Creepy."

He laughed. "You read it and you know what it says."

"I didn't see the text. I'm totally in the middle of a wedding rehearsal right now."

Of course she was. He couldn't expect her to stop

working just because he'd reached the goal.

"Where are you going? Can I walk with you?"

She gave him a smile. "I like your persistence, Lieutenant, but I'm just going up to the garden to get Tessa's kids. They're supposed to be in this wedding, and Bridezilla, er, Jill Peyton wants to see them to make sure they match."

"Each other or the decor?"

"What did your text say?"

"Five."

He saw the slow deepening of color in her cheeks. "Chapters." It was a statement, not a question.

"That's right." And they both knew what that meant.

She gestured toward the house. "Setting the mood with the melodic and romantic strains of *Rock Hard*?"

He just laughed. "Guilty."

She put a hand to her ear. "Oh, yes, there's my favorite line. 'Take it, take it, let me break it.' You know what he's talking about in that line, don't you?"

"I have a pretty good guess."

"But I bet you're wrong. Listen to the next line."

"I don't have to," Nick said. "I know it by heart: 'Your treasure is mine to trash.' Which is not, by the way, how I feel."

Laughing, she kept walking, but he stayed with her. "The whole song is about this God-awful amethyst statue—that's the 'rock hard' he's talking about. My mother bought it in Kyoto and insisted on keeping it in the center of the living room table, which blocked Dad's view of the TV."

Nick's jaw dropped as he processed that impossible piece of information. "You're kidding me." He'd thought it was about, well, sex, of course.

"Swear to God. Believe me, my dad is not the badass you like to think he is."

He considered that, letting the news filter through everything he thought he'd known about Donny Zatarain. "I like that about him."

"Talk any more about him, Nick, and I'm going to think that's the only reason you're being nice to me. *Again.*"

He slipped his arm around her shoulder and eased her into his flank, a move that felt utterly comfortable and remarkably sweet. "How about a proper date tonight?"

"I can't. I have a mountain of work for this wedding, and then I have to read five chapters by my new favorite author."

Squeezing, he got her to look right up at him, her lips so close he could almost imagine how they'd feel. "Read them with me. I'll cook for you."

"You'll read over my shoulder, stress out, and then strip naked and go swimming."

He put one hand in the air, Boy Scout style. "I swear I will not read, I will cook. I will not stress, I will relax. I will not strip naked and go swimming, I will…"

"You will what?"

Closing his eyes, he kissed her, long and slow and deep.

In the background, Donny Z answered for him.

Gonna shatter you with my love. Break you in two with my love.

"He's really talking about a statue?" Nick asked as they broke the kiss.

"Yep."

"Mmmm." He put his mouth over his ear. "I'm not."

He could have sworn he felt her melt a little in his arms.

Years ago, when Willow taught herself to appreciate

everything *other* than food, she'd discovered the sheer bliss of having all five senses treated to something wonderful at the same time. Right this moment, she thought with a smile, every one of her senses was having the time of its life.

Her taste buds were enjoying the pull of vanilla and oak blended into a fine, chilled white wine. The plush leather sofa where she reclined embraced her like a cloud, every inch of her body in the perfect, most comfortable position. The whole villa smelled of tangy onions and sizzling beef, and the lilting strains of Tchaikovsky's Piano Concerto No. 1—he'd asked what she liked—danced over her ears, relaxing her.

She looked up from the laptop resting on her stomach to peek into the kitchen, separated by a long granite-topped bar. And there, her sense of sight was getting the best treat of the night.

Nick Hershey…cooking with the same intensity he gave everything. He wore a loose linen shirt that fit snugly over his incredible shoulders, and an expression that said he was keeping his promises about not stressing.

Since she'd arrived, he'd let her read, after a few kisses and a toast to the next five chapters. Somewhere along the way, they'd started using "five chapters" as code for steps in her march to losing her virginity.

It was a wonder the laptop didn't topple when all those butterflies took flight in her stomach. Lifting her head to take one more sip of the crisp, clean wine and another look at the sexy chef twenty feet away, Willow forced herself to stop thinking about senses and sex and concentrate on his book.

She moved the cursor back up to the top of the page and re-read the paragraph where Gannon shared a little bit of his childhood with Christina. She read the words carefully, a few key phrases jumping out.

A home full of laughter. Two sisters he loved. Mom and Dad itching for grandchildren to fill up their empty nest.

She couldn't help comparing this to what she knew about his family. Had he mentioned sisters? No, a brother. And when he talked about "home," he'd never referred to where he grew up or his parents.

"Why is this woman frowning?"

She looked up to find Nick a few feet away, looming tall, his outstretched hand holding an olive between two fingers.

"Why is this man watching me read?"

"I bring an appetizer." He took a step closer, then knelt between the coffee table and the sofa, popping the briny Kalamata in her mouth. "Careful, there's a pit."

"Mmm." She could feel her brain slip into calorie counting—ten per Kalamata olive—and she shook her head to get the thought away and enjoy the salt on her tongue.

"And she's shaking her head."

She took the pit out of her mouth and handed it to him, the act ridiculously intimate. "Just trying to make myself think about the taste and not the cost."

He lifted his brows. "Dinner's on me, unless you count having to read fifty-three pages of drivel."

"It's not drivel," she said.

"Then why are you frowning over..." He inched closer to see the screen. "Ah, he's telling her about his childhood."

"Which is remarkably white bread in flavor."

He dragged his gaze from the screen to her face, his features shifting enough to somehow let her know how much he liked studying her. How did he do that? It was a gift, one she enjoyed every time he looked at her.

"I'm taking that is not a compliment."

"Well, I don't know much about these things, but his ideal childhood doesn't make for super-compelling reading.

But I guess you're following the muse's instructions to stick with the truth."

He didn't answer for a moment, but then pushed up, fast. "Steak will be cooked perfectly in less than two minutes. Just enough time for you to finish that scene and join me on the patio for dining alfresco."

He stepped away before she could reply, and Willow turned back to the book and read the rest of the exchange. Clean words, easy to visualize, story seemed to be moving forward. He'd checked all those boxes, but missed the emotional one.

And she had a feeling she knew why.

Outside, he set a table next to the pool with a view of the bay, a few votive candles, and fresh glasses of wine.

"So, you probably don't want to ruin this lovely, romantic setting with my questions about your crappy childhood."

He closed his eyes briefly as he pulled out a chair for her. "Only if you talk about yours. Seems fair."

"You not only know about mine, you know my parents quite well." She settled into the seat and took a moment to admire the filet mignon, rice pilaf, and green salad. Simple, healthy, and delicious. She looked up at him. "This looks amazing, by the way."

He gave a humble nod and took the other seat, giving her an unobstructed view of the bay, and him.

"I don't know your parents," he said as he sat down and put a cloth napkin on his lap. "I know *of* them. I wanted to meet them, of course, but as far as I knew, they never showed up at our dorm."

"They sent a limo to bring me home on the rare occasions I wanted to go there." She sliced into the tender beef, inhaling the aroma to enhance the experience. "You weren't telling the truth about Spencer Gannon's backstory, were you?"

"I was telling *his* truth."

"Which we've established doesn't make the best writing in this book."

He chewed for a minute, wiping his mouth before responding. "My truth is not the stuff of great fiction."

Except they'd kind of established that it was. "Your parents?" she asked.

He shrugged. "Not the lovebirds yours are."

The memory of Ona shopping in a high-end lingerie store flashed in her mind. She hadn't really given the near brush with Mom a second thought, but it had occurred to her why her mother would be shopping for over-the-top lingerie. She considered sharing that with him, but that would open a can of "why didn't you talk to her?" worms that would definitely wreck the steak.

"They are affectionate," she said instead. "My dad can't keep his hands off her, actually. That part of his persona is true." She scooped some rice onto her fork, but kept the utensil poised in the air as she looked at him. "This isn't about me and my parents, Nick. I want to hear about the Hershey family."

"Let's just say it couldn't be more different from yours."

She rolled her eyes. "Will you forget mine and tell me about yours?"

"I can't," he admitted, nothing but dark seriousness in his eyes. "In fact, that might be part of the reason I was such a fan of your dad."

"Because he was married to my mother?" She couldn't help letting her voice rise in disbelief. "I thought it was his music."

He laughed and nodded. "I love Z-Train's music, no

doubt about it. But I used to scour *Rolling Stone* and those other magazines for anything about Donny Z, and every single time I saw a picture of him with his wife, they were kissing."

She shrugged. "Welcome to my world. Like being the daughter of a couple on a permanent honeymoon. When the bedroom door opened, rapture rolled out every morning."

"What's wrong with that?" he asked.

"I didn't say anything was."

"You don't have to. It's obvious you hate the idea."

She abandoned the rice for a deep drink of wine, and a chance to corral her thoughts. But they were all over the place, and not nearly as delicious as the food or company. "Whatever," she finally said. "I'm not letting you derail this conversation. Didn't your parents kiss?"

He snorted a laugh and sliced his steak with a little more force than necessary. "I can honestly say I never saw them kiss, touch, smile at each other, or come out of their bedroom with anything remotely like rapture. In fact, from the time I was ten, my mom slept on the couch and only went in their bedroom to dress."

That sounded...sad. "They didn't get along?" she asked.

"Oh, no. They were way past not getting along. They pretty much hated the sight of each other, fought constantly, and on one memorable occasion, exchanged blows."

She gasped. "Seriously?"

He gave her a tight smile. "Don't knock the permanent honeymoon, Willow. I have to believe love in the air beats hate in the house."

She didn't know what to say since, obviously, he was right. A long, silent moment passed as they ate and sipped wine.

"They're divorced now," he said softly.

Not surprising. "Very sad, but that's probably better for everyone. And you said you had a brother in Manhattan Beach? Any other siblings?"

"Jessica, my older sister, who I rarely talk to. She's on her third husband, and she's only thirty-four." A little bit of heartbreak came through with every word. "Apparently, she learned too much from my parents."

"You don't have to be exactly like your parents," Willow said. "I couldn't be more different from my mother, much to her horror and dismay."

He eyed her across the space that separated them. "Any chance you'll ever patch things up with her?"

"Doubtful." Maybe it wouldn't wreck the dinner to tell him about the near miss with her mother. If she was ready to sleep with the guy, and he already knew her situation, why not be honest? "As a matter of fact, I just managed to avoid her in Naples."

His eyes widened. "You saw your mother?"

"I didn't actually see her, but we were in the same place."

"But you didn't talk to her?"

She placed her knife and fork at angles on the plate, denying herself the second half of the steak. "Nick, I told you I'm not close to her. I have no real desire to have a big reunion in the lingerie shop."

He looked long and hard at her. "I have to ask you something, Willow."

She swallowed, bracing for the same litany of questions and well-intentioned advice she'd received—and rejected—from her friends. "Yes?"

"What exactly did you buy at the lingerie shop?"

She laughed. "Wouldn't you like to know?"

"You have no idea." He pushed back from the table. "Stay there. I'll get this."

"Save my steak. It was amazing."

As he scooped up his plate and hers, he bent over and kissed her on the forehead. "So are you."

The compliment warmed, along with the fact that talking about their families hadn't ruined the beautiful mood. So she leaned back, sipped some wine, and watched the moonlight dance on the gulf, knowing exactly what she wanted to do next.

"Any chance I could talk you into a walk on the beach tonight?" she asked when he returned.

"Every chance." He stood behind her chair, placing his hands on her shoulders. He leaned all the way over, his cheek next to hers. His fingers slipped lower from her shoulders to the bodice of the thin cotton dress she wore, grazing her collarbone, then inching lower. He brushed the rise of her breast and then gingerly lifted the fabric to see right into her cleavage.

"The new lingerie?"

She let her head drop back with a laugh. "You're not going to let that go, are you?"

He dipped his finger in a little bit, sliding along the lace of her bra. "Not a chance. Let's take that walk, Willow."

Somehow, despite her shaky legs, pounding heart, and slightly curled toes, she managed to get up and let him lead her to the beach.

Chapter Nineteen

Willow's hand was slim but strong in Nick's, a feminine hand with long fingers and no rings, easy to thread into his and comfortable to hold. Neither one talked as they walked barefoot across the sand, drawn to the river of gold cast by the moon on the Gulf of Mexico.

She rolled up her light linen slacks so they didn't get wet, but even that look was somehow womanly when she walked. Her hair was down in soft waves around her face, accentuating her fine cheekbones and almond-shaped eyes. Another thing feminine about her.

"You're staring at me," she said.

"I was just thinking about how girlie you are."

She let out a soft hoot. "Gussie would disagree. Now, she's a parfait of girliness."

"She wears a lot of makeup and wild wigs, yes, but there's something so feminine about you." He curled their joined hands around her back, for the pure pleasure of feeling more of her body next to his. "Was that because you were raised by a model?"

She shot him a look that he couldn't quite read, but he could feel the ice in it. "No."

"I mean, she's—"

"Why are you so obsessed with my parents?" She broke away, taking a step backward. "Believe me when I say you are killing my romance mojo every time you bring up my mother."

Why? he wondered. "Well, I sure don't want to kill that."

"Then kill your curiosity about my parents. They're not even in my life anymore, and I'm happier than I've ever been. But every time you mention her, I...I..." She turned away and looked toward the water. "I certainly don't feel worthy of...this."

The catch in her throat tore at his heart. "Willow, are you serious? Worthy of me? You're worthy of *ten* of me." He reached for her, but she hesitated, searching his face. "Why does she make you feel that way?"

She relented and took his hand, slowly letting him pull her back into his side. "Because I let her," Willow said softly. "And I know I shouldn't give her that power, but the longer and more aggressively I can avoid her, the more I gain the control I need to let that go. Does that make sense?"

Not really. But some of the shit he'd dealt with in war didn't make sense, either, and she'd listened.

They took a few more steps along the sand, the light of a bonfire flickering toward the north, and the dim lights of the resort to the south. But here, they were completely alone. Except for the ever-present celebrity parents who seemed to haunt her.

"So, how long do you plan to avoid her?"

"Long as I can. So far, it's been a breeze. Maybe the need to avoid is mutual. No, no maybe about it. She hates me."

He froze mid-step. "How can you say that?"

"Okay, maybe hate is the wrong word. What would be the word for a feeling of utter disappointment that the one thing you wanted most in the whole world turned out to be exactly the opposite of what you thought it would be, and every time you looked at it, your heart broke because you'd done everything right, but it turned out wrong?"

He laughed at the run-on, but not the sad sentiment behind it. "I'd call that...Charlie Foxtrot."

"What?"

"It's a military expression we use to mean a clusterfuck, which is basically when everything comes together and goes wrong." He'd been involved in a few. "But not usually a way to describe a mother-daughter relationship."

"It's a perfect way to describe it," she assured him as they reached the frothy white water, each little bubble pearlescent in the moonlight. "Everything about me went wrong for her. My weight, my attitude, my personality. My whole essence was not what she wanted, and looking at me was a constant reminder and embarrassment. She named me Willow, for God's sake, clearly having different expectations for me than I produced."

He turned her to face him, lightly lifting her chin, and suddenly having the clearest understanding about her that he'd had yet.

"That explains so much about you," he whispered. "And I promise you, Willow Ambrose Zatarain, that..."

She started shaking her head, making him stop his romantic and heartfelt speech. "Ambrose is not my middle name."

"You said you dropped Zatarain and used your middle name as your last name."

"A version of my middle name, which is actually Ambrosia," she told him, giving him a wink. "My dad picked it and then wrote a song about me."

He drew back, jaw dropping. "*My Sweet Ambrosia*? Holy shit, that song's about you?" He knew he sounded like a teenage boy, but he didn't care. "That is my all-time-favorite song, ever. Ever."

She laughed, looking skyward as if she couldn't believe him. "I thought *Will Ya, Will Ya* had that honor."

"That's my favorite rock *anthem. My Sweet Ambrosia* is the best ballad in rock history. It's about *you*?"

"Well, me when I was an infant."

The melody already threaded through his brain, as familiar as his name. "I must have listened to that song ten thousand times."

"That makes two of us."

She was Sweet Ambrosia? He still couldn't wrap his head around that.

The nectar of the gods, delicious and divine, making all who drink her beauty live for all time.

"It's not like any other song of his," Nick said. "There's something so haunting about it, like he was in physical pain with how much he loved Ambrosia."

She laughed and pulled away, dragging her hand down his arm and capturing his fingers in hers. "He might have been. He says he wrote the lyrics while singing to me one sleep-deprived night, desperate for me to stop crying."

Beautiful lady, precious and pure…

He closed his eyes, walking with her, feeling the hit directly to his heart. That song had always spoken to him, deep inside, stirring him.

"Hey." She tugged on his hand. "You were about to make some major romantic pronouncement prior to learning that I'm the subject of a song."

Not a song. *The* song. "I was." He eased her back to him. "I was about to say that all that I've learned about you tonight makes me certain I've initiated the right optempo for you."

"Optempo?" She lifted her brows, confused. "Navy SEAL-speak?"

"Operation tempo is the pace at which a military plan is unfolded."

"I am now a military tactic, Lieutenant Hershey?"

He wrapped her tighter into his chest. "A critical operation that must be handled with"—he slid his palms up and down her back, enjoying every curve under his touch—"experienced, caring, capable hands."

Her eyes fluttered closed with a sigh. "You have those."

He hoped so. "I'll call it Operation Sweet Ambrosia."

She curled her fingers around his neck and tunneled them into his hair. "I sure hope the optempo isn't too damn slow."

"It will be just right," he promised with a kiss. "Here's my attack strategy." He put both hands on top of her head. "Tonight, my area of control is from here..." He smoothed her hair as he moved his hands down her cheeks, over her neck, and to her shoulders. "To here..." Down her arms to her fingertips. "And here." Back up by way of her waist. "To here." And slowly, over her breasts, the nipples puckering as he lingered a few seconds before sliding back up to burrow his fingers in her hair. "All that is my personal target zone to infiltrate and gather intelligence."

"Intelligence?"

"I'll need to find your hot zones and vulnerabilities." He kissed one, right on her neck, then worked his way up to her ear to whisper, "So I really know exactly how to implement the most effective campaign to complete Operation Sweet Ambrosia."

She let her head fall back in pure resignation, a gorgeous smile on her lips. "Get to work, Lieutenant."

It really was a beautiful song. At least, it was when Nick hummed the melody to *My Sweet Ambrosia* and held Willow so tight and secure she could have fainted and not hit the sand. She'd always liked the song, of course—how could she not?—but the piece took on a new meaning now. She used to think of it as a lullaby. On Nick's incredible lips, it became a love song.

He walked her back to his villa, stopping only to kiss intermittently and brush the sand off their feet. By the time they reached his door, her heart was power-pumping in anticipation of what would happen next.

More kissing, she soon discovered, this time with him pressing her against the front door of the villa.

"Let's go inside," he murmured, sticking his key card in the lock.

"One condition."

He inched back, a question in his expression. "I'm in charge of this operation."

She laughed softly. "I'd expect nothing less, but—"

"We're not, you know, finishing things up tonight."

She tamped down a curl of disappointment, even though she wasn't surprised. "I know, but that wasn't my condition."

He opened the door and guided her in. "Name it. And you only get one."

"No Z-Train in the background. I can't...you know...with my dad's voice screaming at me."

Laughing, he kissed her and closed the door. "You know? You *don't* know, that's all I'm going to say, but I agree to your request."

"No, I don't know, Nick..." She closed her eyes and leaned against the door, angling her head so he could continue his kisses on her throat. The masculine scent mixed with the smell of salt air, teasing her, making her dizzy. "But I'm willing to learn."

"You're doing okay for a rookie." He guided her across the room. "Here, on this loungie thing."

This "loungie thing" was a Hollywood-style chaise tucked into the corner of the room. He pulled her down so they could lie side by side.

"Kiss me more, Nick."

He obliged with a long, lingering, sweet kiss that demanded she sink a little deeper into his amazing arms, ripped muscles holding her tight, his masculine chest pressed against her. Sparks ignited between her legs, sharp and bright and aching for pressure. Unable to resist, she pressed against his erection, moaning at how glorious the contact felt.

He dipped his head, sucking lightly on her throat, flicking her collarbone with swift, sweet licks. His hand moved slowly over her V-neck bodice, skimming the top of her breast, threatening to flip open the oversize buttons that kept her linen top closed, but he didn't.

She kissed his temple, his soft hair, and got her mouth over his ear, but he still held her gingerly. He slid off the chaise to kneel on the floor next to her.

"Turn around," he ordered.

She didn't quite get it. "What are you doing?" she asked.

"Staying focused on my target area. Turn around so your head is down here. On your back."

The orders sent an unnatural thrill through her. He meant what he'd said when he said he was in charge. Without arguing, she switched her position, laying her head on the flat bottom half of the chaise and folding her knees so her feet tucked under the headrest and cushions there.

"Close your eyes." He knelt on the floor at the end of the chaise, facing her.

"This is not like any foreplay I've ever heard of."

"Shhh." He scooped up a handful of her hair and let it fall off the end of the chaise, no doubt spilling into his lap. "I'm not like any man you've ever heard of, either."

That was for sure. Her reply was just a sigh as he played with her hair. Stroking it, finger-combing it, lightly caressing her scalp.

"That feels good. But I can get this at the hair salon."

He laughed softly. "Woman, you need to shut up and enjoy every single moment of this."

She smiled at his upside-down face. "Sir, yes, sir."

His mouth pressed on her forehead, gently, but the warm contact surprised her. "Listen to me, Willow Ambrosia." He gently rubbed her temples. "When I am finished tonight, I will have kissed, touched, tasted, licked, sucked, and appreciated every inch of my target zone."

"What will I do?"

"Drown in pleasure."

"Mmm." She was already halfway there.

"Discover exactly what turns you on."

Everything he did turned her on.

"And…" He closed her eyelids with a sure hand. "When I'm finished, you will see yourself as the beautiful, sexy, sensual, desirable, and smokin'-hot woman that I see every time I look at you."

Something cracked inside—some ice around her heart,

maybe? Or maybe it was the wall of protection she'd erected for so long she couldn't remember life without it. Or perhaps it was her willpower to say no to anything.

She didn't know, but all Willow could do was hope she didn't shed a tear while Nick Hershey gave her a gift she'd feared she'd never get or deserve. Adoration.

He'd moved to her ears, licking one slowly, nibbling the lobe, hot breath like a tropical breeze that lifted the hairs on the back of her neck.

"Sweet ears," he murmured. "And lucky you, they both work."

He kissed his way back over the top of her head, pausing to inhale a handful of hair. "What is that? Strawberry? Lavender?"

"It's goat milk," she said. "A local girl makes it on her farm here and sells it at the spa. I think this is called Vanilla Sunrise. Her boyfriend names them all."

"Nice." But he didn't pause long, flicking his tongue over her temple and down to her other ear. "Can you hear me, Willow?"

She barely nodded, capable only of digging her fingers a little deeper into the plush velvet under her.

"Listen carefully, okay?"

Another nod.

"Every single time you doubt your beauty or worth or value or sex appeal?"

She didn't answer, but only because the lump in her throat was growing too fast. How did he know she doubted that stuff? How did he know she fought demons daily that told her she had none of that? She hadn't told him.

"You remember that just looking at your goddamned ear gives me a hard-on."

Her fingers relaxed a little, aching to dig into something

other than the chaise. She managed to swallow despite a bone-dry mouth.

"Okay," she said. "Now where are you going?"

He chuckled softly. "Your throat."

Oh. Could she take that? She arched her back to offer him access, and he took it by planting his kiss right on her pounding pulse. "Someone's fired up," he teased.

"You should feel my heart." *In fact, please do. Now.*

"Getting there, baby. First, I like this." He leaned over her face, his bare chest against her lips.

"When did you take your shirt off?" And what else did Mr. I Love to Get Naked take off?

"While you were thinking about other things." He licked the tender spot between her collarbones, which felt great, but she was completely assaulted by the pressure of his granite-like muscles over her face, the scent of soap and man and sea air clinging to him like she wanted to. She reached up and closed her hand over his head, pushing his mouth down to her chest, wanting his incredible abs in her face so she could lick every crevice and cut.

"I'm getting there, sweetheart," he promised. "Not quite yet. There's all this delicious territory."

He splayed his hands over her breastplate, and she did the same on his cheeks, pulling him to her face for an upside-down kiss. It was as awkward and dizzying as it was perfect, his tongue finding new access to her mouth, hot and wet.

Lifting his head, he started on the wide, stylized button of her top. She used the break to get her breath, to look up and see nothing but masculine neck, the angles of his chest, a hint of dark hair he must shave, and sexy, taut nipples.

She lifted her head and kissed whatever skin her lips could find, her ears hammering with a wild pulse, her whole body already rising and falling as if he were on top of her.

"War is hell," she muttered, making him laugh and kneel all the way up. "Where are you going now?"

"Approaching the target by the side." As he scooted around to her left side, she was both relieved and disappointed he still had his cargo shorts on. But the thought was short-lived as he finished with her first button, kissed the rise of her breast and then opened the second.

"Ahh, a pretty bra you bought just for me."

Why deny it? "You like baby blue?"

"It matches your eyes." He spread her blouse wide after finishing the last button and stared at her breasts. Normally, she'd burn with embarrassment. Especially on her back, knowing that didn't exactly display optimum perkiness.

But the only burn she felt was from his eyes as he stared at her, his jaw slack enough for her to know he liked what he saw, his next breath a tad ragged.

"Damn, Willow, I'm honored." He finally dragged his gaze to meet her eyes. "You put down some cash on that pretty bra."

She laughed, so not expecting that. "Worth it?"

He answered by lowering his face to her cleavage, then closing his teeth along the top of the bra. "Tastes expensive." He reached under her, easing her back up so he could reach the hooks. "I'll be careful."

She didn't reply, still trying not to pant and to somehow keep from lifting her hips, too, because, she wanted him…there.

But he simply unlatched the bra, with one easy, experienced flick of his fingers, then repositioned himself, kneeling closer, looking up at her.

"You could join me on the loungie thing, you know."

"I like this view. And if I get up there, it's all over."

Exactly. "And you want to drag this out."

What he dragged was the side of her top, sliding it back so he could get her arm through the hole. "That's not why I'm doing this. I'm a huge fan of fast and furious sex."

Her heart slipped at the thought of fast and furious sex with him. She bit her lip to keep from begging.

"But I told you, I'm in charge of the optempo." He got the other arm out and gingerly removed the top altogether, laying it neatly on the floor next to him. "We have many, many years of missed foreplay to make up for, Willow."

She knew he meant *she* had years to make up for, but let herself roll around in the pleasure of the "we" anyway. They did have years to make up for.

"We should have done this back in college."

Her jaw loosened in surprise at the statement.

"Don't you agree?" he asked.

"Well, yeah, but... Nick, we don't have a missed history or anything."

He looked hard into her eyes, his smoky and dark with arousal. "We do have a missed history, Willow. Yes, I was nice to you because of your dad, but I also liked you. You made me laugh. You were real, and all those other girls were fake."

She considered that, liking the sentiment, somehow believing it, or at least talking herself into believing it. "How did you lose your virginity, Nick?"

He didn't answer, instead ran his finger over the lacy trim of the high-end bra that lay loose on her now, brushing her skin, but also concentrating on each little loop and flower on the lace. "Some girl whose last name I don't remember. I was a junior in high school, a hormone time bomb, and I met her at a football party. We were a little drunk and..." He shrugged, lifting a shoulder. "Stupid."

"Bet it wasn't stupid at the time."

"It wasn't much of anything, I'm afraid." He smiled. "It wasn't what I want your first time to be." He lowered the lace, revealing more of her breast. "I want your first time to be so incredibly special that every time you think of it, you can't help but smile."

She smiled then. "You know what I want my first time to be? Soon."

"Not yet, Little Miss Impatience."

She gave in and rocked her hips, glaring at him. "I'm dying down there."

He knelt up, revealing a huge tent in his cargo shorts. "Me, too."

"Well..."

He shook his head. "This is my operation. You want a siege. I want..." He slid the bra strap down her shoulder, moving the cup away to reveal her hardened, swollen nipple. "An indirect counteroffensive." Closing his eyes, he leaned forward and took it in his mouth, sending a white-hot spray of pleasure through Willow's body.

"Nothing offensive about that," she whispered, instinctively clutching his head to press him harder. He licked a circle around her nipple then put it between his teeth, nibbling oh-so-softly, making every cell dance with fire and forcing a cry out of her lips.

He kissed his way over to the other breast, holding her securely from his kneeling position, cupping and caressing, getting her bra off with remarkable ease, leaving her upper half as naked as his.

He didn't miss an inch, sighing and sucking and stroking her until she no longer fought the waves that rolled between her legs, letting her hips rock in a natural rhythm, aching and screaming for his touch. But he refused, giving one hundred and ten percent to her breasts and throat and mouth and oh, back to each distended, aching nipple again.

"Nick, I have to, I have to…"

He took her hand, prying the fingers from the velvet, and sliding her hand into her pants. "Do what you want, baby. I've got this territory to control."

He controlled everything. Including her hand as he nudged it down between her legs, and she couldn't fight. She touched herself, shocked at how slick and wet and pulsingly ready she was for his hand and his body.

"Nick, I want *you*." Not her hand, *his*.

"When we're ready, you'll have all of me."

Damn it, she was so, so ready. He squeezed her breast and sucked some more, dragging his tongue across her nipple over and over again. Losing control, she rubbed her sweetest spot, knowing exactly where to touch to make herself come, but never, ever having it happen with a hot, wet, skilled mouth and masterful hands touching her somewhere else.

He kissed her mouth, murmuring instructions into her lips.

Telling her what he could do, what he would do. Her imagination exploded as she closed her eyes and dreamed of the night—very, very soon—when he would fill her with his enormous and sexy manhood.

"Inside," she muttered. "I want you…"

He chuckled softly. "You're gonna make me come, baby."

And just the thought of it, the image of him out of control from merely making love to her breasts, put her over the edge, making her spiral and moan and finally give in to the best orgasm she'd ever given herself.

Fiery, numb, twisty, achy, perfect.

She couldn't take an even breath for ten minutes, and the

whole time he continued his upper-body assault until she was certain there was no inch of his territory unassaulted.

In the best possible way.

Including, she thought with a wry smile, her heart, which happened to fall dead center in the middle of his target zone.

Chapter Twenty

Nick stayed firmly on the floor, not trusting his own body one minute on a skinny piece of furniture that wasn't a bed or a sofa with Willow. His hard-on had gone way past discomfort into pain, but that finally subsided like the bright pink flush on Willow's chest.

She didn't talk, kept her eyes closed, and didn't seem to notice a strand of her hair caught in her lips.

He plucked it out gently, stroking her cheek, full of wonder and amazement and no small amount of man-pride. She might have used her hand, but he got her there.

"Nick," she finally whispered.

"Hmm?"

"Can you go write five more chapters? They can be short. A page each, tops."

He laughed softly, trailing a finger from her chin to her chest, watching her shoulders quiver in response. "Not satisfied yet, Willow?"

She turned to face him. "You're not."

"I'm fine. This wasn't about me."

"Why not? I'm an equal opportunity virgin." She nestled her face into his hand. "And I want more."

He stared at her for a long time, memorizing every angle,

every beautiful slope, every detail of her face. "There will be more," he promised.

"At the risk of sounding whiny and desperate, when?"

He laughed again, leaning in for a kiss on the cheek. "You don't get it, do you?"

"I believe that's at the crux of my problem."

"I mean, you don't get why I'm doing this."

She sighed, closing her eyes. "You want to make my first time special. You want to have a real connection so I don't have a vacant, empty feeling when it's over. You want to make up for turning me down in college. And..." She narrowed an accusing eye at him. "You want me to stick around long enough to be your muse until this book is done, so you're dragging it out."

He considered every single reason, nodding slowly. "Actually, all of those things are true, but you're missing one, and it's the one that matters most to me."

She thought for a while and then lifted a shoulder. "I have no idea."

"I want you to know..." He stroked her cheek then flattened his palm on the side of her face, holding her so she had nowhere to look but into his eyes. "That whoever made you doubt how incredibly gorgeous you are inside and out was wrong. Any guy can take your virginity, Willow, and I'm sure you could have a line of willing guys to pick from. But I want to be the one who makes you realize you can not only take off your clothes and be perfect, you can drop that shell of protection you wear like a coat of armor, too."

She stared for a long moment, long enough for him to see her eyes mist up. "It was my mother," she finally said.

He knew what "it" was, and he wasn't at all surprised about her mother.

She sat up and looked around for her clothes, the move so automatic, he could have predicted it was coming.

"You don't need to cover up to tell me this."

"Yes, I—"

He pushed her back down. "Just talk."

"Naked?"

"The only way to fly," he teased. "And you're not completely naked, and there's nothing about your upper half I don't know." He smiled and licked his lips. "Quite intimately."

"Oh, Lord, you're sexy," she whispered on a moan. "Will you at least come up here and lie with me so I don't feel like my girls are on display?"

"Let's do better. Let's lie in bed."

Her eyes widened. "I thought..."

"We can share a bed together and not give in to temptation, can't we? You're the queen of resisting temptation."

"Not where you're concerned."

He stood and held his hand to her. "You are not leaving me tonight."

She didn't move, eyeing him. "You want me to spend the night?"

"Yes." He reached for her hand to help her stand, then pulled her into an embrace, the shock of their bare chests touching electrifying him all over again. "I'm not saying it's going to be easy on the optempo, but I don't want you to leave."

Before she could argue, he walked her down the hall to the master bedroom, which was dark except for the soft blue glow of the pool lights outside the French doors. He guided her to the bed, but she hesitated.

"Let me use the bathroom to freshen up first."

He released her and watched her walk to the en suite, the pale light highlighting the muscles in her back and the feminine lines of her body as she walked away in nothing but loose, light slacks. How long would those last?

Long, because he was determined to do this right.

He turned down the bed, changed out of his cargo shorts into a pair of boxers and lay on top of the comforter, waiting for her. His body—specifically, the lower half—was more or less under control, but he wasn't the least bit sleepy. For a moment, he glanced at the desk where he'd put his laptop, dark and silent.

What was the next scene? he wondered while he waited. It was time to write Christina's farewell. Would that bird fly or crash?

The bathroom door clicked open, and Willow stepped out in a white Casa Blanca-issued bathrobe.

"You're cheating," he said. "You covered up what I just *uncovered.*"

"I'm cold."

"Then let me warm you, but why do I have to lose the territory I already won?"

Laughing, she came to the bed. "It's your war games, Lieutenant. Ten minutes ago I was ready to complete Operation Deflower."

"Not until I know the inside as well as the outside."

As she reached the edge of the bed, an unreadable expression settled on her features.

"What?" he asked. "You have a problem with that?"

"No, but I don't get you." On the bed, she curled her legs under her, wrapping herself in a little protective hug. "Why don't you want to, you know, do the deed and forget all the ancillary stuff?"

The question actually hurt, surprising him. "Because

you're worth more than that?" He shouldn't have made it a question, but it seemed so obvious, he was surprised she didn't realize that.

"But it's so..." She closed her eyes and dropped her head. After a second, she looked up. "I don't like to be manipulated."

"I'm not manipulating you." Was he? Hell, he thought he should get a freaking medal for being as legit as they come.

"Because," she continued, "that's another thing that led me to have this...what did you call it? Coat of armor."

"Who manipulated you?" he asked.

She gave him a look that said she couldn't believe he didn't know.

"Your mother?" he guessed.

"Not that I want any part of her in this bedroom or discussion or, frankly, my life, but since you are so hell-bent on knowing me on the inside, yes, my mother. Ona Zatarain, who would give Machiavelli a run for his money and then insist he have a full-body makeover afterward."

"How did she manipulate you?" he asked.

"How *didn't* she, is a better question." She gave a sharp laugh. "Starting with naming me for exactly what she planned for me to be—a clone of her—then fighting and squeezing and correcting and insulting and pummeling me to try to get that to happen."

His gut squeezed as he leaned closer. "Did she hit you?"

"No, *no*," she corrected quickly. "Bad choice of words. She tried to"—she mimed the action of someone kneading dough or clay—"make me into what she wanted me to be. My earliest memory is itching. Itching in clothes I didn't want to be in, itching in situations I didn't like, itching to be free of her."

Neither spoke for a moment as she plucked at a thread in the terry robe.

"I figured out somewhere around, oh, twelve or thirteen that I could stop the itching by eating." She whispered the last word, closing her eyes as if it shamed her. "For one thing, food was comforting, for another she couldn't exactly come right out and say I shouldn't eat—what mother could do that, right? But I knew it drove her crazy that I didn't have her legendary control when faced with a box of candy."

"It was certainly a safe way to rebel, considering other things a kid could do to her body," he said.

"Well, it's not safe to get that overweight, and I'm not sure I was rebelling, per se. But I could control what I put into my mouth. She couldn't stop me and, Lord in heaven, she hated every pound I packed on." She looked up with a sad smile that barely reached her eyes. "And by the time I was a sixteen or seventeen, I knew I'd found the secret to getting her to leave me the hell alone."

"She ignored you?"

"Most of the time. When she didn't, we'd fight about my weight, and she'd fling words that stung like 'disappointment' and 'disgusting' and 'humiliation.'"

"Didn't your dad help you?" Surely the man who wrote *My Sweet Ambrosia* for his infant daughter wouldn't sit back and let this kind of abuse happen.

"In some ways, he did. I was always closer to him, which pissed her off more because she wanted to be like some celebrity mom trotting her perfect offspring through LA and New York. But, of course, she couldn't show me to anyone, because I was, you know, eww. Fat."

She let the word fall on the bed with a thud, and Nick wished he could scoop it up and throw it out and take away her pain.

"But to answer your question, there's something you need to know about my dad. He is wholly and completely and down-to-his-last-cell in love with my mother. That's not an act. That is the truest, closest, strongest bond between two people I've ever seen."

"Wow. I can't imagine what it would be like to be raised in an atmosphere of love like that. I told you what I had—the Bickersons."

She lifted a shoulder. "You know what they say about the grass. Your parents fought, but mine lived in a cocoon where no one else could ever squeeze in. And when push came to shove, Dad chose her side every single time. And me?" She gave him a big smile and surprised him by leaning over and slowly falling on the bed next to him. "I chose chips and chocolate."

He reached for her without thinking, pulling her closer in a natural move. "So did you have to go to shrinks to figure this all out and get yourself so healthy and in shape?"

"A little. A few. I didn't really like counseling, though I've worked with some trainers who were natural psychologists. Honestly, I didn't need to dig deep to find the root of my issues. One day, when I was about to turn twenty-six, I'd been at their house, and it had been a particularly ugly blowout. Some magazine was there doing a photo shoot, and they wanted pictures of me, and she…" Willow bit her lip. "She refused to let them take any. I overheard her telling one of the photographers that I had mental issues, and they wanted to keep me out of the media for my own safety."

Her voice cracked, and he tightened the embrace, wishing he could do anything to take away that heartache.

"But it was the turning point I needed," she reassured him. "I left the house, stopped for ice cream on the way, and threw the gallon out of my car before I got back to Canyon Country, where I lived in virtual isolation. She was still manipulating me, and all I was doing was suffering with a two-hundred-and-sixty-pound body."

She cuddled closer, comfortable with her tale now, maybe lost enough in the telling that she forgot they were on a bed side by side with nothing but a bathrobe separating their bodies. Nick forced himself to forget it, too, much more interested in the inside of this complex, damaged woman than the outside right then.

"I started dieting the next day, and I wish I had a story about what an uphill challenge it was, but honestly, losing a hundred and twenty pounds that I didn't want was easy. And it wasn't that tough to avoid seeing her all this time, either. Except for that near run-in on the mainland, we just never connect. I've seen my dad now and again, but really, not for the last two years, so he doesn't know how much weight I've lost. I like it this way."

"Don't you ever want to talk to her? I mean, why not mend the broken fences as adults?"

"No," she said simply. "If she loved me now because I'm not fat, I think I'd hate her even more for being such a hypocrite."

"What about your dad? Will you see him?"

Another shrug. "Probably. I kind of miss him, because he's such a character, but they're a package deal, and I don't...I don't..." Her voice cracked again. "I don't want to have anything to do with her."

"What if you get married or have a child or..." It seemed so final, and really sad.

"If I never see her again, that'll be fine. That'll make me...happy." But she sounded anything but.

"Are you happy, Willow?"

She looked up at him, her eyes misty and full of...well, not happiness. Those eyes looked like pain, regret, and a whole lot of wishing things were different. "Right now I am," she whispered. "Here, with you."

"C'mere." He pulled her all the way into him, stroking her arm over the robe. "You don't have to talk anymore."

"Mmm."

She felt leaden in his arms, like she'd just carried a ton of baggage and dumped it in pure exhaustion. They didn't talk or kiss, but Nick caressed her hair over and over and over until she breathed evenly with sleep.

She was ignoring the truth like he did when he tried to rewrite history. The only difference was, she was helping him face that. Could he help her? When he was sure she'd drifted off, he slipped off the bed, inexplicably energized, and went to the laptop to see if he could unload a little more of his own baggage.

Chapter Twenty-One

During a rehearsal, the bulk of the hard work fell on Ari's shoulders, and tonight's walk-through was no different. With the kitchen completely ready for the dinner service and the dining area staged and ready on the sand, Willow was in a holding pattern. She stayed on the fringes of the festivities, observing the rehearsal with Gussie.

"I'd bet a bucket of Bit-O-Honey this marriage won't last," Gussie murmured. "All you need to do is look at that groom's weak chin. No chin, no balls."

Willow stifled a laugh. "I'm not your gambling partner, Gus, she's down there." Willow gestured toward Ari, currently in a deep conversation with the bride, Jill Peyton. "I don't know who has the balls, but Jill definitely wears the pants in that relationship."

The wedding party was small, but included the darling "matched set" of Emma and Edward, who were doing their best not to be too bored, but twice little Edward had picked up a seashell and turned to find his mother off on the side to show her his treasure.

Finally, Tessa stepped away and walked across the sand to join Willow and Gussie.

"I think we'll be better off if he can't see me," Tessa said as she approached. "He's determined to show me every shell he finds."

"They're amazingly well-behaved for little children asked to play a part with a bunch of strangers," Willow said. "Stand here, Tessa. We have a bird's-eye view, and Gussie's snark is worth the price of admission."

"Who can be cynical at a wedding?" Tessa asked, sidling up next to Willow.

"The wedding planners," Gussie told her.

"Haven't you heard?" Willow teased. "We're the most cynical of all."

"I guess you have seen the dark underbelly of the wedding process," Tessa said.

"Enough to know we'll never have one, right, Willow?"

Willow opened her mouth to agree, but inexplicably nothing came out. Why did Gussie cling to that silly pact so much, anyway? Would a wedding be the worst thing in the world to have?

"Willow?" Gussie prodded.

"Yeah, that's our deal," she finally said. "We've seen enough of these things to know there would only be nightmares ahead."

Tessa shook her head, a smile on her face. "When I married Ian right on this beach, it was..." She laughed again. "Well, you guys were here."

"We certainly were," Gussie said. "I'll never forget how you fainted."

"And then your groom disappeared," Willow added.

"Or how you sent us off in a hot-air balloon ride so we didn't find out the whole thing was a sham." Gussie looked at Willow. "Why would we ever be cynical?"

Tessa laughed again. "I had extenuating circumstances."

"They all do," Willow assured her. "But we don't hold that against you."

"Still, no weddings for us," Gussie said. "They're for the family anyway."

They sure were. And that had been Willow's driving motivation behind agreeing to the pact. She had no interest in a wedding that would mean a reunion she didn't really want to have. As the other two women joked and talked, Willow sneaked a peek over her shoulder, able to see part of the patio and the barrel-tile roof of Artemisia.

Not that talk of weddings and families made her think about Nick, or anything. Truth was, everything made her think about him. She'd had a hell of a time concentrating for the few days since she'd last left his villa.

It had been dawn when she'd slipped out after a remarkably sound sleep. Nick had written almost all night, woke her with kisses and coffee at sunrise, and promised her he'd have another five chapters finished very soon.

He'd texted her his progress, and the last she'd heard, he'd completed four chapters. One more and...

"What the hell is she doing here?"

Willow turned to follow Gussie's stunned gaze, zeroing in on a woman striding along the walkway to the villas, ponytail swinging, a phone to her ear, her freakishly thin model's body moving at a rapid gait.

"Misty Trew isn't due for her walk-through for two more weeks," Gussie said. "The last thing we need is the clash of brides tonight."

Or the clash of a roommate in Nick's villa. There went Willow's five-chapter plans.

"I'll go see what's up," Willow said, stepping away.

"And keep her away from Jill," Gussie warned. "I hate when brides compare notes."

Willow gave a quick nod and hustled toward the small bridge, crossing in time to meet up with Misty.

"Well, this is a lovely surprise," Willow called out, congratulating herself on sounding genuine.

"Willow!" Misty sounded surprised, too. "Hey, I gotta go," she whispered into the phone, loud enough for Willow to make out her words. "No, *now*. I seriously have to go." She planted a smile on her face as she tapped the phone and regarded Willow. "I wasn't expecting to see you here."

"Well, I work here," Willow reminded her, coming closer.

"Out on the beach on a Friday night?"

"There's a rehearsal tonight and a wedding tomorrow, so if there's anything we need to do for you, let me know so we can squeeze it in to the—"

"No, nothing," she said quickly. "I'm here to see Nick. I have to talk to him. Have you seen much of him? Spent time with him?" Each question sounded a little too interested, like a cross between worry and curiosity.

"A little bit." Like all night recently. "He's doing a lot of writing."

"Good, good." She continued walking, and Willow fell into step with her.

"Does he know you're coming?" Willow asked, knowing she sounded just as interested, worried, and curious.

"No, I'm going to surprise him."

Willow laughed. "You better knock. The man loves nothing more than living and working naked."

That earned her a sharp look complete with raised eyebrows. "Really."

"I mean, that first day when I…" She felt her cheeks warm. "He swims a lot and is staying alone, so…"

Misty waved it off. "No worries. I'm not interested in

what he has to show me. I just want to quickly talk to him about"—she swallowed and added a cool smile—"something."

"So you're not staying tonight?"

She slowed her step. "I'm with friends in Naples, so, no, I'm not staying." She waited a beat, holding Willow's gaze. "Are you?"

Willow blinked in surprise. How was she supposed to answer that?

Fortunately, she didn't have to, because Misty reached out and surprised Willow even more by taking her hand. "Not my business, is it?"

"Actually, no."

Misty's smile grew warmer and less shaky. "He seems like a good guy," she said. "So, if anything gets, you know, weird? Don't blame him."

What the holy hell was that supposed to mean? "Weird?"

"Just…" She flicked her fingers as if to brush off the whole discussion. "Nevermind. You'll understand soon enough." She gasped softly. "Shit. I didn't say that."

Willow just stared at her, her heart sinking. "I'm not following a thing you're talking about, Misty. Is something going on with you? Problems with your wedding plans? Your brother? What are you trying to tell me?"

She sighed, shaking her head, her expression utterly unreadable. "Nothing at all, except you should know that you are one very lucky girl. And I hope you don't blow the opportunity when it's handed to you."

Willow remained utterly clueless. "The opportunity for…"

"Love."

Love? Why would Misty say that? Unless… "Misty, is Nick's being here some kind of setup?"

She gave a nervous laugh. "Well, you might say that, yeah. And I really have to talk to him, so—oh, look." She pointed to the beach. "The girl with the ever-changing hair is waving for you. They must need you over there." Her gaze scanned the whole event staging. "That canopy is so pretty."

"That's what yours will look like," Willow said.

"Yeah, nice." She took a few steps away and gave an awkward wave. "See ya." Without another word, she continued toward the villa, leaving Willow with no chance to ask for any clarification.

Not only was that bride completely disinterested in weddings—all weddings, including her own—she was hiding something. Something important. Willow watched her slender figure disappear in the direction of Nick's villa and wondered if somehow she'd be better off not knowing what it was.

He needed a beer. Hell, after what Misty Trew had told him, Nick needed a few of them. Silent, he walked to the refrigerator and pulled one out along with another cold bottle of water for his guest. She'd downed the first one during her rapid-fire confession that had just knocked him on his ass.

After a swig, he rounded the counter to give Misty the bottle, but didn't sit down.

"So there's no wedding."

"There's a wedding, sort of. But it won't be mine. It's a very small, private service for Ona and Donny to renew their vows."

He let that sink in. "So I'm here...why?"

"To write a book, as far as I understand it."

But that wasn't why he'd originally come here. "You had me fly to Florida for a weekend to preview a wedding site even though you knew there wasn't going to be a wedding? Did Jason know this?"

"It was Jason's idea," she said. "He thought you could use the break and wanted to help you. He thought you were getting depressed over the medical leave and thought the trip would be good for you. Honest, he did."

She had to claim honesty, because everything she'd told him before today had been a lie.

"And when you decided to stay and make a month of R&R out of it, Jason was so sure he'd done the right thing."

So sure he didn't tell me the truth. Nick ran his thumb over the label on the bottle, thinking how much that sounded like something Trew Blue would do. Always worried more about the next guy and thinking he knew what was best. And, to be fair, the experiment worked. Nick had been happy, writing, and…falling for Willow.

His heart dropped at the thought of her and all she'd confided about her parents. Who would be here to renew their vows in less than two weeks. "I have to tell Willow."

Misty shot up instantly. "You can't, Nick! I promised Ona. This is so important to her, you have no idea. She's been planning this, moving heaven and earth to make it happen."

"I understand she's a master manipulator."

Misty shrugged, unfazed. "Ona knows what she wants and goes after it, that's true. But what she wants is to reconcile with her estranged daughter. How awful is that?"

"It might be very awful, for the estranged daughter."

"Or it might be wonderful and make everyone happy."

Doubtful, after all Willow had told him. Even if it did end up as one big family love fest, was it his place to hide what was going on from her? Absolutely not. "She'll be furious if she finds out I knew and didn't tell her."

"Not if there's a happy ending and she and her mom are close again."

Again? "From what Willow has said, they've never been close. In fact, there's a lot of hurt between them."

"Exactly!" Misty exclaimed. "Trust me, Ona knows that. She's desperate to fix it. She's not doing this on a whim. She nearly drowned, and when she was saved, she decided there was nothing more important than to have a relationship with her daughter. A good, solid relationship. She's even tried, but Willow always has an excuse why she can't see her parents."

"That's her right, Misty. I can't step in and change that."

"No one is asking you to, just not to stop it from happening."

"Telling her isn't stopping it. She has to be here for the event, whatever it is." But even as he said the words, he could see the look in Willow's eyes when she talked about her determination not to see her mother or anyone from her past. She would find a way to leave, he knew it.

"It could ruin the most important moment in either of their lives," Misty said, the amount of compassion in her voice surprising him.

"Why is this so important to you?" he asked. "You don't know Willow, and it's a pretty big inconvenience for you."

She looked at him, not answering right away. "Hasn't my brother told you about our parents?"

Had he? "Your parents"—searching his memory banks, all he could come up with was a reference to a stepmother— "are divorced?" he guessed.

"He didn't tell you about what hell it was living with Brenda?"

"Your stepmother? Hate to break it to you, Misty, but Navy SEALs don't generally sit around and whine about their stepparents."

She didn't smile. "Well, let me whine for him. We were raised by a horrible, selfish, hateful woman after our mother died. Jason went into the military to escape. I started modeling, and when I met Ona, it was like finding the mom I never had. She's been so good to me, so kind and supportive and wonderful. I had no idea a mother could be like that."

It was Nick's turn to stare and be confused. "Why wasn't she like that with her own daughter?"

"That's the point," she insisted. "She *knows* she was wrong not to try to accept Willow as she is—or was. She wants to take all the blame. That's why she's coming here, to beg for Willow's forgiveness and start a new relationship."

"Why make it so complicated with this big fake wedding and secret...service?" he asked. "Or whatever it is they're doing."

"Renewing their vows," she supplied. "Ona wants everything to be perfect, like a chance for the three of them to bond and become a family again."

What kind of lunatic was this woman? He already despised her based on what Willow told him. Why would he help her? "Sorry, Misty, but I don't owe her any loyalty, so I'm going to tell Willow and let her decide what to do."

Misty's shoulders fell, and raw disappointment darkened her expression. "Jason told me I could count on you. He said you're dependable and—"

"He's right. You can depend on me to tell Willow."

"He said you owe him a favor."

Damn it. "I'm doing it by being here."

"You were doing it by coming here for a weekend, but staying here and getting involved with Willow and ruining

215

everything for someone I love is not a favor to anyone." She crossed her arms and let out a huff of a sigh. "I'm only asking you to let it go. If you weren't here, if you had gone back when I did, this wouldn't be an issue. But Jason called me and told me I had to tell you so you weren't pissed off when the time came and there's no wedding, and he also promised me you would keep the secret."

"But he doesn't know"—*that I'm about to relieve Willow of her virginity*—"that we've grown close."

"I gathered that. What if you grow even closer?"

"And?"

"And...you fall in love. And get *married*?"

What? He couldn't even think of a response to that.

"She won't have her own family at her wedding," Misty said smugly, certain her argument made sense, only nothing made sense right now. "Or what if one of them gets sick and is in the hospital? She won't visit them. What about when she has a baby? Ona and Donny can't be grandparents?"

All of that did sound pretty brutal. "But—"

"All the more reason for you to want her to reconcile with her mother, Nick. Don't you see? You'd be helping her and me. Mostly her. Every woman wants a relationship with her mother, and doesn't Willow want her mother to see how great she looks? How she's lost weight and conquered her demons?"

He had to agree, except for the fact that her mother *was* the demon. "I'll think about it," he finally said. "I can't promise anything, but I'll...I'll put out some feelers, and if I think there's a chance that this might be the right way to go, I won't say anything. But, damn it, Misty, she's going to hate me if she finds out I knew about it."

"Then pretend you didn't. I certainly won't tell her."

He closed his eyes and took another long pull on the beer.

"I'm not going to lie."

"And wait until you meet Ona and Donny! They are the best."

"I always wanted to meet him," he admitted. But not like *this*.

Misty scooped up her bag. "Then meet him. Come to dinner with us right now over in Naples, where they've been staying all month. I'm sure they'd love to meet you."

He didn't think twice about how to answer that.

Chapter Twenty-Two

"Looking at your phone doesn't make the texts magically appear." Gussie elbowed Willow and added a grin. "Go over there. He's expecting you."

Willow put her phone down and picked up some table coverings to fold. Around them, the Casa Blanca staff broke the beachfront dining area after the last of the Peyton-Orinson wedding party left to finish the night in the bar or walk the beach.

"He didn't reply to my text. If he's deep into writing, I don't want to bother him."

Gussie rolled her eyes as she disassembled a seashell centerpiece. "Yeah, 'cause guys hate to be bothered by a booty call."

"It's not a..." Willow laughed. "Yeah, okay, it is. Except..."

"Except what?"

She sighed and lined up the linens. "I really like him, Gus."

"That makes booty calls all the more pleasurable."

"That makes the booty calls all the more...not bootyish, if you know what I mean. It makes it *real*."

"Ahem." They turned at the sound of Ari's fake throat-clearing from behind them. "I know what you mean." She held out her hand to Gussie. "Root Beer Barrels, you are mine."

Willow sighed, fighting a laugh. "Why do you two gamble on my love life more than I do?"

Ari snapped her fingers and pointed at Gussie. "Hah! I told you. She didn't say 'like life.'"

"It's an expression, Ari, she's not in love."

Willow's jaw dropped as she followed the volley of the conversation, not believing it. "You guys are betting whether or not I *love* this guy?"

They looked at each other, silent and guilty. Finally, Gussie shrugged. "I'm betting against it, if that counts for anything."

"I'm certain that even if you don't now, you will," Ari said. "I believe the universe has preordained this."

"I don't know what's worse," Willow whispered on a sigh. "That you believe the universe preordains things, or that you"—she turned to Gussie—"have bet against me."

"Against love," she corrected. "I'd bet my life on you, Willow, and you know it. I don't think you're..." Her voice faded out, and Willow leaned closer, dying to hear the rest.

"I'm what? Ready? Worthy? Lovable?"

"Willow!" That came at her in unison.

"How can you say that?" Gussie set down the centerpiece and came closer. "You're the most lovable person I know."

Willow angled her head, communicating her doubt. "Then what do you think I'm not that Nick Hershey could or should have?"

Gussie shook her head, reaching out her hands to place them on Willow's shoulders. "Before you tackle love or a mega-serious relationship or, hell, even a casual fling, you need to deal with the devils on the inside, and not just the ones that you slayed in order to lose weight. I mean the ones that keep you entirely shut off from your past."

Willow stared at her, letting the words fall over her heart, and knowing exactly what—and *who*—Gussie meant. She turned to Ari. "What do you think?"

She lifted a shoulder. "I think that what's going to happen will happen, and you can't change that, but..." She gnawed her lower lip, carefully choosing her words. "I do think that you've built a wall around yourself for protection and that man might take it down. Are you ready for that?"

"A wall? What kind of wall?"

"One built out of Wasa crackers and determination," Gussie cracked. "With a little denial to keep it standing."

"Denial?" Willow sputtered the word. "Because I denied myself chocolate cake?"

"I don't think chocolate cake caused you to be unhappy, Willow. I think you were unhappy and turned to chocolate cake."

Like that took Gussie *or* a shrink to figure out. Willow swallowed the retort since they were obviously trying to help, no matter how much she didn't like it. "And what does this have to do with my having a fling or relationship or whatever you call it with Nick?" she asked.

"Look, you can ignore all this. It was a silly bet," Ari said. "We love you and want you to be happy."

"I am happy," Willow insisted. Why did people seem to doubt that? "Although I'd be happier if I were naked with Nick and not having this conversation."

"Then forget what I said," Gussie said. "Just go over there."

Willow handed Gussie the last tablecloth and looked down the beach toward Nick's villa. From here, it looked completely dark. Her heart rose up to her throat as she imagined him in there, alone. Asleep? Writing? Underwater? Waiting for her? Didn't matter. She was going.

She scooped up her phone and snagged her shoes and bag from another table where she'd left them. "The safest bet?" she asked with a smile. "I won't be home tonight."

The privacy gate was locked, so she walked around the side of the villa to the front entrance on the path, glancing in windows. Pitch black in there.

Had he gone somewhere with Misty? Was that why he hadn't texted back?

At the front, she knocked and waited. And remembered that, in her bag, she had a master key that she'd used to put the welcome basket in Jill Peyton's villa. Without giving herself time to think too much about it, she pulled out the card key and unlocked the door.

"Nick?"

The villa was completely dark and silent.

"Nick, are you here?"

Stepping inside, she switched on a table lamp, which flooded the place with a golden light, but revealed nothing else. She passed the kitchen and headed to his bedroom, which was also unlit and unoccupied. He wasn't on the patio, either.

So much for her booty call. Disappointment pinged, but his laptop was on the bed, a little green light flashing like it was still on. Had he been writing? Would reading be an invasion of privacy or a welcome assist from the muse?

Unable to resist, she touched the keyboard, and the computer flickered to life, the now-familiar double-spaced paragraphs of Nick's book flashing on the screen. She'd checked the word count and realized he'd already knocked out another twenty-five pages.

She tapped the keys to get back to the last chapter she'd read and within a minute, she was lost in a war in the Middle East, deep inside the head and heart of a lonely lieutenant. It was almost as good as being inside the head and heart of Nick Hershey. Especially when she reached the last part he'd written, a quiet, intimate scene with Gannon and Christina. On these pages, the journalist used her talent for getting people to reveal their most personal information and got the Navy SEAL to talk about his childhood.

Not a memoir, huh? As she read about "Gannon's" parents, she fought a smile at how thinly disguised this autobiography really was. So he had decided to be honest. Like Nick's, his character's parents lived together in a loveless marriage. But the fictional Nick didn't brush that off as though it didn't affect him. On the contrary, Nick's alter ego on the page revealed how deep that pain ran in his heart.

She'd love to talk to him about that. She'd love to have this same conversation that Gannon and Christina had, but...he wasn't here. So she satisfied herself by re-reading the scene five times until she'd practically memorized it.

Donny Zatarain put his hand on Nick's back and nudged him toward the lobby after they finished an incredible meal at the Ritz-Carlton's five-star restaurant. The little bit of guilt he'd felt for dining with Willow's parents behind her back had mellowed with the wine, along with his curiosity about what this world-famous couple was like.

They were funny, relaxed, and crazy in love with each other. They wore their wealth and fame with the ease of aristocracy, and kept the conversation light and comfortable.

It wasn't until dessert and coffee that Misty explained that Nick thought he should tell Willow about Ona's planned surprise.

Ona said simply that she didn't want that to happen, and the dinner ended shortly after that.

"Can we talk privately?" Donny asked softly.

"Of course."

"On the patio." He led Nick down the wide lobby hall, past darkened shops closed for the night. For a moment, Nick tried to grab hold of the knowledge that he was side by side with his rock hero. He glanced at Donny, still surprised to see a mellowness in his idol's demeanor that was nothing like the videos and concerts. He seemed...old. And wise. Much wiser than Nick would have ever imagined from this burned-out rock star.

Outside, most of the tables and sitting areas were empty now, with only a few guests lingering on the wide veranda, the only light from flickering candles and up-lit potted plants.

"Over here." Donny guided him away from the only other group of people chatting around a table in high-backed rattan chairs. When they reached the edge of the patio, the older man put his hands on the balustrade railing and looked out at the blackness of the Gulf of Mexico.

"There are two things in the world that matter to me," Donny said, surprising Nick when he pulled out a pack of cigarettes and a lighter. "Well, three." He added a sly smile and narrowed his eyes as the flame flickered. "Do you mind me smoking?"

"No, sir."

"Don't call me that. And if you tell Ona I smoked, I'll kill you. And if you tell *anyone* I love to golf, I will have your balls removed."

Nick laughed. "Your secrets are safe. What are the two things that matter to you?"

"No, *who* are the two things," he corrected. "One is that woman in there." He pointed in the general direction of the restaurant. "And one I suspect is in here." He pointed in the general direction of Nick's heart.

Oh, boy. Was he about to get the "if you touch my daughter" speech? Because, shit, it was too late.

"What did I say to give you that impression?" Nick asked.

Donny chuckled. "'It's not the words that spill your secret, the trick is in your eyes.'"

Nick recognized the lyric immediately. "'Don't expect me not to keep it, it's lies that I despise.'" Nick finished the line from one of his favorite songs without blinking. "*Secrets and Lies* is one of your best works, Mr. Zatarain."

"Donny. And, meh." He shrugged. "That whole album was weak."

"*Zero Hour* is a fantastic album," Nick argued, tamping down the excitement that he was actually discussing Z-Train's music with Donny Z himself. "I mean, it's not *Zenith* or *Zephyr Blows*, but most of the tracks are amazing."

Donny nodded, looking ahead. "I didn't bring you out here to evaluate my body of work, Nick. I know you're a fan from what you said at dinner."

He swallowed, a little chastised. "You want to talk about your daughter?"

"I always want to talk about Willie, but not about your..."

"Relationship?"

He looked at Nick. "Do you have one?"

Shit. What was he supposed to tell her father? *I'm relieving your daughter of her virginity.* The whole idea of it was preposterous on every level. "We've been spending a lot of time together, and she's helping me on the book I mentioned."

"Has she talked about us?" he asked, the vaguest hint of hope and fear in his voice.

Yep. "A little. Well, obviously, I'm interested in you, and…"

"What about her mother?"

Oh, she really hates her mother. "Very little about, uh, Mrs. Zatarain."

Donny inhaled slowly, making his nostrils quiver as he let out a long tendril of acrid smoke. "I want to make something very clear to you, and I need you to assure me that you understand."

A reply seemed unnecessary.

"This scheme of my wife's can't fail. It matters more to her than her next breath, *and it can't fail.*"

"But what if Willow isn't receptive to a reunion or reconciliation?" Nick asked. "I mean, part of what will make it succeed is out of your control, isn't it?"

"Willie's always been out of my control," he said wistfully. "And she sure hasn't been controlled by her mother."

"Then what makes you think this time will be different?"

"I don't know," he admitted, his voice rich with honesty. "But I do know this. We only have a shot with the element of surprise in our favor. If Willie knows this is happening, she will leave."

"Maybe not," Nick said. "She works at the resort, so she can hardly disappear, and I think she'll give you a chance." But even as he made the statement, he knew it wasn't true.

"She'd give *me* a chance," Donny said with a soft snort. "She won't give her mother the time of day. And I can't really blame her."

Wow, it must have been brutal in that household growing up. "Do you want me to talk to her?"

"No." He turned, his eyes sharp. "I want you to do the opposite. Do not tell her we're coming. Do not tell her Ona wants a reconciliation. Do not *ruin* this."

But if he didn't tell her, what would he ruin? Anything they have. Any chance of something more. Their relationship would be up in smoke like the cigarette in Willow's father's mouth.

So would a decision not to tell her be yet another selfish one?

"She's a grown woman," Nick said, "and has a right to prepare for whatever your wife has in mind."

"Oh, she'll prepare, all right. She'll pack and haul ass to some 'conference' or a wedding or something that will sound perfectly acceptable and real, but will, in fact, be Willie's form of running away from home." He balled his fists, giving the air a little frustrated punch.

Nick didn't reply, waiting in the heavy silence for more honesty from his rock 'n' roll hero. Who was, it appeared, just another husband and father with family issues.

"You have to understand how important this is," Donny finally said, crushing his cigarette butt under his shoe. "Please, *please*, don't say anything to her. I want this family whole again. I want..." He worked to swallow as if something were strangling him. "I want my wife to be happy and my daughter, too. Neither one of them will ever be whole without a...a healing of this wound. Sorry if I sound like some new-age shrink, but it's true."

"I understand," Nick said, knowing he sounded like he didn't.

"But your loyalty is to my daughter."

"I don't know her that well," he said. "I'm trying to," he amended quickly. "I'm hoping to…"

"What are you hoping to do?" Donny asked.

Nick wasn't at all sure how to respond.

"Maybe I don't want to know," Donny said quickly.

"I really like her and—"

"Well, I really *love* her," the other man shot back. "So who has more at stake? A young man trying to get laid with the least amount of white water before he ships off to his next assignment, and has nothing but a memory of a nice month on the beach, or a family that desperately needs and wants old heartaches to disappear?"

How the hell could he answer that? Because, shit, Donny Z was right. Absolutely dead-on-the-money right. Wasn't he?

"The chance to make up her past treatment of Willie is the only reason I still have Ona. The *only* reason she came back."

"I heard, at dinner."

"No, you heard Ona's side of the story," he said. "You heard about how she lost consciousness and saw 'the light.'" He used air quotes and looked skyward. "Whatever the hell that means, I don't know. What I do know is this: She was dead. Flat-out, no heartbeat, no breath, no pulse, no *life*." He whipped that last word at Nick. "And then, she was back. Alive. And different. With new priorities, and an entirely different outlook on her life. I want Willie to know *this* Ona." He grabbed Nick's arm. "I am convinced, beyond a shadow of a doubt, that they will love each other like I love them."

That love was so powerful that Nick could swear he felt it, and saw it in the steel-blue eyes so much like his daughter's. Donny's changed color when he grew passionate, too.

"You cannot, in good conscience, get in the way of that. Not if you care for my daughter." Donny squeezed a little tighter. "You do care for her, right? I'm not misreading that?"

"I do," he admitted.

"Enough to help her get over the darkest part of her past?"

Surely he owed her that, when she was helping him to do the same thing? "Enough for that," he agreed. "More than enough."

Donny's face relaxed in relief. "Thank you. Now, how about next time I got the Train together, you come and jam with us?"

The question threw him, so far out of left field he didn't know how to respond.

"Didn't you say you play the drums, Nick?"

"A little, I…" Was he trying to bribe Nick into silence? "Not well enough to play with your band, Donny."

"Pfft." He flicked his hand to the door. "We're so old, it's painful to listen to us now. Thank God for all that technology and smoke and mirrors on stage. I'd love to, you know, thank you for being so understanding with a chance to jam with your favorite band."

In other words, Donny Z was buying his silence. "That's not necessary, sir."

"Call me sir again, and I rescind the offer." He laughed, giving Nick a nudge. "Come on, young lieutenant. Say good night to my beloved wife."

Chapter Twenty-Three

"Hey, Sleeping Beauty." The deep male voice pulled Willow from her dream, the warmth of lips on her cheek making her eyelids flutter but not quite open. "What a nice surprise to find you in my bed."

Nick. She practically purred when he kissed her jaw and throat, his weight pressing down on the mattress and making her dip a little closer into his body as he settled next to her.

"On," she murmured. "Not in."

"A technicality." More kisses, lingering right under her ear. "Did my writing put you to sleep?"

She liked that he didn't get all bent out of shape that she'd let herself in and taken the liberty of reading his work. And she liked…that. Right when he kissed her…there.

"No." She moaned a little as he turned her on her back and worked his way to her mouth for a kiss. "The rehearsal dinner wiped me out. Where were…mmmm." The question faded into his mouth, the kiss sending a roll of thunder in her chest as her heart went to work warming her blood and sending it off to dormant, sleepy places.

Like her arms that already felt heavy with the need to wrap around him and her breasts that tingled with the desire for him to touch her and the taut ripple of need right between her legs where the first sparks started to ignite a fire.

She was wide-awake now.

"Did you read what I wrote?" he asked in between peppering kisses over her breastbone, his hands gripping her ribs and waist so tight it was almost as if he didn't trust where they'd go if he relaxed.

"Every word. Some five times."

He stopped kissing her, leaning up to look into her eyes. "Seriously?"

"Oh, why do I tell you things that make you think about something other than this?" She pulled his head back to her, getting his mouth right back on hers where she wanted it.

He obliged with a long, wet, sensuous kiss that melted her and did the absolute opposite to him. As his erection grew against her, Willow couldn't stop herself from reaching down, dying, aching to touch him.

She closed her hand over the tent in his pants, pressing hard against the ridge, both of them sucking in loud and simultaneous inhales of surprise and pleasure.

"Willow..." Her name was ragged on his lips.

"Shhh," she whispered. "If you say you haven't written enough for this to happen, I will push that laptop off the bed, break it, and tell you how wrong you are."

He chuckled into the next kiss, but that faded into a groan as she stroked the length of him again, vaguely aware that the fabric of his pants felt nicer than his usual worn camo shorts.

"Why are you all dressed up?" she asked.

This time, he responded with a long kiss and put his hand over hers, adding pressure on his hard-on. "I went...oh, God, Willow."

"Out to dinner?"

"Mmmm. Yes." With an effort so strong she could actually feel him fighting his desires, he pulled away from the kiss and lifted her hand off him. "We're going too fast."

Frustration zinged. "I hate to be old school, but isn't the girl supposed to say that?"

"You know why." He settled into a position that separated their hips, but kept one hand on her face to talk to her. "I didn't write enough for us to go to the next step."

She rolled her eyes.

"Hey, we had a deal."

"I think what you wrote must have taken a lot of effort, so it counts as more pages."

He studied her for a minute, then asked, "You read the Gannon Tells All scene?"

She nodded. "It was powerful, Nick."

He didn't answer, but she could read the truth in his eyes.

"Did—does—it bother you that your parents had such a crappy marriage?" she asked.

He blew out a breath, puffing his cheeks and falling back on the pillow. "About as much as it does Gannon."

Which was a lot. "Gannon says it made him determined not to fall into the same 'pit of despair.'"

This time he rolled his eyes. "Maybe that phrase was too melodramatic."

"No maybe about it, but it was telling."

"What does it tell?"

"That you hide a lot of pain."

He shrugged. "Everybody hides pain, Willow. You do and I do. I try not to let it own me."

But did he succeed? She wanted to know more, but with Nick, it was always easier to talk about the character than the real man behind that character. "So Christina takes that to mean he won't settle for anything less than a perfect, fairy-tale, impossible-to-achieve marriage. Is she right?"

"No. I think what he's trying to tell her is that the key word there is *impossible*."

She sat up a little, surprised at how much that admission bothered her. "What makes you think a happy marriage is impossible? I saw one every day of my life."

His eyes shuttered closed for a second, as if that hurt or bothered him.

"Don't be jealous. You know there were other problems," she added.

"You could fix those," he said.

She gave a soft snort. "That would require giving my mother a lobotomy and personality transplant. Never going to happen. I've learned to deal quite well with my childhood issues, but it doesn't seem like you have. Surely you're not going to give up on the idea of marriage because of your parents?"

He turned away, denying her the chance to read the truth in his eyes. "Your mother's getting older, and people change. Why don't you give her a chance?"

It was so obvious why he was changing the subject. This was too painful for him to talk about. "Because nobody changes that much, and I gave her a chance for twenty-six years," she said. "She's out of chances." She reached for his chin, turning his face to force him to look at her. "So which is it, Gannon? You won't settle for less than perfection or you won't try on the chance you'll miss?"

"I'm not Gannon," he mumbled.

"I'm not going to dignify that with a response. Answer my question."

But he didn't, holding her gaze. "I don't think you really have learned to deal with your own childhood issues."

"That wasn't my question," she fired back, burning for a different reason now. "Leave my damn stupid mother out of this conversation. In fact, leave her out of any and every conversation we ever have. Why are you being so evasive?"

"Why do I have to leave your mother out of every conversation?"

"Because the very thought of her sucks every drop of happiness out of my heart. Is that reason enough?"

For a long time, he looked at her, scrutinizing her expression. She didn't flinch. Let him see that she meant that, and maybe it would be enough to drop the topic of Ona Zatarain, once and for all.

"You should give her a chance."

Or not. She pushed up, hard and fast. "You should give marriage a chance."

"With you?"

She gasped, swinging around to face him. "Holy hell, is that why you're acting so strangely? You think I want to..." Embarrassment burned her cheeks. "I want sex, Nick. Just a good old-fashioned deflowering. Nothing more. You're the one who keeps trying to load it down with some kind of *significance*."

He pulled her back down next to him. "I want you to be happy."

"Then let's stop all this chattering and forget your six stages of foreplay and..." She leaned over him and kissed him, dragging her hand back down to his crotch, which clearly hadn't gotten the message that they were arguing.

He agreed silently, intensifying the kiss and slowly sliding his hands over her back and ass, pulling her hips against his. "Willow," he whispered into the kiss. "I don't want you to hate me."

She closed her eyes and let those words slide over her, as

warm and welcome as his touch. Did he really think she'd hate him because he didn't believe in marriage and probably wouldn't ever commit to a woman? Did he really think the loss of her virginity meant that much?

"You're sweet," she said. "And I could never hate you."

"But you will." He sounded so damn sure. "When...this is...over."

When this is over.

Well, at least she knew exactly what she was getting into and that this was a fling. She tried to be comforted by that knowledge, to let her body take over at this point, to think about nothing except the way his large, strong hands felt as he caressed her backside and dug into the fabric of her dress, inching it higher and higher.

But way in the back of her mind, she wished Christina was right, and that he was a man who wouldn't settle for less than perfect...and not a man who would run fast and hard when things got serious.

Because, deep inside, she knew this wasn't *just sex.*

Except, he was already thinking about...*when this is over.*

Nick knew Willow would hate him. She would despise him for staying silent. She would scream at him when she found out he'd known her parents' plan. He was playing with emotional fire, and he himself was the kindling.

Damn it. His body betrayed him by not caring a bit about that. His dick slammed against his pants, engorged with need, and his hands found their way right under her dress and up her thighs. Sweet, smooth, silky thighs that he wanted wrapped around him until he screamed for mercy.

Would taking her virginity make the whole explosion that much deadlier when the time came? Because there would be an explosion, he had no doubt.

"Stop *thinking*," she demanded with a laugh.

"How do you know I'm thinking?"

"Your hands go still." She kissed his neck and put her mouth over his ear. "Considering how difficult it must have been to write some of those pages and, really, how good they are, you've earned—we've earned—another step on the pleasure ladder."

He laughed. "The pleasure ladder?"

She gave him the eye. "You're one to talk, Mr. Pit of Despair."

"That was pretty bad," he agreed.

"But this…" She put her hand over his and guided him up her thigh. "Is so, so good."

How could he fight this? Which made him more of a complete shit? Denying what she wanted—hell, what they both wanted—on principle because he was keeping something from her? Or letting this go its natural course and then letting her find out what he'd done?

So who has more at stake? A young man trying to get laid with the least amount of white water before he ships off to his next assignment and has nothing but a memory of a nice month on the beach, or a family that desperately needs and wants old heartaches to disappear?

"You're thinking again."

"Sorry."

"Don't be, just…touch me." She led his hand between her legs. "I want you to touch me."

And he wanted to. Every single burning, frying, electrified cell in his body wanted to. He stroked her thigh, making her sigh and moan. "You like that," he whispered.

"Stating the obvious."

"I like it, too." He let his fingers go higher, reaching a silky, lacy, tiny piece of lingerie that barely covered her. Kissing her, sucking her tongue into his mouth, he stroked the wet silk.

"Isn't it your turn?" she asked, reaching down to grip his erection again. "I want to give you pleasure, Nick." She started to push down, kissing his chest, trying to turn so she could get her head lower.

He couldn't let her do that. He couldn't let her put him in her mouth when he'd just gone against everything she wanted and now he had this secret.

"No, not yet. Not...that," he said. She looked disappointed, and it twisted his heart. "This is still for you."

"Why do you get to make all the rules?"

He shushed her with a kiss and another stroke of her panties then easily slid inside to touch her soft, wet center. "Because I can do this to you."

She gasped, shuddering against him. "Oh, yes, you can."

"And this." He stroked a circle, gratified by her response. "And this." As her hands dug into his shoulders, he slid one of his fingers into her.

"Yes, that."

She was so tight, he moved carefully and slowly, but with every stroke, she rocked harder against him, each breath tangled and tight, the sweet smell of her sex intoxicating him. It was like he lit a match, and she sparked fast and furious, clinging to him.

"I want you inside me," she murmured.

"I am inside you."

"Not the right part."

He slipped another finger into her. "How's that?"

She inhaled sharply. "A tease, but divine."

"I'm not teasing you, Willow." He rubbed lightly, then found the place that made her throat catch, and took advantage of the knowledge that gave him. He intensified the pressure and pace and then started kissing her again, cupping her breast with his other hand. That was all it took, making her let out a soft whimper, then a cry, then a low, long moan of surrender.

He knew better than to think—and risk slowing his fingers. Instead, he let himself feel everything, every sweet, sexy, sensual second of intimacy, holding her while she shattered with an orgasm brought on by only his touch.

Damn, sex with her was going to be amazing.

Followed by…her finding out that he was a lying, secret-keeping douchebag.

She would hate him. She would hate him.

The words echoed with the same rhythm as her panting breaths, finally slowing to something resembling normal.

"Nick?"

"Yeah?"

"I'm sorry we had that little argument." She stroked his face, her eyes still partially closed, as if it took too much effort to open them all the way.

"It's okay."

"I didn't mean to jump down your throat about my mother."

He inched back. "I thought you wanted no mention of her, especially here in bed."

Her fingers rested on his cheek. "Please understand that the only way I can deal with the future is by knowing I am completely finished with the past, and that means her."

But she wasn't finished. He could see it in her eyes. There was so much unfinished business and pain. And if his job—the one he'd taken on—was to give her pleasure, then didn't that include the kind of pleasure she'd get when she finally resolved her issues and got to know her new, changed mother who, in some weird way, had actually *had* a personality transplant?

If he told her, she'd find an excuse not to be here. He knew that, as well as her father did.

If he didn't tell her, she would hate him. He would lose any chance he had with her.

He knew what he had to do. It was a no-brainer. He had to make a decision that would hurt him, but heal her. He had to make an unselfish decision this time.

Chapter Twenty-Four

Willow rounded the harbor, crossing the street and jogging back toward her house with a strong, steady pace that matched the hard-rock selections she'd found on a Pandora station she loved for running. Sweat dribbled down her back, and her thighs burned for the last two miles, but she didn't care.

She hadn't run for days. She hadn't done much of anything for a week and a half, except think about Nick, be with Nick, laugh with Nick, revise scenes with Nick, and find ever-more-innovative ways to give each other pleasure without…

It had to be soon. Somehow, they'd reached the agreement that "it" would happen when he finished the book. And since she hadn't heard a word from him in two days, she had a sense that he was nearly at that point.

A familiar bass line started up the next song, and she could practically see the look of pain on Graham Senate's face when he closed his eyes and played the chord, getting the expected scream from the crowd for Z-Train's *Will Ya, Will Ya*.

She'd never hear the song again and not think of walking in on Nick, bare naked and belting out the worst version she'd ever heard. How far they'd come in these weeks since then. A warm, comfortable sensation filled her chest as she slowed her pace a little to hit the rhythm of Michael Brooker's incredible drumbeat. She should tell Nick that "Uncle Mike" was her godfather. He'd love that.

And then Donny Z's voice filled her ears with the low, long intro that got the song rocking. He played the part of a sex-crazy rock 'n' roller so well, but Willow would bet everything she had and more that not once in their entire marriage had Donny Z even thought about cheating on his wife. How many rock stars could say that? In all those years. Thirty years. This month, she realized. Holy heck, in a week.

She didn't hear her own voice softly singing the song, her father's throaty, world-famous voice screaming in her ears.

She couldn't help belting out the first stanza. "Gotta know if it's real, gotta know if it's forevah."

"No foolin' around, for worse or for bettah!" One strong arm wrapped around her from the back, making her stumble and yelp as someone pulled out one earbud and sang the next line right in her ear.

"Nick!" She half-laughed, half-shrieked as he turned her around and held her steady. And she needed that help, because every time she saw him, she felt a little bit weaker.

"You're singing our song, baby." He punctuated that with a kiss that lasted a few seconds too long.

"How'd you find me?"

"Gussie told me she saw you leave for a run, and I know your route." He swiped some hair off her face. "God, you're freaking hot when you sweat."

She laughed softly. "What are you doing up so early?"

"Look at this face." He pointed to his eyes. As if she needed the suggestion. She could look at his face for days. Months. More. "I haven't slept yet."

"Not at all?"

He gave her a slow, easy grin and tugged her a little closer. "But guess what I wrote?"

She knew. A tingling of warm expectation worked its way through her. "Tell me."

"The two prettiest words in the English language." He leaned closer to the ear without a bud in it. "The end."

She leaned back, her mouth agape. "You did? How did it end?"

He swallowed visibly. "Badly. But only for me. I hope that means the book's good."

"Oh, Nick." She reached up to cup his whisker-rough face in her hands. "Was it hard to write?"

"It was cathartic. And I have to thank you, Willow. You forced me to face some demons in the past, and in the process, I learned a few things."

"Like?"

"Like sometimes a decision changes the course of your life, but you can't spend the rest of it wallowing in regret. Writing about it, about how it all happened and why, that helped a lot."

She stroked his cheek. "That's good, Nick."

He closed his eyes and pulled her closer. "You know what 'the end' also means, don't you?"

Chills exploded down the nape of her neck. "And that means…"

He put the earbud in his right ear. "My heart's right here…" Her father was singing the bridge notes. "Saved just for you."

Nick put his mouth right over hers without kissing to sing, "So say yes, woman, that's all you gotta do."

Willow practically melted into the street, despite how horrifically off-key he was. "I really ought to get you to meet my dad someday. You're such a fan."

She could have sworn Nick froze at the suggestion. Probably from sheer excitement. She really should bite the bullet and see her dad. She could introduce them. The thought made her even dizzier, and by Nick's expression, he felt the same.

"Does it mean that much to you to meet him?" she asked, a little amused and even in awe.

He didn't answer as if the idea actually rendered him speechless.

She just laughed, but he surprised her by moving them along at a faster pace.

"What's your hurry?" she asked.

He gave her a *get real* look. "We have *stuff* to do, Willow."

She smiled. "Stuff? That's what you call it?"

"A lot of stuff. You have to read and critique the end. I'm not sure about it, you know? I…told the truth." His voice nearly cracked, and so did something in her chest at how hard that must have been for him. "And then I have to get things ready for us," he added quickly.

She elbowed him. "What's to get ready? Roses on the bed? Candles in the room? How epic do you want this deflowering to be?"

"Epic," he replied. "What's your schedule today?"

"Light on my end, but Gussie and Ari have a lot to do for Misty's wedding next weekend. You didn't forget about that, did you?" she asked with a laugh. "It was the reason you're here."

He closed his eyes as if the very idea pained him. "I did not forget."

"When's Misty getting in? Has she told you?"

"Sometime in the next few days." As they reached the driveway of her house, he slowed his step and gave her a long, serious look. Maybe too serious.

"What is it?" she asked.

"Willow, about the wedding..." He looked away, clearly gathering his thoughts.

"Don't worry, Nick. I know it's the last thing on your mind, and I'll never tell Misty how much you didn't do. We had enough instructions to pull this thing off. Honestly, it's such a small affair, and she seems to care so little about the details..." That wasn't what was bothering him. Because whether or not they had lace napkins or the right wedding favors wouldn't put that look of—pain? worry?—something dark in his eyes. "What's the matter, Nick?"

He took her hands, one in each of his, and pulled her closer. "Maybe we should wait for, you know, until after the wedding."

Wait? She bit her lip, mostly to keep from screaming.

"I want to be sure that everything is right, the timing, the place, and, well, us."

She wasn't sure what that had to do with the wedding, or what needed to be any "righter" about them. Every time they touched and kissed, one or both of them exploded. In fact, she may be a virgin, but she wasn't dumb. Not having sex would be strange at this point, considering how intimate they'd been.

"If we waited," he continued, "then you could be sure it's me you want."

What else did she need to say or do for him to know? "Nick, I *am* sure."

"You might change your mind, and then you'd have lost your virginity to me and—"

She clamped a hand over his mouth and got very close to him, narrowing her eyes in a pretend warning. "If you turn me down again, Nick Hershey, after all we've been through, you will break my heart into a million pieces. You don't want to break my heart, do you?"

He kissed her fingertips. "That's just it. I don't want to, and I'm afraid I will."

She searched his face, trying to figure that out. Why did he think that having sex would break her heart?

Because he assumed she'd want...more. And this was the guy who was willing to not ever get married in case he ended up in a loveless union like his parents.

"From the beginning, Nick, I've told you that I wanted to lose my virginity. And I want to lose it with you. I'm not asking for anything more." More would be nice...but she wasn't going to give up sex with him to get "more" in writing.

"I know, I know, but you deserve...better." His voice hitched a little, nearly undoing her.

"There is no better," she said softly, lifting up on her toes to kiss him. "And let me make you this promise."

He looked at her expectantly and unsure. "What?"

"I promise that no matter what happens, no matter how we feel afterward, or what the future holds or doesn't, I will not blame any unhappiness on you. You've been amazing, carrying me through each step like you really, truly cared about me—"

"I do."

She put her finger on his lips. "I know. You've proven that. So no matter what happens, I will know that everything you've done is because you care about me."

"That's so true, Willow." He sounded desperately sincere, and it touched her.

"Then don't worry. I couldn't give my virginity to a more special man, and I couldn't be happier." She stepped back and held out her hand. "Now give it to me."

"What?"

"The thumb drive with the rest of your book."

He laughed, shaking his head. "How do you know I have it?"

"Please. I know you. Give."

He reached into his pocket and took out the tiny drive and put it in her palm, closing his much larger hand around hers. "You really promise that, Willow? No matter what happens, you know that every single thing I've done or, for that matter, not done, is because I really care about you. You promise to believe that?"

"I promise." She eased her hand out of his and looked at the drive. "Is this going to make me cry?"

"That's not," he said. But then he looked at her like he was finishing that sentence in his head. The book wouldn't make her cry, but something would.

Was he going to leave her and break her heart? Maybe. Probably. But it didn't matter. She couldn't stop the way she felt about him any more than she could stop breathing.

"I'll be over tonight," she told him. "Get the rose petals and candles ready."

He smiled and watched her as she walked into the house, knowing that he was trying to let her down gently and that this brief sexual interlude was all they were ever going to have. She squeezed the thumb drive, holding tight to the little piece of him she did have.

It would have to be enough, then.

Trying to stay busy, Nick made some arrangements and phone calls and didn't finish until he had everything he needed for tonight to be perfect.

Except the one thing he needed most: the balls to tell Willow the truth.

He paced the villa, in and out of the patio, staring at the horizon, digging his fingers into his hair and dragging his hand back with each heavy sigh. He couldn't do this. He couldn't lay Willow down on that bed and make love to her and a few days later have her find out that he was the world's biggest dick...for "her own good."

She hated to be manipulated, and that's exactly what he would be doing. Still, her father's words echoed, so familiar since they'd been haunting him for ten days.

So who has more at stake?

Willow. Willow was the one who had the most at stake.

A young man trying to get laid... No. He wasn't a young man trying to get laid, despite what Donny Z thought. Nick's game with Willow had gone way past a "favor" to help her lose her virginity to something...more.

...with the least amount of white water before he ships off to his next assignment and has nothing but a memory of a nice month on the beach...

Donny was wrong there, too. Nick didn't care about creating "white water" because there didn't have to be any if he told her the truth. Nothing but a memory of a nice month on the beach? Sorry, but they'd sailed past *nice* a few weeks ago. He cared about her. Deeply.

...or a family that desperately needs and wants old heartaches to disappear?

Wasn't there a better way than ambushing her? Man, how could he have been so blind? He not only had to tell Willow, he had to help her deal with the shrapnel to the heart after the Z-bomb detonated. But how? When?

Tonight, of course. But he knew what he had to do first.

He moved like a man going into combat, certain and fast.

246

Grabbing his phone, he clicked onto the Internet, got the phone number he needed, and dialed.

"Ritz-Carlton Naples, how can I direct your call?"

They'd never connect him if he asked for a celebrity, but he distinctly remembered the room number when he and Misty had visited. "Suite 1601, please."

The phone was answered on the third ring, a soft, female voice. "Hello?"

Shit. He wanted Donny, not Ona. "Is Donny Zatarain available?"

"He's not here at the moment. Message?" He recognized Ona's distinct inflection and had no doubt Donny had relayed everything he and Nick talked about on the veranda that night.

"When do you think he'll be back?"

"Is this Nick Hershey?" Ona asked.

"Yes, ma'am."

She cleared her throat lightly. "Perhaps I can help you. Is there a problem with my daughter?"

Yes, there was a huge problem with her daughter. But this woman was the master manipulator, and he didn't completely trust her. "I really need to talk to your husband."

"About?"

Now what? Lie or suffer the consequences? "He'd mentioned my jamming with the band and…" The lie caught in his throat, his brain buzzing too loud to even come up with a good rationalization.

"And that's why you're calling?"

No. It had nothing to do with that. He hesitated, rooting around for something that wouldn't be a lie, but wouldn't be the truth he wasn't ready to share. "Among other things."

"He's golfing."

"Can you have him call me when he gets in?"

"My, it sounds urgent." He could hear the smile in her voice. "Are you sure there isn't anything I can help you with?"

It would be so easy. But he'd made his assurances to Donny, not his wife. He should have this conversation with him. "Do you have a pen? I'll give you my number."

"Of course, go ahead."

He recited the number and then paused, waiting for her to say good-bye.

"How's Willow?" she asked, the question throwing him.

"She's..." *Beautiful. Funny. Sexy. Perfect.* Everything he ever wanted in a woman. Holy, holy shit. When did that happen? "She's great."

Ona laughed softly. "I know she is, Nick. Is she happy?"

"She is now," he said quickly. But won't be when she finds out he was party to *this* operation.

"Does she laugh a lot?" Ona sounded like she really cared.

"All the time," he assured her.

"I always loved her laugh," Ona said. "It's musical with that little lilt when she catches her breath."

"Yeah, I love that, too." In fact, he loved...everything about her.

"Oh." She barely whispered the word. "You love her."

"I...I..." *Can't admit that right now.* Not yet. Not until he made everything right, then he'd figure out how he felt. "She's an awesome woman, Ona."

After a long beat of silence, she said, "I'll tell Donny to call you. Good-bye now." She hung up, leaving him feeling incredibly hollow and frustrated. Probably the way she'd made Willow feel her whole life.

Without having any writing to do, he felt a little lost. And he couldn't do anything until he talked to Donny, so he pocketed his phone and took a ten-mile run up and down the beach.

Afterward, he was still anxious. Stripping down to nothing on his patio, he set his cell phone on the table and dove into the pool, making sure not to stay under too long to miss Donny's call.

He kicked hard, easily getting from one side to the other before much of a thought formed in his head. Of course, the only thought he had was…Willow.

Willow who made his body burn with desire and his heart heavy with affection. Willow who somehow got under his skin and in his head and helped him see the futility in rewriting his past. Willow who…deserved to know the truth.

He shot up for air, his eyes closed, the jangle of his phone so loud it stunned him.

"You want to take this?" He opened his eyes to stare up at Willow, who held his phone out to him. Did it say Donny Zatarain on the screen? Guilt and fear squeezed.

"Not now," he said. How could he? "What are you doing here?"

She turned the phone over and looked at the screen. "You sure? It's an LA phone number. Maybe your brother?"

Shit. *Shit*. "No, no. Just put it down. He can wait. Are you okay?" he asked. Had she somehow figured out his secret before he could tell her?

She set the phone on the glass tabletop and turned to him. "I want to talk about your book."

"You do?" He wiped some water out of his eyes to get a better look at her expression and read her feelings. "Did you like the end?"

For a moment she didn't answer, but stood very still, looming over him. She had her hands on her hips, a long, tight red skirt accenting her narrow waist and curves. Her chest rose and fell with each inhale and exhale, her breasts nicely outlined in a tight, cotton button-down blouse tucked into the skirt.

"It couldn't have been easy," she said, taking a single step along the side of the pool, the click of one very high heel and then the other like a clock ticking down to…trouble.

"What couldn't have been?"

"The helicopter scene. You were right. It made me teary." She took a few more steps, rounding one corner, her gaze on him, her fingers on the top button of her blouse. And then the second. And then the third.

"It…did?"

"I thought you handled it beautifully." She slid the blouse out of the skirt and let the fabric spread open, revealing a sleek cream-colored bra of sheer lace. So sheer, he could see the dark circles of her nipples and feel the first surge of blood to his lower half. He moved in the water, hoping it would cool him off.

He couldn't do this until he told her the truth.

"I especially loved that last kiss." She slipped out of the blouse, letting it flutter to the patio, continuing her slow, predatory strip-walk around the pool. Helpless, he stayed rooted in one spot, doing nothing but pivoting to follow her.

"You know what you did, don't you?" she asked.

She reached around to unzip the skirt, the zipper making a slow, scraping sound.

He tried to swallow. "I'm not sure." Of anything.

She turned around, giving him a view of her backside as she very slowly slid the skirt over her hips, revealing tight, taut, round ass cheeks covered by nothing but a lacy thong in that same sweet cream color.

The skirt hit the ground, and Willow stepped out of it,

still in her sexy, black high heels, her crazy-hot thong, and her too-sheer-to-think bra. Nick drank in every curve, every line, every single sexy inch of her. She kicked the skirt away, reached up and flicked the hook of her bra, and turned again, inching the straps down her arms to show him her beautiful breasts.

"You let her go."

"What?" He couldn't even begin to follow the conversation. "Let who go?"

"Christina. Charlotte. The past." She was topless now, naked but for the thong and, shit, those shoes that screamed for sex. Sex he couldn't and wouldn't have until—

The phone rang again, freakishly loud and horrifically intrusive. She raised an eyebrow. Maybe. It was hard to get all the way up to her face with the heavenly view of her body.

"Ignore it," he managed. "What do you mean...I let her go?"

"You're over her. She died in the book, as she did in real life, and Gannon was able to own up to what happened and tell her family at her service."

"I never did that." He didn't want to talk about Charlotte now. His body was humming with need, and his heart was heavy with shame, and his phone was screaming with a call he had to take but...

She stepped out of the thong, leaving it on the patio.

"You did it in the book, though." She took a few more torturous, fully naked steps, then reached the stairs in the shallow end that led into the pool.

Very deliberately, she toed off one shoe, then the other. And started her descent toward him.

"The book ends beautifully, Nick. You didn't need me at all."

Oh, but he did. He needed her so much that nothing could stop him from reaching his hands out for her. One touch, then he'd tell her. Then he'd spoil this perfect, sexy, electrified seduction, but he had to.

"I want to know how you did it. How did you come to terms with the past without actually rewriting history?" She came into his arms as smoothly as the water, folding into his embrace, pressing her gorgeous body against his, the chill of the water making her shudder slightly in his arms.

"I met you." He didn't even know where that came from, but it was the absolute truth.

She looked up at him, confusion in her baby-blue eyes. "Me?"

"You." He kissed her forehead and hated what he had to tell her, but not all of it. Not this part. Tipping her chin back, he took a long, long look, appreciating what would surely be the last affectionate gaze he received. "I never met anyone like you, Willow. I'm absolutely, completely, and totally smitten. You inspire me and excite me and"—he closed his eyes—"deserve better than me."

She tightened her grip around his waist, laying her head on his chest. "Better? I thought you were over it, or at least on your way, after writing all that."

"I'm in a better place as far as what happened in Afghanistan," he replied. "But I have to tell you something—"

"Hello! Hello, anyone home?" The woman's voice echoed from inside, yanking them apart.

"Don't any of the maids knock at this place?" He spat out the question. But Willow was already scrambling away. Of course she didn't want some Casa Blanca staff person to see her naked in the pool with a guest.

"Where are you, Nick?"

Who *was* that? Misty?

He opened his mouth to ask Willow, but she was climbing out of the pool, scooping up clothes and shoes, and darting to the French door that led to the master bedroom. There, she turned, an unreadable expression in her eyes.

Then she stepped inside and pulled the door behind her, disappearing inside before it latched.

"Are you out here?" Ten feet away, a woman stepped out from the living room French doors, placing her hands on her hips precisely as Willow had. In fact, she looked exactly like Willow at that moment.

Which wasn't really a surprise, since she *was* Willow's mother.

Chapter Twenty-Five

W illow's pounding heart drowned out the voices on the patio as she entered the cool air of the bedroom and tried to inventory what clothes she'd managed to grab—everything but her blouse, which had been too far away to snag. Damn, that was close. Imagine the rumor mill if one of the housekeepers had walked in on them. It could have put the Barefoot Brides out of business.

As her pulse slowed and she slipped into her underwear—the set she'd been saving for "D-Day,"—a woman's voice floated in from the patio.

"...important I talk to you in person, Nick."

Willow froze. That wasn't one of the housekeepers. Cripes, even worse. Management? Still wearing the bra and thong, she took a step closer, careful to stay out of sight.

"So you just walked in?"

"Misty left me her key."

Misty? Who *was* that? The voice sounded familiar, but—

"You will not tell my daughter what we're doing, young man. You will *not*."

Willow froze, quite literally deadened by the voice.

"You made a pact with my husband."

No. *No.*

"Like hell I did!" The splash of Nick climbing out of the water and his angry response barely registered. Her brain went blank, her body numb, and somewhere in the back of Willow's head, a dull throb started to thump and make her shake.

"I know why you called Donny, and I had to come here and stop you!"

What?

"Put this towel on, please." The order was so...Ona.

This wasn't happening. Any moment Willow would wake up in a cold sweat, bathed in relief that this was a very bad dream. *Please, God.*

"We made a *deal* at dinner."

A deal? Willow grabbed the wall to keep stable. She tried—and failed—to make sense of what she was hearing. Ona and Nick made a *deal*?

"You were going to play along, let the plans proceed, and give me a chance to do the one thing that matters most to me. Have you told her yet?"

"No." Nick's voice was so soft and Willow's heartbeat was so loud she almost didn't make out the word.

"Thank God!" High heels tapped on the patio, much faster and more determined than Willow's striptease a few minutes ago. A lifetime ago. "Then we still have a chance to make this work. But only if the element of surprise is on our side."

"I'm going to tell her."

"No, you are not." Ona ground out the words, sounding very much like she had when Willow was fourteen and reached for her tenth cookie.

"Yes, I am."

255

"If you tell her…" Her mother's voice faded as she no doubt dug for the worst punishment she could inflict.

"I *am* going to tell her."

Willow moved in as if in a trance, every muscle engaged and active except the one between her ears, which stayed numb. Opening the French door, Willow stepped outside into the sunshine and locked her gaze on Nick standing with just a towel around him.

"Tell me what?"

"Willie!" Next to her, Ona came closer, but Willow refused to even turn her head an inch.

"Tell me *what*, Nick?"

"Look at you!" Ona's hand touched her shoulder, but Willow shook it off, rage coursing through her.

"Willow, you have to understand—"

"*I* have to understand?" She cut him off, too angry to let him finish. "I don't understand anything except that I hate being manipulated. What is this pact you have with people you claim to have never met, Nick? What is this deal you made behind my back?" Her voice rose, but she didn't care. She didn't care that the mother she hadn't seen in years was five feet away or that she walked outside in nothing but a bra and a thong. She didn't care about anything but how her heart was shattering so hard in her chest she could actually feel sharp pieces stab her.

He was in some kind of partnership with her mother?

"I didn't make a deal."

Ona choked softly. "That's not how I understand what Donny said."

Donny! He'd met her father? After all that…talk? All they'd shared? He'd just held her and kissed her and took her almost there with that lie right between them?

"How is this possible?" she whispered, her voice ragged.

"Willie, you look amazing!"

She turned to slice her mother with a look. "Don't call me that. My name is Willow."

Ona flinched, sending a different kind of stab into Willow's chest. No, she would not succumb to guilt. She was not the guilty party right here.

That person was standing in front of her in a towel, dripping wet and miserable.

To think that, moments ago, she was about to lose her virginity to him.

Oh, damn it *all*, she'd wanted that so much. And now…

"Willow." He stepped forward, nothing but abject pain in his eyes as he got between her and the pool. "I was about to tell you that your mother is coming, that she's behind Misty's wedding that isn't a wedding at all, but that—"

She shoved him with every ounce of strength she had. Stunned, he flailed his arms, his step faltered, and he tumbled right back into the pool with a splash.

"Oh!" Ona stifled a laugh, hand to mouth.

Willow looked at her. "What is it, if not a wedding?"

"Dad and I are renewing our vows, Willow. And you and I are going to be a mother and daughter again."

She was aware that Nick sputtered to a stand in the pool, silent while she considered all the possible responses to that statement.

"No, we're not ever going to be mother and daughter again, and"—she turned to Nick—"we are never going to be lovers."

Without waiting for their responses, she went back inside and slammed the French door, snapping the lock. She pulled on her skirt, stepped into her shoes, and grabbed a Navy SEAL T-shirt from the back of his chair.

It was all of him she'd take. He could have Ona and

Donny and whatever shred of memories they'd made together.

Nick heard the front door slam like a rifle shot. Funny how he could hear things he didn't want to hear—like the sound of a door across the house—and didn't hear what he really needed to hear. Like, he should have listened to his conscience when it screamed, *Tell her the truth.*

Instead, he'd listened to Donny Zatarain and now—

"She'll be back."

Nick swiped some water from his eyes and blinked up at the woman standing on the patio. Slender as a reed, her narrow shoulders confidently back, her ash-blond hair pulled straight off her face in a stark style that revealed virtually no wrinkles for a woman in her fifties.

"You don't even know her," he shot back, climbing out of the water and grabbing his own towel this time, whipping it around himself furiously.

"That's at the core of this, don't you see? I need to know her. I need her."

"No, no, damn it. *I* need her. And now she's gone. I've lost her." It was his fault, all his fault, but that didn't stop anger from bubbling up at this woman.

"You can manage a way to get her back."

He shut his eyes. "Not everyone wants to *manage* people, Ona. Don't you know that's what she hates?"

She stared at the door where Willow had disappeared a few moments before. "What she hates is me." The statement came out heartbreakingly pathetic, the tone enough to quell some of his fury at her.

"And me," he added. "I should have told her the minute I found out the truth. She thinks we're in cahoots now. And nothing could be further from the truth."

"So you tell her."

He slumped into the nearest chair. "If I ever see her again."

Ona rounded the table and took a chair across from him. "You'll see her again. This is meant to be."

Oh, please. "I suppose this all became apparent to you while you stepped into the great beyond and had your life transformation?"

She smiled as if his sarcasm had no effect. "Actually, it all became apparent to me when I saw the agony in her eyes when she said good-bye to you. She's in love. So that makes two of you, which is usually just the right number."

Confused emotions mixed with an adrenaline dump, burning his chest. At least he thought that's what was burning his chest. Maybe it was…no. *No*.

"I don't *believe* in love." Right? *Right*?

"Your loss," she said quietly. "Because Willow does, and she loves you."

"It's lust," he said simply. "We both feel it all the time."

"But you haven't acted on it yet."

Her know-it-all tone was starting to irk, but he supposed she could infer that fact from what Willow had said.

We are never going to be lovers.

The searing in his chest grew worse at the echo of her words. He looked down at his lap, watching a droplet of water fall from his hair and get absorbed into the towel, trying to get his head around the fact that he was talking to Willow's mother, not her friend. How much to share?

Nothing, if Willow had a say in this.

"It's really not your business," he finally replied.

She let it go, slipping a slim leather bag off her shoulder and opening it with an officious snap. "I can't believe how much she's changed," she mused, fishing through the bag. "I've never seen a person transform herself so completely," she continued, fishing in the bag for something.

"All it took was getting away from you," he said quietly, still nursing his anger at the unexpected arrival that ruined everything.

What would have happened if Ona hadn't shown up? Guess he'd never know.

"Ah, here it is." Sliding a photo out of her bag, she placed it on the table. "How does a person go from this to"—she jutted her chin toward the French door—"that?"

He didn't want to look, really. Willow had told him that she'd gotten rid of any pictures from the past, so she wouldn't want him to look at this one.

"It's almost impossible to believe," Ona said, nudging the picture closer, forcing the issue.

He glanced, disinterested. "Not if you know her," he said. "She does whatever she sets her mind to." He waited a beat, then stared at Ona. "And she set her mind to never seeing you again."

She closed her eyes, the target hit. "I don't blame her."

A tendril of sympathy wrapped his chest, enough to make his gaze shift to the picture in front of him. Holy shit.

"Is that how you remember her?" Ona asked.

Was it? Against his will, he reached for the photograph, lifting it to get a better look. He'd expected to see a fat girl, that was all. An overweight, unhappy, lost girl who'd somehow managed to find herself in the last three years. A girl he recalled being nice to in college, first because she was a breath of fresh air, and then because she had a famous father.

Or had he been attracted to Willow all along, from day one, but convinced himself otherwise? What if that history had been different? Where would they be today?

Sure, the girl in the picture was heavy, but her eyes still gleamed blue, and her smile belied any unhappiness. She looked to be in her early twenties, the backdrop of the Eiffel Tower telling him exactly where this was taken.

"She looks beautiful," he said. "Her fire is on. Her smile is real. Her heart is right there in her eyes." He brought it closer, absently grazing the edge of the photo with one finger. "She's looking at the camera as if she loves the person who's taking the picture." She'd looked at him like that...back then and now. But not anymore, he thought glumly. He'd never see that expression again.

"Her father took her on a tour with him to Europe," Ona said softly. "I wasn't there, as you can tell by the joyous look on her face."

He lifted his gaze to look at Ona, the last shreds of his anger fading at her sad, sad whisper. "There was a reason I didn't tell her the truth, and it had nothing to do with a deal I struck with your husband."

She waited, silent, gnawing on her lower lip.

"I thought that she needed to have some kind of reconciliation with you. I've gotten to know her, and she carries around a freight train of baggage where you're concerned. She says she's happy, but I don't think she is. I thought that if she could start over with you, then..."

Ona leaned forward, her eyes glistening with tears. "Help me, Nick. Help me get my daughter back."

"I did. And it cost me any chance I ever had with her." But then he'd known that was going to happen when he decided to withhold the truth, hadn't he?

They both sat silently for a second, lost in their thoughts, the two-dimensional image of a woman they both loved—

Nick shook his head. Did he love Willow? What would he do if he lost her now?

"Your phone is ringing," Ona said, gesturing toward another table where he'd left it.

Of course, he didn't even hear it. Why was his hearing clear one second and gone the next? Pushing up, he walked to the phone.

"It's probably your husband returning the call."

"No." She shoved her chair back and stood, too. "I never gave him the message."

He threw her a look as he reached his ringing phone. "Always pulling the strings, aren't you, Ona?"

She closed her eyes with a guilty look and lifted her hand in good-bye, slipping through the living room door as quietly as she'd arrived. Nick looked at the caller ID, hoping for one name, but seeing something he'd never expected.

Lt. Commander Doug Seaton. He tapped the phone and put it to his ear. His good ear. "Lieutenant Hershey speaking."

The clipped baritone of Nick's commanding officer was both familiar and unsettling. This was it: his fate.

As he listened to the decision based on the hearing test he'd taken a month ago, Nick slowly sank back into the chair and tried to accept what he'd dreaded all along. Central training. Illinois. Desk job.

Of course the Navy didn't want to keep paying him to live at a resort and write novels, did they?

As he listened to his crappy fate and future, he picked up the picture of Willow her mother had left behind. All he could see was the image of a woman he loved...and lost. Once more, he'd gambled on someone's fate and made the wrong choice.

Chapter Twenty-Six

For the second time in one day, Willow reached the harbor in record time, blinded by sweat and exhaustion, but freakishly charged to run another five miles before going home to bed. Run and sweat and refuse to think.

That was all she was capable of tonight.

She'd stumbled through the day, told her tale of woe to her closest friends, who'd been so supportive they hadn't even placed bets on the situation, and then finally got into her sneakers to escape the pain that engulfed her heart. She'd long ago learned that physical pain could sometimes erase all the other kind.

From where she stood, she could see the lights of the Victorian-style beach house where she lived, but they didn't call to her for comfort and rest as they usually did. The girls would want to talk. Or, even worse, Nick could be there, waiting for her with his excuses and apologies and rationalizations.

And hard, hot body that was *supposed* to invade hers.

With a grunt, she adjusted her earbuds, kicked up the volume on her music, and started to run again.

As much as she didn't want to think about anything, one

thought kept pounding at her brain with as much force as her feet on the pavement.

She *still* wanted to have sex with him. Even now, when she was spitting mad and truly hurt. Her body ached for that one chance, and now she'd never have it. On top of all the upheaval and heartbreak, she'd just wanted to get laid. By Nick. And only Nick. Whoever her first lover would be, he wouldn't be Nick, damn it.

How could he do that to her? How could he lie so easily and pretend...

She slammed her feet as though the pavement was his heart and she could do to it what he'd done to hers.

Fury fueled every step, a bitter, familiar, resentment-infused anger that made Willow's blood sing. She rounded a corner at the bottom of her street, slowing enough to make a decision whether to run home, shower, and cool off, or start the whole five-mile loop over again.

Definitely start over—

A man stood in the shadows of her driveway. She caught the silhouette, moving slowly. Waiting for her.

Of course Nick would be there. He'd ambush her with kisses and sweet talk, groveling with apologies and promises. Then maybe he'd take her...to bed.

A slow, low heat rolled through her, and it had nothing to do with how long and hard she'd run. What did that make her, other than slutty and stupid and maybe a little desperate to do it?

It.

That's all sex was. A two-letter pronoun that could mean nothing, anything, or everything. *It* could be mind-bogglingly beautiful lovemaking that left a person's soul soaring with joy. Or it could mean up-against-the-wall toe-curlingly hot sex.

And, honestly, the hot wall sex was *all* Willow had ever wanted when she asked—both times.

It was Nick who'd turned the whole event into something bigger and more meaningful than she'd ever had in mind. She wanted to *do it*. He wanted to do *It*. But now, nobody was doing anything except Ona, who was probably gloating that she'd orchestrated a dramatic conclusion to Willow's one and only brush with love.

No, no. Not love. *Sex.*

Willow shook off the frustrations and jogged up the street, bracing herself for the encounter.

"Hey." She called out to the shadow behind the hibiscus tree. "I know you're there."

He didn't step out, probably waiting to see if she'd attack.

"You want to know the worst part? The very worst part about all of this?"

He still didn't answer.

"I'm *still* a freaking virgin, Nick. You dragged the whole thing out so long and now I—"

"No way."

She froze the second she realized it wasn't Nick, then letting out a low, long grunt of disbelief when she recognized the gravelly voice and slightly aged posture.

"A virgin? At twenty-nine? You can't possibly be my daughter, and if you are, don't let anyone know. I'd be the laughing stock of rock 'n' roll."

Oh, great. Just great. Could her day get any worse?

Her father stepped out of the shadows, arms extended, and Willow almost gave in to the need to throw herself into the arms of the one member of her tiny family she actually missed and loved. Except...when push came to shove, he was always on her mother's side, and no doubt that's why he was here.

"Hey, Daddy," she whispered, using the little girl's name because...because it felt right. "What are you doing here?"

"Finding out more about you than I could have imagined. C'mere, sweet Ambrosia."

Oh, why not? She let herself be folded into his hug, and a rare and completely uninvited lump formed in her chest as sadness swamped her. Why had she let so many months and years pass without seeing this man?

"I'm sweaty," she apologized, but didn't pull away.

"You're skinny," he replied, giving a squeeze and then putting both hands on her waist. "Holy hell, woman, where did you go?"

She finally inched back, the streetlight casting a yellow glow on his wrinkled face, but adding to the glimmer that always danced in his eyes. His hair stood up in the front, the sides nearly hitting his shoulders, a pink diamond twinkling in one ear. Her father, the world's sweetest rock star.

"Dad." She took another hug of his wiry frame. "I've missed you."

"Not enough to come home."

A litany of old, lame excuses played in her head. *I've been busy. You guys were traveling. I had weddings every weekend.* She tossed them all aside for the truth. "I couldn't handle it. I'm sorry."

He broke their embrace, but kept his hands on her shoulders, looking hard at her. "Look at you, girl. You look like a freaking model."

She rolled her eyes. "And you know how much I want to be one of those."

"How about a virgin? Do you want to be one of those?"

"Not particularly. And, God, does the free world have to know my dark secret?"

He gave her shoulders a squeeze. "I hope not, because,

damn, that would annihilate my reputation."

"I know, right? What kind of self-respecting rock god raises a twenty-nine-year-old virgin?"

"Apparently, this one." The soft hint of pride in his voice touched her heart.

"How'd you find me out here?"

"I knocked on your apartment door, and when you didn't answer I went upstairs and met a pretty girl with pink hair."

"Gussie. She's one of my business partners."

"What's she trying to cover up with all that makeup?" he asked.

She just smiled at him. "I forgot how you know people so well."

"Oh, I do," he agreed. "It's my superpower. How about we walk and talk while you cool down?"

"Of course, but you aren't going to change my mind about Mom."

"Oh, she'll change your mind all by herself, believe me. She'll tell you what happened while she was up there and how she met God or Saint Peter or some such nonsense and had a vision about you and woke up with a new purpose in life."

Willow stopped mid-step. "What?"

"Your mother died, honey."

She blinked at him, unable to even process what he was saying.

"Oh, she'll tell you she didn't. She has quite a story, and I swear one of these days she's going to sell it and make another fortune."

"What happened to her?" A cold, numb feeling tingled in her limbs. Ona had nearly died? Or had died? "Why didn't anyone tell me? When? What was it?"

He gave her a sideways smile. "You sound pretty

concerned for a girl who just claimed she wouldn't ever change her mind about her mother."

She shook off the admonishment. "Dad, what happened to her?"

"She drowned in the ocean during her morning swim."

"*What*?" The numbing turned icy, freezing her blood and hollowing out a hole in her chest. "I just saw her today."

"She's not dead now, but she was." He brushed back some of his long hair, the heels of his boots tapping on the pavement as they headed toward the harbor. "She was utterly flat-lined."

But obviously she had survived, so Willow exhaled. "Oh, Dad. How did you bear it? You must have lost your mind."

He snorted. "That would be putting it mildly." Then he gave her a smile and hugged her a little. "You know, I think you're the first person to think about me in that situation. Everyone who hears the story is all enraptured with Ona's account of her trip through the light and the visions she saw. Oh, wait until you hear about the rainbows that wrapped around her, each color a different degree of warmth." His tone was rich with sarcasm.

"I take it you're not buying that?"

"I don't know. I wasn't on that side of things. I didn't come here to tell you that story." He slowed as they reached the open docks of Pleasure Pointe Harbor, stopping to let the clanging of sail rigging punctuate his comment. "I wanted to tell you what happened to me."

She studied him in the dim light, doing a quick inventory of his lines—there were definitely new ones. Worry lines between his brows that must have formed while he sat in some emergency room waiting area.

"Oh, God, Dad, why didn't you call me?"

"Honestly, it happened so fast and was so chaotic while

they were trying to revive her, I didn't think to call you. Then she woke up and insisted I not tell you a thing."

And, of course, he did what Ona wanted.

She wrapped her arms around him again and held him tight. "I'm sorry, Dad. I'm sorry you went through that alone."

He took the hug, but she could feel him shaking his head. "No, no. Didn't come here for pity or your apologies."

She didn't quite understand why, but she let it go. "When did this happen?"

"Six, seven months ago."

Oh, God. She'd had no idea. She should have—

"Hey." He tapped her chin, reading her expression as he always had. "Regrets are for idiots. Don't bother with them."

She tried to take that advice, but she couldn't help feeling like shit. "I'm the worst daughter."

"She was no picnic as a mother." He guided her to a bench that faced the long wharves with sailboats and pleasure cruises lined up, a yellow glow from a dock light illuminating the area. "But here's the thing, Willie."

She didn't cringe at the name for once. Yes, it reminded her of her old fat self, but that was what her Dad called her, and it sounded right.

"What's the thing, Dad?" she asked, taking one of his hands between hers and holding on to it.

"Life is so fucking short."

She just looked at him.

"One second you're here, living, working, singing, bitching, golfing, laughing…loving. And the next, you're watching a corpse be wheeled into an ambulance, and everything that you thought mattered…poof." He made his fingers explode. "Gone."

"God, Dad. How did you keep it out of the media?" At

least if she'd read about her mother going to the hospital, she would have gone home.

Or would she have stayed and...stewed?

He laughed at her question, and she knew the answer. Money, of course. "And while she was wrapped in rainbows and making deals with the Big Man, I realized that nothing—and I do mean *nothing*, child—matters in this world, because it's over in a blink of an eye."

"I know that, Dad, but—"

He held a hand up to silence her. "The people you love and the people who love you, no matter how piss-poor a job they do of showing it, are all you have in this life." He took her hands this time, squeezing. "If she had died—or, if she had stayed dead, because she was gone—you would have spent the rest of your life despising her for how she treated you."

Yes, she would have. She planned to, in fact.

"Then you would have gotten older and maybe had a child of your own." He angled his head and lifted one of his brows. "You do know you have to actually have sex for that to happen, right?"

She elbowed him. "Finish."

"Well, when you are a mother yourself and you make all manner of dumb decisions because you don't know any other way to do a job that is really too hard for anyone, then..." He took a deep, slow inhale to elevate the drama of his pronouncement. "Then you probably would wish you had made up with her before she died."

"Maybe I would or will, Dad, but you don't understand how trapped she made me. I spent more than half my life— which doesn't seem short when you're in the middle of it— hating myself because I couldn't be what she wanted me to be."

"No one can be that," he said. "Even I can't be what she wants, but you won't be find me running away, avoiding her, and hating her. You'll only be free to be and love yourself—and someone else, I might add—when you forgive, forget, and be a family again."

"I'm free," she said, sounding defensive. "I'm completely free for the first time in my life. Free of the weight, literally and figuratively."

"Are you? Is that why you've never fallen for a man long enough to unload that virginity you carry around like a big ol' suitcase?"

"You don't know how I carry it around."

He grinned. "Did we not just discuss my superpower of knowing people better than they know themselves?"

"I appreciate what you're trying to tell me, Dad."

"Do you?" he asked. "Because if there is one simple, single lesson I can impart to you, it's this: Don't waste time, because you don't have any time to waste." He frowned and tilted his head. "There's a song in there somewhere."

She stared up at the night sky, all the day's thoughts muddled in her mind. "What would you have me do, then? Act like the last thirty years never happened?"

"They don't matter, Willie. What matters is the next thirty years or days or, possibly, minutes. They may be all you have." He took her hand again and looked into her eyes. "Use them wisely."

He was right, of course. And how could she most wisely use the next thirty minutes?

Nick.

The thought hit her like a hammer to the head—and heart. Nick. *He* was how she should use her next thirty minutes...or maybe thirty hours. Nick was all she wanted. Maybe it *was* just sex, but damn it, she wanted that.

She shot up. "You know what, Dad? You make a lot of sense."

A smile tugged at his lips as he reached for her hand. "Music to a father's ears, those words."

"You're right. I'm going."

He stood next to her. "Fantastic. She's waiting at the Ritz in Naples."

"Let her." Willow worked a crick out of her neck, her own broad smile pulling. "I gotta go somewhere else, Dad."

"Where?"

She reached down and kissed him on the cheek, then started backing away. "No time to waste. I've got some baggage to unload." And only one man in the world could do that job. "You understand that, don't you?"

She saw the moment the realization hit his eyes, followed by a wry smile. "I'm afraid I do."

Chapter Twenty-Seven

Nick kicked the volume up to an ear-thrashing level and pressed the soft sides of the noise-canceling headphones over his ears. What difference did it make now? The Navy made its decision on his future, and he sure as shit didn't need to baby his deaf ear anymore.

Donny Zatarain howled while Mikey Brooker hammered the drums and Graham Mitchell's bass line thrummed a vibration down through Nick's bare body.

This is it. This is love.

He opened his mouth to sing the words, but nothing came out. He couldn't sing that song ever again. *This wasn't love.* He'd blown that chance.

He stuffed a pair of camos into the bag and reached for the last of his clothes in the drawer. He'd be packed in ten minutes and out of here when the sun came up the next day. Off to the shithole of a desk job.

Come and take it, don't ya fake it, we can make it...

But they couldn't make it. They couldn't even fake it.

As much as he wanted Willow—physically, emotionally, mentally, and whatever the hell other way he could have her—they couldn't make it.

The guitar wailed as Donny screamed the next line.

Will ya, will ya be my girl?

He stopped packing long enough to air-drum the riff along with the band.

Will ya, will ya...

He imagined the concert when Donny proposed to Ona, thinking of the man wailin' on the song, getting on one knee, and the whole stadium screaming, "Will ya, will ya..."

He sucked in a deep breath so he could howl the amended lyrics. "Marry meeeeee—"

The headphones snapped off, silencing Donny's scream, but not Nick's. He whipped around, arms out, eyes wide as he met familiar blue ones.

"Hey."

Willow.

She stood with one hand on her hip and the other holding out the headphones, the reedy screech of the song still coming through.

"Do you never knock?" he finally asked.

"Do you never dress?" She let her gaze drop over his body, lingering below the waist where, of course, his cock twitched under her scrutiny.

She didn't wear much more, a tank top, sports bra, and very short shorts. Her skin glowed with the flush of exercise, and the tendrils falling from her sloppy ponytail were damp with sweat.

"Did you run here?" he asked.

"No, but I was running. I need a shower." She handed him the headphones and stepped past him, glancing over her shoulder to take another look at his ever-hardening johnson. "You're fine the way you are. Just, you know, get what you need."

What?

He watched her head into the bathroom, but then she

froze. Slowly, she turned to the bed and looked at the open duffle bag and then she shook her head silently, disappearing into the bathroom. Fifteen seconds later, the shower was running.

No fight? No attack? No demand for an explanation or some epic groveling for his mistake?

Because he would have done all that and more for...

Just, you know, get what you need.

She meant condoms, no doubt. Not candles or champagne. Not soft music and sweet promises. Not what he'd wanted for her—and for him.

She just wanted to...

He squeezed his eyes shut, wiping out every word for the act that came to mind. That's *not* what he wanted, damn it. Not like this. *Not like this.* She deserved better. Hell, *they* deserved better.

He marched into the bathroom without knocking. Steam already filled the small room and fogged the glass of the shower. He yanked that door open, too.

She sputtered, pulling her face from the waterfall, soap suds sliding over every inch of her. For a second, he forgot what he wanted to say, because she was so damn naked and wet and gorgeous.

"Yes?" she asked, somehow managing to arch a brow despite the water on her face.

"No," he replied.

Confusion flickered, and that dissolved into disbelief, which faded into...hurt.

Shit. "I mean, not yet."

She let out a soft grunt. "I've waited long enough, Nick."

"I know, and I don't want to wait either, but, Willow, we can't fall into bed and have sex with all this...this business between us."

She closed her eyes, reaching for the wall as if she needed support. "You're turning me down...again?" She barely whispered the question.

"Willow, listen to me." He twisted the faucet to turn off the water and grabbed a towel from the rack, handing it to her.

She held the towel in front of her. "Really? You're going to put me through the same thing you did years ago?"

"You know damn well this is different."

"Do I?" She pressed the towel against her chest. "I'm not going to beg, Nick. I gotta have a shred of dignity."

Then he had to tell her the truth, no matter how vulnerable it made him.

"Willow, I really, really care about you. And I know you're pissed as hell at me for what happened with your mother and this wedding that isn't even a wedding. And I don't want that hanging between us the first time."

She clutched the towel so tightly her knuckles turned white. "You have got to be kidding me."

"Would I kid about his? When this first started, and you wanted me to be the one to take your virginity, I thought I'd make it special and meaningful. I didn't know...this would happen. I didn't know I'd want it to be meaningful for me, too."

Her eyes flashed, hot and hurt, and then instantly, her expression went blank. "Fine." She reached to close the shower door, but he stopped her.

"That's all you're going to say? Fine?"

"Yes. Fine." She tugged at the chrome handle.

He stared at her. "Don't you have anything else to say? You understand? You believe me? You feel the same? You're still mad about your mother?"

"Yeah, that one. C'mon, Nick, this is mortifying enough. Leave me alone."

"Mortifying?" He spit the word out. "I just told you that I care about you. That this *means* something to me now."

She looked away, staring at some distant point as though it pained her to even look at him. Was she really going to shut him out *now*?

"Don't you understand?" he asked. "I can't just fall into that bed and…and mindlessly *do it*."

She let out a dry cough. "Apparently not, no matter how many times I ask." Each word was loaded with sarcasm and pain.

Damn it! He reached for her shoulder. "You and I both know this isn't just sex anymore."

She finally looked at him. "You have no idea how much I want to believe you."

"Then why don't you?" He narrowed his eyes as the futility of the argument squeezed his guts.

"Because you went behind my back, you sided with my mother, and you lied to my face. How can I trust you?"

"But you're willing to sleep with me."

She shrugged a shoulder, her color rising as his point hit home.

"And about what happened, Willow. I'm sorry. I made a decision that I thought was best for you."

Her eyes sparked like gas flames. "*You* decided what was best for *me*? Do you have any idea, any inkling at all, how much I hate manipulation like that?"

"I do, and I was completely wrong. But I had to make a choice of who to hurt—you or me. So I chose me."

She nearly choked. "You? I was the one who—"

"Your reconciling with her is more important than whatever happens with me. Because nothing can really happen with me if you don't make things right with her first." Didn't she see that? "I want you to be happy, Willow."

"I am happy," she insisted. "I'd be happier if I weren't the world's oldest living virgin."

He gave a dry laugh. "Believe me, I'd love to do my part, but, Willow, I want more than that now."

Inhaling slowly, she closed her eyes. "You're doing it again."

"Doing what?"

"Deciding what's best for me."

"What's best for *us*." He leaned into the shower. "Dry off, put a robe on, and let's talk. I want to explain my side of what happened."

She swallowed hard. "I can imagine your side. The blind side. That's where my mother puts everyone."

"That's true, but we still need to talk."

"About what?"

"About all that shit that's holding you back. I want to help you. Like you helped me come to terms with what happened in Afghanistan. Because until you're truly and genuinely free of that, I honestly don't think you can give me what I want from you."

"I can't give something you won't take," she said.

"I want more than your body," he said simply. "I don't know when that happened, but it did. And now I'm not going to be satisfied with less."

Very slowly, she inched back, as if his words finally hit her heart. "Then what do you want from me?"

He swallowed hard, knowing this was it. He'd lose her or not when he admitted this. But he couldn't lie.

"Everything," he whispered right before he closed the shower door. "I want everything."

Goosebumps blossomed over every inch of Willow, her skin turning to ice while her heart folded in half and his parting words melted with the last of the steam.

Strictly to stay warm and think, she tossed the towel and turned the water back on, letting the stinging spray wash all the confusion away. Why was she confused? It was very clear what just happened: Nick turned her down…again.

The punch of that reality was tempered by the next thought: He said he wanted *everything*.

Was it possible he meant that? Or was that just the nicest rejection ever offered from a man who was obviously packing to get the hell out of Dodge? Because, no matter how you paint and shade that rebuff, it was still a flat-out *no*.

Oh, God. And it still hurt, no matter what he said.

Of course, part of her—the whole, healthy, unscarred little part of Willow—wanted to not only believe him, she wanted to go out there, talk the hell out of this, and maybe even have that same kind of conversation with her mother. Not a Band-Aid conversation, either. A real one.

But the other part—the big, fat, scared, insecure, protective, desperate-for-control Willie—wanted to run. And run. And run some more.

She pressed her fingertips against the cool tile, her thoughts whirring.

What exactly did he mean by *everything*? He meant the kind of love he said he'd always wanted but didn't believe in. He meant forever.

Or, a little demon in her heart suggested, he meant to let her down with the least amount of pain.

Which was it? Well, there was only one way to find out.

She stepped out of the water, realizing how breathless she was as she dried and wrapped the towel around herself to face her moment of truth.

She turned the knob and opened the bathroom door, peering into the dark and empty room. Walking toward the bed, she noticed the open, partially packed duffel bag again. One foot out the door before they'd even talked.

No, no. She tamped down that thought, determined to give him the benefit of the doubt. Maybe he'd been redeployed. She didn't even know. Just as she was about to call his name, a scuff and a sigh from the patio caught her attention.

She spied him standing in the moon shadows, dressed in baggy shorts now, his hands in the pockets as he stared out toward the water of Barefoot Bay.

She took a long moment to drink him in, letting her eyes adjust to the darkness until she could see his profile, his shoulders, his chest rise and fall with another sad, deep sigh.

Why was he sad? Because maybe that *wasn't* the nicest rejection in history. Maybe he really, really did care about her and wasn't willing to have meaningless sex just for the sake of having it. Wasn't that better than what she'd been asking for?

So much better! She quietly put a hand over her mouth, clamping down the sudden urge to run to him, instead of away, and promise him…everything. Her heart slammed against her chest at the thought of how close she was to real happiness. Not pretend happiness—the way she had been living. But real, true…joy.

True love.

Taking a steadying breath, she dropped her hand, and her fingers landed on his duffel bag. She glanced down at the neatly folded T-shirts and shorts. She touched the soft cotton of one of his favorites, a Z-Train shirt, of course.

She rubbed her finger along the collar and touched the edge of…something. A card? A …photo. What picture was he packing from his month in Barefoot Bay? What memory was he taking away?

Unable to resist, she slipped it out, surprised to feel the matte finish of an old-school photograph that—

The Eiffel Tower caught her eye. Angling the picture toward the ambient light, she hissed in a soft breath when the image became clear and all the blood and hope and *joy* evaporated as quickly as they'd arrived.

Fat Willie Zatarain just as unattractive, unappealing, and unsexy as she could be. She swayed a little, looking at an image she'd worked so damn hard to erase from her brain. She closed her eyes, but couldn't unsee it.

How did he get this? Why did he have it in his bag?

As if she didn't know.

Thank you, Ona. Sabotage successful.

Her mother had managed to stop everything with one picture, one stark reminder that Willow would always, always be that fat girl to him...and to herself.

No damn wonder he turned her down. *Again.*

She let the picture flutter to the floor, then went straight back into the bathroom where she put her running clothes back on with shaky hands, refusing to look in the mirror for fear of seeing Willie Zatarain.

He was still on the patio when she stepped back into the room. She softly cleared her throat, but he didn't turn.

Defective hearing or...not?

It didn't matter. But just in case, she held back her sob until she was out the front door and halfway down the path.

Chapter Twenty-Eight

"I'm scared, Donny."

Ona's admission earned an amused glance from her husband. "I think it's possible that, in thirty years, that's the first time I've ever heard you say those words."

He was probably right, because the bone-deep terror that gripped her gut and seeped through her veins right now felt entirely foreign. Fear wasn't an emotion that had a hold on Ona Zatarain. Regret, remorse, guilt, and an ocean of sorrow had their way with her most days, but very little scared Ona.

After all, she'd broken the code on death. Now, if she could just earn the forgiveness she didn't deserve but so profoundly needed, she could concentrate on the one that mattered most: love. Would that be possible today?

Of course! Nothing was impossible. Hadn't she learned that firsthand?

Donny steered her across the lobby of the upscale resort, slowing their steps and guiding her toward a mosaic wall.

"What are you doing?" she asked.

"We're fifteen minutes early, babe."

"But she'll leave," Ona said, imagining how the wedding planners would plaster smiles on their faces and make up some excuse for Willow's absence from their scheduled meeting.

Donny angled his head. "How many times have you told me this is meant to be? Predetermined? As seen in your dreams?"

"It wasn't a dream," she muttered, staring up at the Moroccan-inspired stones, half of her head thinking about her daughter, the other half imagining an entire summer collection in those gorgeous blues and golds. "But our daughter is like liquid mercury, and you know she'll slip out of my grasp."

He nudged her. "Not if you grab her now."

Ona turned just as Willow came through the lobby doors and headed to the registration desk, a sea foam green dress skimming her lovely body, her posture as confident as if she were sailing down a runway.

"Oh." The soft exclamation slipped out as she drank in her daughter from a distance, trying to memorize every angle of her face, the tilt of her head, the way her wheat-colored hair picked up sunlight through the windows.

Seeing her near-naked at the villa yesterday had been such a shock. Ona really hadn't had much time to appreciate the sight of her—not just her newly sculpted body, but *her*.

"She's a beauty," Donny whispered, fatherly pride in his voice.

"She always has been." Ona's voice hitched as her throat squeezed. *But I was too dumb and dead inside to see it.* "Let's talk to her."

Donny didn't move. "Don't ambush her out here."

But even her husband's determination couldn't stop Ona from moving forward, magnetically drawn to her daughter, arms already aching for that first embrace. Just as she took a step, Willow turned and looked directly at Ona.

For a second, time stopped. Willow's eyes flashed ever so quickly, just a glimmer of panic that was almost instantly wiped clean, replaced with an icy calm. She straightened her back, lifted her chin, and gave an infinitesimal nod, as if to say...*Game on.*

Oh, why was it always a fight with them?

Not anymore. Willow wasn't the only one who'd changed. Her transformation might be more obvious, but Ona had transformed, as well. She'd created a new person, too. But Willow would have to be willing to take some time to get to see that Ona.

Please, God, give me that opportunity.

Ona strode so fast across the lobby, she heard Donny swear softly as he hustled to keep up with her. Halfway there, two more women came out of the door to the side of the registration desk, flanking Willow as if she'd called for support.

The other wedding planners, Ona assumed, quickly taking in the dark, exotic beauty of one and the over-stylized vibrancy of the other.

The dark-haired one whispered something to Willow, who gave a quick shake of her head and smiled. As she expected—fake, plastered-on smiles from Willow and her close friends, who stood with her in solidarity against the evil mother.

Ona's heart slipped a little. She had so much wrong to make right.

"Welcome to the Barefoot Brides," Willow said. "We're so glad you're here."

And a fake, plastered-on greeting. Undeterred, Ona closed the space, holding Willow's gaze. The petite girl with a platinum wig reached out her hand, and Willow did a round of stilted introductions.

"Let's go back to the Barefoot Brides's office," Gussie suggested.

Where there would be no chance of privacy. Ona shook her head. "I want to talk to you, Willow." The name seemed formal and unfamiliar on her lips, but Ona was determined to make it clear she'd accept her daughter's obvious desire not to be called Willie anymore.

"Absolutely," Willow said with more of that phony, accommodating tone. For the first time, Ona noticed the shadows under her daughter's eyes and some puffiness on the lids. She'd been crying. Ona's heart dropped so fast and hard it was a wonder they didn't all hear it hit the ground. "We can talk in our office."

"No," Ona said. "I'd like to go outside and talk alone."

For a few heartbeats, nobody spoke, the pause just as awkward as it could be. Willow and Ona looked at each other—and the others looked at them while everyone waited. This was it. She'd say yes or no, and Ona would have to accept it if it was no.

Willow's eyes shuttered slightly as if something hit her. She'd not only been crying, Ona thought, she was tired. Weary and spent. Her chest tightened with the need to help her daughter, who still teetered on the fine point of an important decision.

Please, Willie. Please.

Willow let out a sigh of pure resignation. "Okay."

Ona's knees nearly buckled.

Donny squeezed Ona's hand and leaned in to kiss her cheek. "Go, Mom," he whispered.

The tiny bit of encouragement was all she needed to walk with Willie—*Willow*, she corrected herself—to the door that led to the beach. On the way, Willow self-consciously smoothed a wrinkle from her dress and tucked an invisible hair behind her ear.

She's as nervous as I am. The realization gave Ona much needed courage as they stepped out in the sunshine.

"How horrible to have a mother who makes you so skittish," Ona said softly.

Willow just smiled. "I'm not skittish." Then she laughed a little. "That didn't take long."

"What didn't?"

"For us to disagree." They crossed the wide patio, threading tables around the pool. Willow paused at an empty one and gave Ona a questioning look, but Ona gestured toward the sand.

"Let's walk," she suggested.

Blessedly, Willow didn't argue. They took a few steps down to the sand, both of them slipping off their shoes before going any farther.

"All the way to the water," Ona said.

Willow turned and sighed. "Is that necessary?"

"Humor me," Ona replied, giving her a gentle prod toward the hard-packed wet sand and the frothy white lace left by the last wave. "Because when I saw you, it was here, and you looked like this."

"When you saw me…" She drew out the words, no doubt ready to roll her eyes or maybe make a patronizing comment about Ona's experience. She was used to the response to her mystical journey. "I take it this was when you were in the hospital?"

"I wasn't in the hospital." At Willow's look, she added, "My body was. The part that matters was somewhere else altogether."

Instead of skepticism, she saw a hint of interest and even a little regret in her daughter's eyes. Encouraged, Ona ventured a little closer to the water's edge, thinking about all the different versions of this speech she'd prepared.

None of them sounded genuine right now. She let some cold water cover her pink-tipped toes and nearly dampen the handkerchief hem of her long gauzy dress. She studied the horizon and the swells that formed the gentle gulf waves.

"I bet I wouldn't have gotten caught in a riptide in water this calm," she finally said.

Willow came closer. "So that's what happened? It must have been terrifying."

Lifting her face to the sun, Ona closed her eyes, basking in rays she rarely let hit her aging skin. Today, age didn't worry her.

"I didn't really feel much fear, because I was unconscious fairly quickly," she finally said. "And, yes, that's how it happened, but I don't think that's what's important. That day I could have been hit by a car or fallen off a ladder or been pulled into the Pacific's undertow. I was summoned, and I had to go."

After a few seconds, Willow asked, "Where exactly did you go?"

"I guess some people would call it heaven or the afterlife or the other side."

"What do you call it?"

She turned to look at her daughter. "There's no name, not in this world. And, really, if I tried with every glorious word in every language on earth, I couldn't describe it to you. The beauty hit senses I didn't know I had. The message hit...emotional places I didn't know a person could feel." She took Willow's hands, surprised by how slender and strong her fingers were. "For an hour, I existed on another plane, able to see everything here, including you. Mostly you."

Her voice cracked on the last word, and Willow flinched

slightly, as if that vulnerability actually hit her.

"And that's why I'm here. To tell you that my…my mistakes were made crystal clear to me. And, honey, I regret every time I put you down, every day I acted like you weren't good enough, every word I spoke that wasn't a mother's love." Her eyes filled, blurring Willow's face. "I don't expect you to fall into my arms and shower me with forgiveness, but I am standing here offering an apology and begging for a chance to start over with you."

The slightest hint of a wry smile tipped her lips. "You know, Mom, you can't rewrite history. I've learned that in the most excruciating way."

"I'm not trying to," she said. "I'm not denying what I did or how I acted. I'm not asking that you forget it. On the contrary, maybe in some twisted way, I've taught you to be a better mother when your time comes."

Willow gave a soft choke, as if she thought that time would never come, but Ona didn't let it take her off track. She inched her daughter closer to make her point. "I'm not trying to change the past or even obliterate it, but I am desperately attempting to not let it own us."

Now she did smile, but there were tears in her eyes, too. "You sound like someone else I know."

Ona suspected she knew who that was. "What do you think?"

Willow nodded, looking toward the water rather than meet Ona's unwavering gaze. "I get that you had an experience that changed you," she finally said. "Dad told me. And I get that you want to smooth things over with me and you felt you had to pull strings and lie to people and make complete strangers complicit in your schemes. So, fine, all that's done. But let's just move on and not dwell on it anymore, okay?"

"No, not okay." Ona reached up to turn Willow's chin, forcing their eyes to meet. "Willow, I cannot erase the mistakes I made with you."

Her blue eyes, so like her father's, narrowed. "And I can't remove the scars they left."

Ona swallowed. "I know I was dictatorial and unrelenting and disapproving and manipulative."

Willow managed a smile. "That pretty much sums it up."

"People change, Willow."

"Not that much. Believe me, I know this is true."

Oh, so much pain in her voice. "This is not just about me, is it?"

Willow stepped back, still averting her gaze. She walked a few paces then bent over to pick up a shell, pretending to examine it. All the while, Ona waited, sensing that whatever weighed on her daughter's heart was one of the reasons the apology hadn't been accepted the way she'd hoped.

"In some ways, Mom, it is most definitely about you." She hurled the shell into the waves and turned a sharp eye to Ona. "*Why* did you give Nick that picture?"

She drew back, so not expecting the question. "What...oh, that picture from France that Dad took?"

"That's what you do, Mom," she shot back. "So, for all your rainbows and talk of the great beyond and promises to change, what's the first thing you do? Drop a little photo bomb on my happiness."

Ona just stared at her, a white-hot horror twisting through her. "How did that ruin your happiness?"

"He...I...we..." She kicked some sand and then let out a long, slow sigh. "I am so freaking tired of this. Why am I blaming you?"

Good question.

"I'm just using you and Nick as excuses, you know that?

I'm trying to take control of my life, and I'm giving it all to you and Nick." She shook her head and wiped her hands as if cleaning her personal slate. "No more. I'm done. Forget the picture. Forget the past. Forget everything."

"You can't do that, Willow."

"I can try!" She whipped around and took off, getting a good five strides in before Ona shot forward and caught up with her, grabbing her elbow.

"And you will fail!"

"Look at me," Willow demanded, opening her arms to invite a full-body inspection. "Do I look like a person who fails? One hundred and twenty pounds lost. Is that *failure*, Mom? But it isn't enough, is it?" Her voice broke with tears.

"Enough for what?"

"To be loved," she admitted on a shudder.

"Willow!" Ona threw her arms around her sobbing daughter and pulled her closer, pressing their bodies together. "How can you say that? I love you. Dad loves you. Your friends love you. And, whether you want to accept it or not, Nick loves you."

The only answer was a shoulder shake with the next sob.

"And I left the picture with him because when he looked at it, that's when I *knew* he loved you." She eased Willow back so she could look in her eyes. "Do you know what he said when he saw it?"

She shook her head.

"He said, 'Her fire is on. Her smile is real. Her heart is right there in her eyes.' But it wasn't just *what* he said, honey, it was *how* he said it. He sounded so much like your father when he's writing a song for me."

Willow blinked at her. "Really?"

"You don't know how much he cares for you?"

She sniffed. "He tried to tell me."

"But you refused to hear him."

"I...I..."

"You can't believe him even though he has given you absolutely no reason not to—and don't you blame him for not telling you about me being here. He really did think he was helping the two of you by helping the two of us."

Willow let out a soft grunt and looked skyward. "What a mess I've made."

"Then fix it."

"Spoken like a true manipulator."

"Willow, there's no manipulation involved. The man is in love with you. And I'm pretty sure that's mutual. Take all that steel armor off your heart and give it to him."

For the first time all day, something that looked like hope lit Willow's eyes. "You think I can?"

"I know you can."

"No, Mom. He's gone, and I blew it. I walked out on him, and it would be impossible to get him back now."

Ona laughed softly. "Nothing is impossible." She put her hands on Willow's cheeks and held her beautiful face very still. "That is the one thing I learned on my journey. Absolutely nothing is impossible."

"Oh, Mom." This time, the embrace was genuine, with Willow's long, strong arms wrapping around Ona and holding her close. "Some things are impossible, but...but..."

"But what?"

Willow leaned back, her eyes red, her makeup streaked. "But I want to try. I *have* to try." She touched her tear-stained face. "Am I a mess?"

"You're beautiful, inside and out."

Willow smiled. "I don't think I've ever heard you say that."

"Shame on me."

"No." Willow shook her head. "No more shame. Not on

either one of us." She grabbed Ona's shoulders and gave her a squeeze. "I gotta go. I have something I have to do." She started to step away, but then she stopped suddenly. And quite unexpectedly, she leaned forward and kissed Ona's cheek. "Thanks. It shouldn't sound weird to say this, but I'm afraid it does. But I'm going to say it anyway. I think I should. I want to."

"Say what?" *Please, please. Say it.*

"I love you, Mom."

And with that, Willow took off across the beach, running full speed with her bare feet kicking up a wake of flying sand. Ona stayed firmly planted, her hand pressed to her burning cheek, her daughter's words echoing in her heart.

She'd never ever heard anything so beautiful in this world or the next.

"I love you, too, baby girl," she whispered.

As Willow disappeared around the resort, Ona lifted her hands to the sky and wept with gratitude.

As Willow ran the length of the beach, her mother's heartfelt apology bounced around her heart and head, welcome in both places. But now, she had to see if there was any possibility Nick hadn't left yet.

She had to tell him—

Hope soared when she saw the front door of Artemisia wide open. He was still there! He hadn't left yet. She slipped through the gate, a dozen different opening lines bouncing around her head. Should she go for funny? Serious? Loving? Sarcastic?

But nothing really formed as she stepped into the sun-dappled living room and heard the sound of...a vacuum...sucking up any bits of Nick's stay that he might have left.

"Hello?" she called.

The vacuum stopped immediately, and a woman Willow recognized as a housekeeping staff member stepped into the hall.

"Oh, hello," the woman said. "I'm almost done. Do you have something to leave for the next guest?"

The next guest.

"Is he gone?" Willow made no attempt to hide the disappointment.

"Oh, yes, long gone."

She felt like she'd been shoved off a cliff. "Are you sure?" She sounded desperate, but, then, she was. "He didn't..." *Change his mind?*

"Oh, you want that little thingy he left behind?" She rolled her eyes. "It's unbelievable how people leave a villa or room and forget something every time. I must find a charger a week."

"What is it?"

"Oh, I don't know. Something electronic. Right there, on the counter."

Willow walked to the stretch of gleaming granite that separated the kitchen from the living area. There was the tiny jump drive she'd handled dozens of times in the past month, his favorite way to deliver pages for her to read. Under it, the picture of Willow in Paris.

Of course, he left that behind.

"Is that what the guy's looking for?" the maid asked.

"I...yeah." Willow slipped the drive in her pocket and picked up the photo. "Did he leave anything else?"

"There was a little box next to the bed," she said. "It had

a few candles in it and what looked like a bag of rose petals, of all bizarre things. I put the candles on the dresser, but I have no idea what to do with the rose petals. Did he want those, too?"

For a second, Willow couldn't breathe.

Rose petals and candles. He really had them. She blinked against an unwanted burn in her eyes. "No, you can just toss them."

"Seems a shame. Don't we have a wedding this weekend? Would make a nice surprise for some newlyweds."

A very nice surprise. She just lifted a shoulder, not trusting her voice right then. Wordlessly, she turned and left, reaching into her pocket to hold on to the only thing she had left of Nick.

As she walked out of the villa, she glanced down at the picture, her stomach clutching at how ugly she'd been. She certainly didn't see fire or light or anything attractive. She flipped the photo to save herself from having to look at it and noticed some writing on the back. Nick's writing. She knew his scribble from seeing it on manuscript pages.

Rewriting History by Nicholas S. Hershey.

With her other hand, she squeezed the jump drive so hard, she could have cracked the plastic case.

Where could she go? Where was the closest computer?

Her parents would be in the Barefoot Brides offices, but she had to read this. Right now.

Back in the resort lobby, she bypassed the management offices and slipped into the darkened business center that very few resort guests used while on vacation. Today was no different. The room was dim and empty, the lone computer set up for guests dark.

She fired it to life, stuck the jump drive in, and opened

the folder. There was only one file—all of the drafts of his untitled manuscript had been deleted. But she opened the one called RH.

Rewriting History.

Immediately, the familiar double-spaced manuscript page appeared, in his favorite font.

Bracing herself for whatever she might find, she read the opening lines.

Rick Hanson put down his copy of The Grapes of Wrath *and watched the co-ed walk through the dormitory lounge for the third time in an hour. This pass, she smiled at him, and he couldn't help smiling back. She had a fire in her eyes that reminded him of a flickering gas flame. The wordless exchange made her stop and take a few steps closer, and something deep in his gut told him his life was about to change for the better...and forever.*

She stared at the words, choking back a sob. She dropped her chin into her hands and leaned closer to the screen, enthralled by this piece of fiction as much as the man who rewrote history.

For the next hour, she read a short story that made her laugh, brought her to tears, turned her on, and, in the end, made her sigh with happiness. It wasn't the truth, but it was the best piece of fiction she'd ever read.

She didn't know where he was or if he would ever be back. But she did know that if she ever saw Nick Hershey again, her first words would be, *I love you.*

Chapter Twenty-Nine

From the parking lot of the Casa Blanca Resort & Spa, Nick could hear the distinctive chords of *Piece of Me*, one of Z-Train's best blaring from the beach. But that wasn't a DJ spinning the tune, he thought as he reached the double glass doors and nodded to a valet.

That was the real deal.

Of course, the Donny and Ona "event" was in full swing. But that didn't change a thing. He'd come to find Willow and tell her what he'd decided in the last few days while he was away. He could have waited until tomorrow morning, knowing that on a quiet Sunday morning, he'd find her in the office, listening to her classical music and getting caught up on work. But he couldn't wait. His flight had landed an hour ago in Fort Myers, and without giving it much thought, he'd rented a car and come to Mimosa Key.

He'd found her apartment empty and decided she must have cracked her shell and come to the party. A swell of pride rolled through him. She'd made the right choice, after all. Would she make one more?

Time to find out.

He veered through the dimly lit lobby and made his way to the back doors that led to the sands of Barefoot Bay.

Halfway there, he heard the final killer note of *Piece of Me* followed by a garbled speaker on a microphone. Then it grew quiet.

As he reached the door, one of the Casa Blanca employees suddenly appeared next to him.

"I'm so sorry, sir, but there's a private party on the beach tonight, and you can't go out there without an invitation."

Like that would stop him. "I'm going—"

The door whipped open, and suddenly, he was face-to-face with Donny Zatarain.

For a split second, neither of them spoke. Then Donny's face brightened. "Holy shit, am I glad to see you. I need a...a...what do you call the guy who's on the lookout?"

"Guard duty."

"Right. And you just pulled it." Donny snagged Nick's arm and yanked him outside, then ushered him away from a hundred flickering torches around a dance floor and bar and the happy chatter of a small, well-oiled party. Only when they were out of sight did the cigarette pack come out.

"Why am I not surprised to see you here?" Donny asked on his first long exhale.

Nick gave an awkward laugh. "Because I'm predictable?"

"Predictable is good," Donny said. "Women love it. Makes them feel secure and in control."

"Is that the secret to your happy marriage, Mr. Z?" Nick asked.

"Depends." He narrowed one blue eye at Nick. "Are you here looking for marriage advice?"

Possibly. If everything went his way. "What I'm here for is a very specific mission, sir."

He got a toothy grin around the cigarette. "I love when you go all macho military on me."

"Then you might not like what I'm about to tell you."

Nick slid his hands in his pockets, still trying to get used to saying these words. "I'm leaving the military."

"Really? I thought you were a lifer Navy SEAL type."

"I am, I *was*," he corrected. "My hearing has improved, but it's still not up to the standards of the military, and I can't get excited about pushing papers after what I trained to do. I think I'm taking a medical discharge and..." He looked out to the black horizon, formulating his thoughts. "I might like to try my hand at writing as a profession." He waited for the expected scoffing.

"Damn straight. I like it."

"You do?"

Donny choked on a puff of smoke. "I'm the last guy who's going to say don't follow your dreams no matter how off-the-wall they might seem to other people. I was pre-med until I dropped out and went after music for my livelihood."

Pre-med? Donny Zatarain? He couldn't even start to wrap his head around that. "Obviously, you've never regretted that decision," Nick said.

"Only when I want to golf without becoming the laughingstock of the *Rolling Stone* editorial department." He grinned. "Nothing wrong with pursuing your creative muse, I say."

And speaking of muses... "Which brings me back to my earlier question, Donny. What's the secret to your happy marriage?"

He nodded, glancing at the cigarette as it neared its last few puffs. "If I told you, it wouldn't be a secret."

Nick slid his hands deeper into his pockets, his fingers closing around his keys and...other things he'd stuffed in there. "But don't you want your daughter to experience that, too?"

Amusement glinted in Donny's blue eyes, along with something else. Satisfaction, maybe. Hope. And a father's love.

"Here's the best advice I can give you, son."

"I'll take anything." Anything that would help him seal this deal and make it last.

"Once a year, take her somewhere she's never been. Once a month, do something new that melts her in the sack. Once a week, stop everything and just listen to her. Once a day, catch her doing one thing you love. Once an hour, kiss her on the mouth. And every minute of every day, be grateful that you got her."

No surprise, it sounded like song lyrics. But it made a lot of damn sense. He tried to imagine his own father doing any of those things, and failed. But not Nick. He wouldn't fail.

"Donny? Are you back here?" A woman's voice floated over the night air.

"Oh, and..." Donny held the cigarette butt out. "Don't think for one minute you're getting anything by her."

"Here. I have a mint." Nick wrapped his fingers around everything in his pocket and retrieved everything in there.

When Donny looked down, even in the dim light, he saw it all. And started to chuckle. "You're serious about this, aren't you?"

"Hell, yeah. Like right now, right here serious."

The older man grinned. "Reminds me of a song I wrote." He popped a mint.

"Donny? Are you smoking?"

He closed his eyes and shook his head. "Damn it."

"The band's ready to play again," Ona called from around the corner of the building.

He looked to the sky. "Sometimes, I'm so sick of singing the same effing songs. It's my own damn do-over wedding, but all anyone wants me to do is sing."

"Well, sir, if you don't mind." Nick put his hand on Donny's shoulder and guided him toward Ona's voice. "I have an idea. But you'd have to agree to help me, because we're going to have to pull a few strings."

Ona popped into sight, smiling. "Oh, I like the sound of this already."

"Woman, you are incorrigible, and I love the holy hell out of you." Donny reached for her and pulled her closer. "C'mere." He kissed her square on the mouth for a good ten seconds. When he pulled away, he turned to Nick and winked. "Got that, kid?"

"Got it."

"This has to have been the easiest wedding we've ever done." Gussie looked out over the beach party with no small amount of pride.

"It's not technically a wedding," Willow said, smoothing the ivory silk of her gown, her very first Ona Z original. "But the ceremony was really nice."

"You cried," Gussie said, giving Willow a playful hip bump. "Don't think I didn't see you."

"How could I not? My dad is a goof, and my mom..." She sighed, looking around for the lithe figure that floated like a ghost in gray gauze around the party. "There's hope for her yet."

"She sure seems genuine," Ari agreed. "And crazy about you."

"Well, she apparently talked to The Big Man Himself," Gussie said. "Even Ona can't argue with Him."

"Do you believe her, Willow?" Ari asked. "She really has a compelling story about her near-death experience."

"It's hard not to buy anything that woman is selling," Willow said with a laugh, still scouring the group for her parents. Where had they gone? "The change is amazing, and I'm willing to try anything. *Once*. I think I've proven that."

Ari and Gussie shared a look, and Willow rolled her eyes. "Oh, you two. Forget it, okay? He's not coming back." As they opened their mouths to answer, she flattened her palms in front of both of their faces. "I don't care if you bet the whole damn Necco Wafer factory. It's over. He is not coming back. And I'm fine with that. I learned a lot from him. I don't think I could have forgiven my mother if he hadn't taught me how to…you know."

"Love," Ari said. "I believe the word is love."

Willow stared straight ahead, not really seeing the crowd mill about and vaguely aware that Uncle Graham and Uncle Mike had climbed back up on the stage to play one more set.

"I believe that is the word," she said wistfully, the statement drowned out as the first screech of a guitar note vibrated the speakers and Gussie gasped.

"I know, they're loud." Willow put her hand to her ears. "It's amazing I can hear a thing." Which only made her think of Nick—something she'd been doing non-stop for days. When would that end?

"No, look." Gussie lifted her arm to gesture, and as Willow followed, her gaze locked on the middle of the dance floor where a small circle had formed around her mother and father.

"What are they doing?" Willow asked.

Another noisy chord, and then the low bass beat started thrumming.

"Garter throw," Ari said. "I thought she didn't want to do that."

The next few notes echoed from the amps, and someone sat Ona on a chair. All three women moved closer to the circle where everyone started clapping with the familiar drum line of *Will Ya, Will Ya.*

"Of course he'd want this song played," Willow said under her breath. A song that would always and forever make her think of—

"Gotta know if it's real, gotta know if it's forever."

She froze mid-step, almost afraid to look at the stage to her right. Because Dad was in front of her on one knee and...*someone* was singing.

"No foolin' around, for worse or for bettah."

Badly. Someone was singing very badly.

The next line faded into the crowd noise as she finally turned, almost unable to process what she was looking at.

Nick Hershey, center stage, a mic in hand, a smile on his face, his gaze riveted to her.

Ari and Gussie each squeezed one of her hands.

"Told you," Gussie whispered.

The band hit the chorus, and the crowd screamed louder than Nick.

"Will ya, will ya be my girl?"

Dad pushed Mom's dress up to her thighs and, oh, God, *really?* He used his teeth to pull the garter down, making Willow put her hands to her face and shake her head. The crowd exploded and so did the band when Donny stood and circled the garter like a silver satin lasso, singing the chorus at the top of his lungs.

Nick stayed center stage, singing his heart out to her. Blood pumped through her wildly, her knees weak, her heart fluttering, her brain incapable of even imagining why he was there.

Except...she knew why.

Donny gathered enough steam to rile the crowd to a frenzy, then he flung the garter over everyone's heads to the stage, where Nick snagged it left-handed.

Another cheer exploded, and Nick gave a slow, sexy, killer smile. And launched into the next verse.

"I'm gonna kiss you every morning, and take you for a ride. We're gonna try new things together, with you by my side."

What? "Those aren't the words," she whispered, her pulse louder than Uncle Mike's drums.

On the dance floor, Dad howled, "Oh, yeah! A new verse!" He raised his fist in a victory punch toward Nick. And then the whole place slid into the chorus.

Will ya will ya...be my girl?

Screaming, clapping, hands in the air, it was exactly like a Z-Train concert, only the Z-man was on the dance floor with his arms around his wife, the two of them beaming at Willow like they knew something...

Will ya, will ya—

Gussie grabbed Willow's arm, and Ari shoved her closer to the stage.

"You guys—"

Then her father was behind her and her mom, both of them pushing her closer like a tidal wave of...

Will ya, will ya—

Still singing, Nick started to the stairs, coming off the stage, holding a microphone, staring at her.

"He's a wretched singer!" Donny yelled in her ear.

"Ya think?" Willow asked, her whole head about to explode from all of this...joy.

But Nick kept coming, his eyes smoky, his smile sly, his voice...oh, so bad. But the crowd saved him, repeating the chorus over and over and over.

Will ya, will ya...be my girl? Will ya, will ya...be my girl?

Until he stood two feet away, all tall and dark and hot and perfect. Willow couldn't breathe or think or move, but surrounded by her best friends and her parents, she somehow stayed standing as everyone and everything but Nick faded into the background.

"I love you." She mouthed the words, knowing he couldn't hear, but he could read her lips.

He just smiled, nodded, and reached into his pocket with his free hand.

"You gotta sing it!" Donny hollered behind her.

The music softened, the crowd quieted, and Nick pulled out a small black box from his pocket. And then he dropped to one knee.

She couldn't even process the perfection of this moment. And suddenly, everyone screamed the words for him.

"Will ya, will ya marry me?" Louder. "Will ya, will ya marry me?" Deafening. "Will ya, will ya marry me?" And all Willow could do was let the tears fall down her cheeks as Nick flipped open the box and a diamond sparkled in the torchlight.

"Quiet! Quiet!" Donny hushed the crowd with his raised hands. Finally, everyone was quiet, all attention on Nick.

Still on one knee, he looked up at her. "Willow, we both know we can't rewrite history, but I love you, and I know we can make an amazing future together. I don't want to do this halfway. I want...everything. Will ya, will ya marry me?"

Willow stood speechless as her whole body tingled with unadulterated happiness. *So this is what happy feels like.* She'd had it wrong all along.

"Say yes, honey," her mother whispered.

"Please, before he sings again," Donny murmured.

Willow nodded and whispered, "Yes." The explosion of cheers was lost as Nick slipped the ring on her finger and stood to wrap his arms around her.

All around them, people sang and clapped and cried.

But all Willow could do was press her head to Nick's chest and listen to his pounding heart. The one that belonged to her.

"You couldn't have written a better ending," she said to him.

"Ending? This isn't the end." He pulled her against him and hugged. "Our story's just starting."

Nick reached over her shoulder and handed the microphone to her father. "One last request, please."

Donny gave a rueful smile and signaled to the band as he made his way to the stage. They started a slow, rhythmic beat and, as if on cue, the crowd backed away, leaving Nick and Willow in the middle of the dance floor, swaying to the haunting strains of *My Sweet Ambrosia.*

She folded into his embrace, wrapped her arms around his powerful shoulders, and listened to the man she loved sing softly, sweetly, blissfully off-key.

Epilogue

"You're not going home tonight," Nick whispered to Willow when the last of the guests had gone and her responsibilities for the event ended.

"Sorry to break the news, but Artemisia's been rented, so I am going home. But I'd like you to come with me."

"Nope."

Her jaw loosened with a soft, disdainful cough. "Don't tell me. You want to wait for the wedding night."

Laughing, he guided her back into the main building of the resort. "I'm not that old school." He put his arm around her as they walked through the quiet lobby to a curved staircase that led up to the hotel rooms on the second floor.

"You got a room?" she asked as they reached the hallway.

"I had some assistance." He stopped at the door with the number he'd been given, slipped the card key in, and slowly opened.

He was rewarded with Willow's soft sigh of disbelief, as they stepped into a room with dozens of flickering candles and a path of roses that led to the turned-down bed, also sprinkled with flower petals.

"How did you do this, Nick?"

"I have friends. Well, you do."

She smiled. "Ari and Gussie?"

"They love you as much as I do," he said, taking her in his arms. With sure hands, he pushed the blond hair off her face and held her securely. "I'm so glad you said yes."

"I'm so glad you asked."

He kissed her, lingering on the sweet taste for a while, sliding his hands up and down the shimmery white dress that clung to her curves and had teased him all night.

"I have something else to ask," he murmured into the kiss.

"Mmmm." She angled her head so he could press his lips on her jaw and throat. "Anything."

"Willow Ambrosia Zatarain." He inched back so he could look into her eyes. "Will you make love with me?"

She lifted a brow. "I've never done that, you know."

A warm rush of pleasure heated him. "I know," he said gruffly. "Which is about the sexiest thing I ever heard." Very slowly, he turned her around. Lifting her hair, he kissed the nape of her neck then slid the long zipper all the way down. The sound cut through the silent room, a long, slow promise of things to come.

Shuddering on her next shaky breath, she stayed still. "No one has ever seen me completely naked before."

His knees almost buckled as the honor and privilege and awe of that hit hard. "Then I'm the luckiest man alive."

The dress fell to the floor with a soft whoosh, pooling around her feet. He closed his eyes, taking one second to appreciate what he was about to see and touch and love. He turned her again to find her eyes were closed, too.

"Are you scared?" he asked.

She shook her head. "Happy. Deliriously happy." She opened her eyes and looked up at him. "I had no idea that anything could feel like…this."

"And this." He touched her face, stroking her cheek, her jaw, her mouth, then drawing a line straight down to her bare breasts. They rose and fell with her next sigh, their gazes still locked.

Still silent, he traveled his finger down her abdomen, over her belly button, into the tiny slip of lace she wore for underwear. "The last barrier."

"Except for your clothes. I hardly recognize you with them on."

He laughed and stepped her back to the bed, easing her down. Standing over her, he undressed while she watched. She bit her lip and looked up and down and up and, well, mostly down. With every passing second, he grew harder.

"There's the man I know and love," she teased. "Bare-ass naked as the day I found him screeching out our song."

He knelt on the bed, studying her, touching, stroking, caressing, kissing. He helped her out of the lacy thong, nibbling on her thighs as he slid it off.

"Our song." He couldn't stop grinning. "Willow's gonna marry me," he sang.

"And Nick's going to make love to me." She sang back, tugging him closer with no small amount of impatience. "*Now.*"

"Yes. Now." He lowered his head and kissed her open mouth, soft as air at first. As she reached up and clung to his shoulders, they both intensified the kiss, the moment like a leaf suspended in air, fluttering to the ground, lasting five, six, seven slow heartbeats.

Finally, they pressed against each other and began the dance.

A caress of skin, a sigh of pleasure, one whispered promise, and another long, sweet kiss, as they rolled and tumbled over velvety rose petals.

The flower scent mixed with the something Nick couldn't identify but already needed. Willow. She folded under and around him, any inhibitions gone as she explored his body with sweet hands and tender lips, kissing his throat, his chest, his stomach.

He threaded her hair as she dragged herself lower and closed her hands, then her mouth, over the length of him, stunning him with the pleasure of her touch.

He hissed in air, closing his eyes and letting raw, rough arousal thrum through him. After a moment, he pulled her back up so they could kiss and touch more, filling his hands with her breasts and bottom, filling his heart with the beautiful sounds of satisfaction that came out of her lips.

Every inch on fire, his body hardened and rocked and vibrated with blood-pumping desire, aching already to be inside her. Had his helpers remembered the condoms he'd asked for?

He opened the nightstand drawer and found them.

"Those girls thought of everything," Willow said with a laugh.

"No kidding." He lifted a handful of Hershey Kisses that had been spilled around the condom box. "Everything."

"Oh, how clever. Hershey Kisses." She smiled up at him. "As sweet as yours."

Kneeling, he tore open the condom packet, then stopped in the act of sheathing himself to look in her eyes. "Willow, you are giving me the most precious honor. I'm...I'm..."

She closed her hand over his shaft. "You're *huge*."

The compliment warmed almost as much as her greedy fingers. "I don't want to hurt you."

"Go easy and we'll be fine." She gave him a Mona Lisa smile and guided him inside her, closing her eyes as he very slowly entered the warm, wet, tight envelope, sliding deeper and deeper as her hips rose more and more to give him access.

Fire licked up his thighs and heat tightened his back and a wicked hot need to thrust squeezed his entire lower half. But he fought the desire, staring at Willow, holding her gaze as he finally hilted himself deep, deep inside her.

For a moment they were perfectly still, suspended, connected, and maybe a little overwhelmed by every sensation that rocked them.

"My darling Willow, you're…" *Mine.* "You're…" *All mine.* "You're…"

She smiled and pulled him down to kiss her. "I'm so happy."

Satisfied with that, he moved slowly in and out of her, letting her get used to him, waiting for her to get completely comfortable and meet his rhythm. Seconds and heartbeats, kisses and soft cries, all of it passed in a haze as each thrust made him burn for more.

She gripped his shoulders and started to lose control, both of them panting and groaning in a syncopated beat. His pulse raged, pounding and screaming, his lungs fighting for every breath, his body lost in the pure, pure pleasure of hers.

"Nick…" She rocked harder, riding him, squeezing him, making the sounds he'd come to know when she was about to go over the edge. "Don't stop," she begged. "Don't…stop."

He couldn't if he wanted to, plunging deep, all worry of pain gone as nothing but raw gratification dragged them both up and up and up to the peak of satisfaction.

She spiraled in his arms, closing her eyes, scraping nails down his back, moaning with each wave of the climax that seized her. He gave in the second she did, arching his back to intensify the feeling as he let go of his control and exploded into her over and over and over again.

Spent and sweaty, he fell on her with his full weight, letting his face hit the pillow so the sounds of her strangled breath echoed in his left ear.

A strange feeling crawled up his back, a sensation of...disbelief. He was too out of it to try and analyze the...awareness. That's all he could think of, that he was hyperaware. He heard her breath, the sound of it filling him. The sound of it—

Sound? In his left ear? He stayed completely frozen while the realization swamped him.

"Nick."

His eyes popped wide, but he stayed still. How was that possible?

"I love you."

"Willow..." He sat up and looked at her. "I heard that."

"Good."

"No, I mean, I heard it in my bad ear." He put his hand over his ear, and even the sound of his fingertips brushing his skin was audible. "My hearing's coming back. Wow, Willow. You healed me."

She touched his face and smiled. "Then we're even."

THE END

311

Enjoy your trip to Barefoot Bay? There are more love stories set on this island! Don't miss a single one.

The Barefoot Billionaires
Secrets on the Sand
Seduction on the Sand
Scandal on the Sand

The Barefoot Bay Quartet
Barefoot in the Sand
Barefoot in the Rain
Barefoot in the Sun
Barefoot by the Sea

And be sure to catch Book Two of The Barefoot Bay Brides Trilogy...Barefoot in Lace, coming in late summer, 2014. Turn the page for a sneak peek at Gussie's story...

Sneak Peek

Barefoot in Lace

The Barefoot Bay Brides #2

Chapter One

"Thomas Jefferson DeMille? Was your mother obsessed with famous people or something?"

Ten feet away, the cashier's question stopped Gussie McBain dead in her tracks, almost making her drop a liter of Diet Coke and a whole bag of Swedish Fish in the aisle of the convenience store. *Thomas Jefferson DeMille?* She stared at the back of a tall, dark-haired man whose shoulders rose and fell with obvious frustration.

"Something," he replied. "Please clear the card, ma'am."

"I can't." Charity Grambling, owner of the Super Min and undisputed Most Obnoxious Human on the small island of Mimosa Key, tapped a credit card on the counter while she peered through bifocals to read another card in her other hand. "Because this credit card does not match this New York state driver's license, so I can't accept it."

"What the hell are you talking about?" His voice was low and gruff, drawing Gussie closer to the exchange. "TJ DeMille, right there."

Gussie bit her lip to keep from letting out a shriek. It *was* him! TJ DeMille, the world's most talented, brilliant, and amazing fashion photographer was standing right in front of her. Was she dreaming? She still couldn't see his face, only broad shoulders in a faded blue shirt with a few thick curls brushing the collar. She'd never actually *seen* TJ DeMille. His face was always behind the camera, not in front of it.

"TJ DeMille on the card but Thomas Jefferson on the license? Thomas Jefferson, *really*?" Charity raised a thickly drawn brow. "I wasn't born yesterday, mister."

"No shit," he mumbled.

Fighting a smile—and a full-body fangirl shudder—Gussie took a few steps closer, finally able to see his square jaw set in anger as he looked down his strong Roman nose at the older woman. His lips were parted as he glared with displeasure at Charity.

"I use my initials in business, and that's a business credit card."

"Sorry." Charity handed both back to him. "We do accept cash, however."

He snapped them from her hands. "Where's your ATM?"

"You'll need to visit the Mimosa Community Credit Union, just at the corner of Harbor and—"

"Nevermind!" He gave a push to a pile of magazines, nearly toppling a bottle of red wine onto a bag of Fritos. He pivoted toward the door and marched out.

"Charity!" Gussie exclaimed when the welcome bell dinged in his wake. "Do you have any idea who that was?" Every cell in her body danced with the desire to run after him and...*fawn*. Or get an autograph. Or actually see what color his eyes were.

"Some New Yorker trying to get by me with fake credit cards." Charity shoved his pile of merchandise to the side, obviously not as concerned with a lost sale as the possibility of stopping a criminal. "What kind of man buys ten-dollar cabernet, Fritos, and girlie magazines, anyway?"

Gussie eyed the cover of the top magazine, instantly

recognizing the masterful camera work of TJ DeMille that somehow managed to make the model look both ethereal and vicious. *Vanity Fair* was a girlie magazine now?

"What kind of man?" Gussie asked. "The man who shot the covers, that's who," she said dryly.

For a second, interest flickered in Charity's unadorned gray eyes, her weakness for local news and notoriety showing. "He did?"

"Yes, so you should have just *given* him the magazine, and asked for his autograph."

She huffed some more. "The only autograph I accept is on the credit card machine. Despite my name, there's no *charity* at the Super Min." Charity pointed to the liter of Diet Coke and bag of candy. "Cash or charge?"

"Cash." While she reached for her wallet, Gussie stole a look out the door, seeing him standing next to a white pickup truck, thumbing a cell phone. Her heart crawled up to her throat again, pounding like a teenage girl backstage at a boy-band concert. Because TJ DeMille was a god in the fashion world, and Gussie an unabashed groupie. She'd loved his work since he burst on the scene a few years ago.

He turned to get a better angle on his phone, shooting a vile look at the store. The unforgiving Florida summer sun poured light over him, making his black hair glisten and emphasizing the shadows under sharp cheekbones. Wow. She'd had absolutely no idea he was so…gorgeous.

Of course a photographer who captured the nuances of beauty would be beautiful himself.

"Cash or charge, or would you just like to stand there and drool all over the magazines so I can't sell them to anyone now that Tommy Jefferson himself had his sweaty palms all over them?"

Gussie instinctively reached for the issue of *Vogue*, the

need to touch what TJ DeMille had just had his very hands on. Once again, she slid a look toward the convenience store parking lot.

Maybe she should run out there and gush about his delicate touch, his clean eye, his—

"Oh, for crying out loud, pay for the soda and candy, please."

Gussie tore her gaze from the man to the beast in front of her. "And the magazines," she said impulsively. "And whatever else he was buying. I'll take it all."

Charity's eyes grew wide behind her bifocals. "And do what with them?"

"Exactly when did that become your business?"

She pffted out a breath. "Everything on this island is my business. Like, why do you wear different-color wigs every day? Someone asked me about it, and I just assumed, you know, chemo or something."

Gussie almost laughed, because how else could you even respond to such rudeness? "So that's what you told them?"

"I told them I'd find out." She leaned way off her little stool to peer hard at Gussie's face. "And all that makeup. What's the deal?"

A slow heat slid up her chest and into her cheeks, which Charity probably couldn't see because of *all that makeup*. She dug for the snappy retort about how Charity could benefit from a touch of mascara and came up with…nothing. Clearly, an encounter with TJ DeMille had killed her witty brain cells.

Reaching into her wallet, she grabbed two twenties and slapped them on the counter. "I'll take it all. His and mine." She scooped everything into her arms, using the magazines to cradle his wine and her Diet Coke.

"What the—"

"Keep the change," she called as she hustled away. The bell dinged as she shouldered the door open, the sound all but drowned out by the growl of an engine.

"Don't leave!" she called out, darting toward the pickup truck. But he was already backing out, sunglasses on, his face turned as he hit the accelerator—hard.

"This is for you!" she cried.

But he was flooring it, the motor screaming. She ran to the truck, just in time to reach it and do the only thing she could to stop him—kick the bumper. The move nearly cost her a forty-dollar armload. "Hey!"

He slammed on the brakes, whipping around to look at her. He froze for a moment, then inched down his sunglasses, disbelief drawing his thick brows together.

"I have...your...stuff." She lifted her arms, making her Swedish Fish fall to the ground and the liter of Diet Coke roll to a dangerous angle on top of the magazines.

He stared at her like she was a complete and total lunatic. Which, right at that moment, was quite accurate. Her impulses would be the death of her someday. Hell, they nearly were once.

He still didn't move.

"Your...magazines," she said, taking a step toward the curb, angling her whole body so the soda bottle was caught by her elbows. "And...wine. I bought them for you."

"You did?" He stayed right in the driver's seat, clearly uncertain of the possible danger of a pink-wigged woman who just spent way too much money for a stranger.

"I'm a..." *Fangirl. Stalker. Crazed admirer.* Right now, she felt like all of the above. "Good Samaritan," she finished, using all her might to hold the Coke with her elbow. "And I kind of hate that woman who owns this place."

Finally, he relaxed into a half-smile, taking the sunglasses off completely as he opened the door and climbed out. "That makes two of us."

He reached for the liter bottle, and she moved to protect it from a fall at the same second, and his hand went right smack against her boob.

He drew back—not terribly fast—but so did she, and she felt the wine slip right between the magazines and her stomach. "Oh!" She gasped, leaning into him to save the bottle from the fall, but it slipped and crashed to the concrete, making them both jump back as red wine and glass splattered all over her sandaled feet and his...oh, man. His crisp khaki trousers.

"Oh, I'm sorry," she cried.

"Are you okay?" he asked, stepping back and shaking some wine off his pant leg.

"I'm...fine." Except for the rain shower of glass over her foot. She lifted her leg out of the mess and the heavy issue of *Marie Claire* toppled, splatting right onto the puddle of wine. "Oh, God."

He inched back again, his smile fading as he eyed her. "This is getting worse by the second."

"I know, I'm..." She looked down and saw a tiny trickle of blood in the arch of her foot.

"You're bleeding."

"I'm fine. I'm..." *A freaking idiot.* "It's tiny."

But he reached for her foot, and she automatically leaned into him, sending the *Vanity Fair* to the same fate. It landed face-up, with the ethereal and vicious model staring up at them.

"Really, I'm fine," she said. "Just take this and..."

He took the last magazine and the bottle of Diet Coke from her hands, and she brushed at the tiny cut, happy to see it was nothing. "I'm sorry for this," she muttered.

"No, no, you were being kind. Here." He handed the remaining magazine—*Vogue* the size of a phone book—back to her. "You should keep this. It's a great issue." When she took it, he returned his attention to her cut, his large hand cradling her foot, forcing her to hold on to his arm for balance. Damn, the man had muscles.

"That's not too bad," he said, finally meeting her gaze. "And wine that bad should definitely kill any germs."

His voice was so low she found herself inching closer just to wallow in the timbre of it. And the sandalwood smell of him.

Finally, he let her foot go, and she had enough balance to stand on her own. Well, nearly enough. TJ DeMille made her downright wobbly.

"I just wanted to do something nice for you," she said, sounding as lame as she felt. "I'm really sorry about your pants."

He shook his pant leg again. "It's par for the course this week, I'm afraid. But that was very kind of you, um…miss…" He let his voice rise with a little question.

"Gussie," she supplied. "Gussie McBain."

"Gussie," he repeated, reaching out a hand. "I'm—"

"Oh, I know who you are."

Thick eyebrows rose in surprise, the look in his eyes—his very sky-blue eyes, she noted—a mix of distrust and uncertainty.

"I mean, I heard you tell…her." She pointed over her shoulder. "Thomas Jefferson DeMille." His name rolled off her lips like she'd said it quite a few times in her life, because, well, she had.

"Just TJ," he said, closing his fingers over her hand in a slow shake. They weren't sweaty at all, she thought fleetingly. On the contrary, his palms were dry and warm and strong and…more wobble-inducing than his smile. "And that was very thoughtful of you since that woman obviously assumed I just arrived from the local prison."

She laughed. "What does bring you to Mimosa Key?" A photo shoot? Her heart danced a little at the thought. She would *kill* to watch him work. He was a master and she was…a dreamer.

"Family business," he said vaguely, the only discernable note one of pure disgust. "Anyway, thanks." He smiled, and she could have sworn the sun shone just a little bit brighter. Gussie couldn't help staring up at him, drinking in the sight of a man who'd previously been nothing but a photo credit…on the most beautiful photos she'd ever seen.

"Is someone going to clean up that mess?" Charity's grating voice broke Gussie's moment of reverie. "Or do I have to call the sheriff and report vandals at the Super Min?"

They both turned to her, and the woman just shook her fried-blond head, shooing them off with one hand. "Nevermind. Go, I'll fix it. You…" She pointed to TJ. "I know who you are now. I made a few phone calls. Just get on your way and take care of that mess your sister left behind. And you." Her finger slid to Gussie. "Lose the wig, and you'd be prettier."

Gussie felt a flush in her cheeks as Charity backed into the store and let the door close.

"Well," she said awkwardly. "Whatever has you on our lovely little island, please don't judge us all by Charity Grambling."

He studied her face and of course, her wig. She should be used to it—she was, really—but his eye was so incredibly trained, the scrutiny nearly melted her.

"I think you're stunning," he said softly.

"Wow, thanks." She tried to laugh, but she sounded as

nervous as he was making her feel. "You, too." Oh, brother. Did she just say that?

"And I owe you a favor," he said, letting her off the hook for the lame compliment. "Really, thank you."

"For a broken bottle of wine and ruined magazines?"

He looked like he was about to argue, but then gave the chips a shake. "You saved my Fritos and, thus, my ass."

His cell phone rang, interrupting them. He pulled it out and angled the screen, that same look of disgust darkening his face. "I have to go. Like the woman said, another mess calls. Good-bye, Gussie." He stepped back to get in the truck, but took one more moment to study her again. "Really, stunning. I mean it. I have an eye for these things."

He closed the door and backed away before she could respond.

Well, no damn wonder he was a gifted photographer. He even made Gussie McBain feel beautiful, and that was saying a lot. Smiling, she stepped gingerly over the broken glass, knowing exactly the favor she'd like to collect from him.

Books by Roxanne St. Claire

**The Barefoot Bay Billionaires Trilogy
(Contemporary Romance)**
Secrets on the Sand
Seduction on the Sand
Scandal on the Sand

The Barefoot Bay Quartet (Contemporary Romance)
Barefoot in the Sand
Barefoot in the Rain
Barefoot in the Sun
Barefoot by the Sea

The Guardian Angelinos (Romantic Suspense)
Edge of Sight
Shiver of Fear
Face of Danger

The Bullet Catchers (Romantic Suspense)
Kill Me Twice
Thrill Me to Death
Take Me Tonight
First You Run
Then You Hide
Now You Die
Hunt Her Down
Make Her Pay
Pick Your Poison (a novella)

Stand-alone Novels (Romance and Suspense)
Space in His Heart
Hit Reply
Tropical Getaway
French Twist
Killer Curves
Don't You Wish (Young Adult)

About the Author

Roxanne St. Claire is a *New York Times* and *USA Today* bestselling author of nearly forty novels of suspense and romance, including several popular series (*The Bullet Catchers*, *The Guardian Angelinos*, and *Barefoot Bay*) and multiple stand-alone books. Her entire backlist, including excerpts and buy links, can be found at www.roxannestclaire.com.

In addition to being a six-time nominee and one-time winner of the prestigious Romance Writers of America RITA Award, Roxanne's novels have won the National Reader's Choice Award for best romantic suspense three times, and the Borders Top Pick in Romance, as well as the Daphne du Maurier Award, the HOLT Medallion, the Maggie, Booksellers Best, Book Buyers Best, the Award of Excellence, and many others. Her books have been translated into dozens of languages and are routinely included as a Doubleday/Rhapsody Book Club Selection of the Month.

Roxanne lives in Florida with her family (and dogs!), and can be reached via her website, www.roxannestclaire.com or on her Facebook Reader page, www.facebook.com/roxannestclaire and on Twitter at www.twitter.com/roxannestclaire.